It was too much would settle dow s like a common man, seeking to wrest riches from the hard, rocky ground of Deadwood Gulch. Sooner or later such mundane labor would wear on him to the point that he would give it up.

When he did, the so-called respectable folks of Dead-wood would be right there waiting for him, holding out a badge, and offering him money and power. And he would accept the offer, as he had in Abilene.

Once Hickok was marshal, it was inevitable that he would try to clean up the settlement. Given his record as lawman, it was highly likely that he would be successful in this effort.

Something had to be done. Deadwood was a golden goose, and Varnes was damned if he was going to let Wild Bill Hickok ruin it.

Berkley titles by Mike Jameson

―――――

The Tales from Deadwood series

Tales from

DEADWOOD

The Gamblers

Mike Jameson

BERKLEY BOOKS, NEW YORK

THE BERKLEY PUBLISHING GROUP
Published by the Penguin Group
Penguin Group (USA) Inc.
375 Hudson Street, New York, New York 10014, USA

Penguin Group (Canada), 90 Eglinton Avenue East, Suite 700, Toronto, Ontario M4P 2Y3, Canada
(a division of Pearson Penguin Canada Inc.)
Penguin Books Ltd., 80 Strand, London WC2R 0RL, England
Penguin Group Ireland, 25 St. Stephen's Green, Dublin 2, Ireland (a division of Penguin Books Ltd.)
Penguin Group (Australia), 250 Camberwell Road, Camberwell, Victoria 3124, Australia
(a division of Pearson Australia Group Pty. Ltd.)
Penguin Books India Pvt. Ltd., 11 Community Centre, Panchsheel Park, New Delhi—110 017, India
Penguin Group (NZ), Cnr. Airborne and Rosedale Roads, Albany, Auckland 1310, New Zealand
(a division of Pearson New Zealand Ltd.)
Penguin Books (South Africa) (Pty.) Ltd., 24 Sturdee Avenue, Rosebank, Johannesburg 2196,
South Africa

Penguin Books Ltd., Registered Offices: 80 Strand, London WC2R 0RL, England

This is a work of fiction. Names, characters, places, and incidents either are the product of the author's imagination or are used fictitiously, and any resemblance to actual persons, living or dead, business establishments, events, or locales is entirely coincidental.

TALES FROM DEADWOOD: THE GAMBLERS

A Berkley Book / published by arrangement with the author

PRINTING HISTORY
Berkley edition / May 2006

Copyright © 2006 by The Berkley Publishing Group.
Cover design by Steven Ferlauto.
Interior text design by Kristin del Rosario.

ISBN: 0-425-20959-8

BERKLEY®
Berkley Books are published by The Berkley Publishing Group,
a division of Penguin Group (USA) Inc.,
375 Hudson Street, New York, New York 10014.
BERKLEY is a registered trademark of Penguin Group (USA) Inc.
The "B" design is a trademark belonging to Penguin Group (USA) Inc.

PRINTED IN THE UNITED STATES OF AMERICA

10 9 8 7 6 5 4 3 2 1

Prologue

Kansas, 1871

Something was wrong. The big bull lifted his massive, shaggy head and looked around, but his eyesight was weak and he saw nothing out of the ordinary. Something didn't *smell* right to him, though. He pawed the ground.

A second later, a .50-caliber bullet weighing seven hundred grains slammed into the bull's side and tore on through his lungs. He was so heavy that even this terrible impact barely staggered him. Disturbed by what had just happened, he blew air out through his nose and tried to walk forward. But his lungs were now filling with blood and an inexorable weakness spread throughout his huge body. His forelegs folded up beneath him, dropping him into a position that made him appear to be genuflecting before some buffalo deity.

He bawled in anger and pain as the awareness that something was dreadfully wrong soaked in on his primitive brain. He tried to push himself up but couldn't do it. Blood gushed hotly from the hole in his side. The other beasts near him in the herd smelled the blood and the scent alarmed their instincts. They began to mill around nervously.

As the wounded bull struggled futilely to get up, he

heard a series of distant booming sounds. The smell of blood was thick in his nostrils. He had no way of knowing if the smell came from the blood pooling on the ground and inside his chest cavity, or if it came from other members of the herd that had also been wounded.

The last vestiges of his strength deserted him. With a groan, he rolled onto his side. His flanks heaved as he tried to draw in a breath that would not come. His muzzle had dug into the rich prairie dirt as he fell. The sun should have been warm on his hide, but he no longer felt it. With a last, rattling wheeze, the buffalo died.

Up on the grassy, windswept hill overlooking the herd, Richard Seymour shook his head and said, "Poor bloody bastard."

The words came during a lull in the firing. One of Seymour's partners, Arthur Ruff, heard him speak. Ruff knelt about five feet away. The barrel of his Sharps Big Fifty rested in a pair of forked sticks that had been driven into the ground. Buffalo sticks, they were called, because they helped steady the barrel of the heavy rifle as the hunter drew a bead on his target. Seymour had his Sharps resting on buffalo sticks, too. He broke open the breech and began to reload, and Arthur Ruff said, "We oughta call you Bloody Dick, the way you talk."

On Seymour's other side, Ab Clifford laughed and said, "Yeah, Bloody Dick, but it sure ain't 'cause you been fuckin' virgins, Seymour! They ain't none in Kansas!"

Further along the line, Ab's brother Walt joined in the gibes. "No tellin' what you did back over there in England, now is there, Bloody Dick? You're one closemouthed son of a bitch."

Finished with his reloading, Seymour ignored the comments. The other men were uncouth, unlettered barbarians, but they were his partners. They had allowed him to come along on this buffalo-hunting expedition, and so far they had treated him fairly. He had made allowances for their so-called wit in the past, and he would continue to do so, even though it got a bit tiresome at times.

Seymour nestled his cheek against the smooth, cool

wooden stock. He had the Sharps's butt tucked firmly against his shoulder so that the strong recoil would be diminished. Even so, his shoulder would be sore by the end of the day.

Also by the end of the day, dozens of buffalo would lie dead on the prairie. The great shaggy brutes just *stood* there. Occasionally, they might break into a stampede if they were spooked enough, but most of the time they simply milled around in confusion and waited for death to claim them.

In a way, they were much like humanity, Dick Seymour thought as he shot another buffalo, a cow this time, with a calf trailing behind her.

For over an hour, the five men—Seymour, Ruff, the two Clifford brothers, and their other partner, John Nelson—knelt on the hill and poured lead down into the herd. There were thousands of buffalo spread over the plains like a huge black, gray, and brown stain. The phrase "dumb animal" might have been coined for them, Seymour had thought more than once, but in their case it referred to their intelligence, not their inability to speak. They were simply too stupid to realize that they were being killed, one after the other.

Eventually, though, the smell of blood, the bawling of wounded, dying animals, and the continual booming of the rifles finally penetrated to the consciousness of enough of the buffalo to start the herd moving. Dust rose from their hooves and mingled with the clouds of smoke that had rolled over the plains all afternoon. With a rumble that started like distant thunder and grew to a tremendous roar, the herd stampeded off to the west.

On the hill, the hunters took down their buffalo sticks and carried their rifles back to the wagons where the skinners waited. The hunters had done their work; now it was time for the skinners to drive their wagons down among the dead and begin their grisly chores. They would labor the rest of the day and then long into the night, working by lantern light as they cut and peeled the thick shaggy hides off the slain beasts. By morning, the backs of the wagons would be filled with stinking piles of buffalo hides. The stripped carcasses would be left on the plains to rot.

The stench of decaying meat, of blood, of burned gunpowder filled Dick Seymour's nostrils for so many hours of the day that it never seemed to go away. He smelled that sharp reek even when it wasn't really there. But despite its unpleasant aspects, there was good money in hunting buffalo. He had arrived in the American West penniless, and he never wanted to experience that again.

It would be nice, though, to smell something for a change that didn't stink.

A field of wildflowers, perhaps.

Kansas, 1873

IN the dim predawn, Dick Seymour awoke with his wife pressed against his back. Her belly was round with the child she carried there, so she couldn't snuggle against him as tightly as she once could. But she tried anyway, and she was close enough so that she could reach around him and rub her hand on his crotch. Still half-asleep, he instinctively began to harden.

When he was awake and fully aroused, he rolled toward her in the thick buffalo robes that were spread out underneath the wagon to form their bed. She turned so that she faced away from him and pulled up her buckskin dress. He rested a palm on one of her ample buttocks, rubbing and squeezing it for several minutes until Carries Water made a little whimpering sound and thrust her hips back at him. Seymour was ready. He entered her, and she caught her breath in pleasure.

When he had first come to America, the idea of having relations with an Indian woman, much less marrying one, never would have entered his head. As he had moved west, the concept had become more palatable. The first time he had heard a frontiersman recite the bawdy couplet "Redskin pussy's good as white, as long as it's nice an' tight," he had laughed like everyone else.

Then he had met Carries Water.

She was a Kansa, a member of the tribe for which this flat, windswept land was named. Among other Indian women, she had offered her services as cook, wagon driver, skinner, and prostitute to the buffalo hunters. She had gone on one trip with Seymour and his partners, and by the time they returned to Dodge City, he had known that he was in love with her, as unlikely as that might seem.

He had asked that she stay there rather than going out with the hunters again. She was offended at first, thinking that he no longer wanted her around because he didn't like her. He'd had to explain that he couldn't stand the thought of knowing that the other men were lying with her. So he gave her part of his share of the profits the group had realized from the sale of the buffalo hides. That made her realize how serious he was, and so she agreed to wait there for him while he went out hunting again to make more money for them.

He already had it in the back of his mind, he supposed, that he would marry her and take her away from the squalid life she had led up until then.

Over the next six months, he went on several more hunting trips while she waited for him at Dodge, living in a small house, a shack, really, that he had rented. He knew the other men laughed about his squaw, but he didn't care. All he cared about was that Carries Water would be there for him when he returned.

Then he came back and found her with her belly swollen from the child growing inside her. His child. She feared that he would turn her out, but instead he took her to one of the local preachers and asked the man to marry them. Indignantly, the minister had refused. He would have no part in joining together a white man, a Christian, with a heathen slattern, he declared.

While the reverend was picking himself up, Seymour took Carries Water's arm and led her away, mustering as much dignity as he could. Unfortunately, the rest of the preachers in Dodge City took the same attitude, and Dick supposed he couldn't knock all of them down.

It was just pure luck that he ran across the Reverend Cassius Stallworth in one of the town's many saloons. Reverend Stallworth no longer had a flock of his own—his fondness for whiskey and women had led a number of churches to dispense with his services—but he'd retained his credentials and, he assured Seymour, his standing with the Lord. For the price of a bottle of Who-Hit-John, Reverend Stallworth had joined Richard Seymour and Carries Water in holy matrimony.

Their daughter was born several months later and was named Rebecca by her father, after his grandmother back in England, and Finds a Flower by her mother, because Carries Water liked the way it sounded. The infant traveled with them on the first trip that Seymour made in the wagon full of goods he had purchased to trade with the Indians. He was no longer a buffalo hunter. He was a respectable merchant now.

For over a year now, Seymour had been trading, mostly with the Sioux. Despite their warlike nature, they accepted him because he treated them fairly and because he was married to an Indian woman. Becky Finds a Flower had grown into a cheerful, bright-eyed toddler, and Carries Water was with child again. She hoped fervently that this one would be a boy, but Seymour didn't really care. He enjoyed his life, he loved his wife and daughter, and whatever fate had in store for him, he would accept it happily.

He cried out as he ejaculated into Carries Water. He tightened his arms around her and ground his pelvis against her soft rump. A warm wind swept across the prairie, rippling the tall grass. The sun peeked over the horizon. It was going to be a beautiful day, and Richard Seymour was that rarest of creatures, a truly happy man.

Kansas, 1875

HE ran through the grass, his heart pounding, his eyes searching desperately. Fear filled his whole being. Not fear for himself, but for those he loved. They had to be here. He had to find them. They had to be all right. Those strident imperatives rang urgently through his brain, clamoring to be made true.

But what he wanted wasn't necessarily what he was going to get, and he knew it.

Blood was crusted on one side of his face where it had run down from the cut on his forehead. He remembered the pain of being struck down, the black sticky tide of unconsciousness that tried to overwhelm him, the crackling heat of the flames as the wagon was consumed. But most of all he remembered the screams, and the ugly laughter of the men.

He had assumed that he was about to die, so when he'd regained consciousness, it had come as something of a surprise to him. Struggling against a terrible dizziness, he had gotten to his feet and looked around, seen the burned-out husk of the wagon and the bloody carcasses of the mules, their throats cut, and he had known that all his work was destroyed, all the effort of the past few years gone for nothing.

But he still had hope. He didn't see any other bodies. And since he could see the tracks that led off through the grass, he followed them, daring to believe that it might not be too late to save those he loved. He could always go back to buffalo hunting and get more money to replace the wagon and the goods it had contained. Only those who lived and breathed could not be replaced.

He called their names as he ran, his voice cracking with his fear. The words were snatched away by the wind and carried whirling across the prairie. He stopped sometimes and listened, hoping to hear a reply, but there was only the ceaseless whisper and moan, sounding almost like a lover.

Then he saw the splatters of crimson on the grass and his fear became terror. He plunged on, tripping a few feet later over the girl. He scrambled up and cried out incoherently, swamped with horror and grief and denial, and then he stumbled on and found Carries Water lying in the grass still clutching the baby, the boy whose birth had been so celebrated by their little family only a few months earlier.

Falling to his knees, he pulled her into his arms and held her tightly against him as he had held her so many other times, but today there was no beating heart keeping time with his, no happy laughter in his ear. There was only the looseness of death and the last faint vestige of warmth that would soon fade away completely and forever.

He clutched her against him and put his head back and howled like a wolf, howled out all the pain and anger he felt at his loss. But nothing would bring them back, it was too late, too late. . . .

"*. . . GETTIN'* late, I said. You gonna sleep the day away, Dick?"

He pried his eyes open, not an easy thing to do since they were crusted over from a night's sleep made even deeper than usual by the amount of liquor he'd put away the night before in Mann's No. Ten Saloon. For a moment there as he'd come out of the dream, he had been back on the Kansas plains instead of in the Black Hills of the Dakota Territory, and it had been a year earlier, on the worst day of his life.

That year had deadened the pain but hadn't made it go away. It was the same with whiskey. He could forget, but only for a while, and then he went back again.

Somebody kicked the cot. "Damn it, get up. We got things to do."

He forced himself to sit up and swing his legs off the cot. He stood up, his head pounding, and swayed a little as he tried to keep his balance.

"What you need is a little hair o' the fuckin' dog. Come on, Bloody Dick. I'll buy you a drink."

"Yes, a drink," Richard Seymour murmured, although every part of his being rebelled against the very idea of pouring more raw whiskey down his gullet. Every part except one.

His memory. The part that had to be stilled and tamed.

Stumbling out of the tent, following the little man in flashy clothes, he was Richard Seymour, former buffalo hunter and trader and loving husband and father, no more.

Now he was just Bloody Dick.

And it wasn't Kansas where he found himself, but rather Dakota Territory, a place called Deadwood to be exact, in July, the Year of Our Lord Eighteen and Seventy-Six.

Chapter One

~~~

"FOR the Lord works in mysterious ways, and we dare not question His wisdom. We know that He has taken this poor girl to be with Him in Heaven, and we may draw comfort from the knowledge that Carla Wilkes is now in a better place."

Of course, most places were better than Deadwood, the woman who called herself at times Martha Jane Cannary and at other times Calamity Jane thought as she sat on a tree stump and listened to the preacher drone on. Deadwood was pretty much a shithole, although she really hadn't been here long enough to form such an opinion. She'd only rolled in with the wagon train from Fort Laramie the day before.

Calamity wished she had a drink. She'd been tapping Bill Hickok's keg of whiskey all during the trip, but it was about empty and she figured Bill might get mad if she drunk up the last of his booze. She didn't want Bill mad at her. What she really wanted, where Bill Hickok was concerned, was to run her fingers through that long, light brown hair of his and to feel his big strong hands moving gently on her body. That thought made her feel womanly down in her belly. Romance always made her go mushy inside.

She wondered idly how big his talleywhacker was. She was willing to bet it was pretty damn good-sized, and she started trying to figure out a way she could get a look at it so she could tell for sure.

"Let us pray."

The preacher's words reminded Calamity that she was sitting on the edge of a cemetery where a funeral service was going on, so she really hadn't ought to be thinking such things. The girl who was being buried had been a whore, but the preacher didn't seem to care about that. He was a tall, gawky-looking sort of gent with black hair and a beard. Like most sky pilots, he was soft-spoken until he got wound up in his preaching, and then he could do some good old hellfire-and-brimstone sin-shoutin'. That was what Calamity figured, anyway. She hadn't heard him go on a real tear yet.

Calamity sat there and looked at the other folks gathered around the newly dug grave. The young fella in the fancy buckskin jacket and whipcord trousers, holding a big creamy hat in his hands, seemed to be the one who was most broken up. Calamity figured he'd been sweet on the dead whore. Next to him stood a well-dressed older woman, probably in her forties but still handsome, with a bunch of red curls under her dark green hat and only a few strands of gray among the red. Calamity had heard somebody say she owned the house where the dead girl had worked.

Behind the redheaded woman and the young fella were half-a-dozen more whores. They had scrubbed most of the paint off their faces and dressed as respectable as they could, but Calamity recognized them for what they were anyway. After all, she was part of the same sisterhood, although she had sworn to herself that she'd given up that profession and from here on out would fuck only for love. She had kept that vow for quite a while now.

Those were the only folks who had come out to mourn for Carla Wilkes, at least openly. One thing about Deadwood, there were hills all around the place, and Calamity still had the sharp eyes of the scout she had once been, especially when she had the bad luck to be sober, like today.

She had spotted a fella standing in the trees on a hill to the north of the cemetery, and another one observing the funeral from a hill to the south. She had no idea who they were or what their interest was or why they hadn't come down to the cemetery, nor did she care.

"Ashes to ashes, dust to dust . . . To the earth we commend the body of Carla Wilkes, and to the boundless mercy of the Heavenly Father we commend her soul."

The young fella put his hat on and stepped forward to pick up a dirt clod from the pile of freshly turned earth next to the grave. He tossed it in, and Calamity heard the hollow thud as it landed on top of the pine coffin. That was a damned ugly sound.

There had been a shoot-out of sorts—hell, a fuckup with bullets would be a better way to describe it—on Deadwood's main street the day before, just minutes after the wagon train had pulled in. A couple of hombres who had murdered some prospector had been killed, and a stray slug had cut down the whore. Calamity had seen the whole thing because Wild Bill had been involved, although the Prince of Pistoleers, the most famous gunman in the West, hadn't fired a shot, and Calamity had tagged along, naturally enough, to keep an eye on Bill. He had to stay safe until he realized that he'd made a mistake marrying that circus lady and ought to take up with a real woman instead. A woman like Calamity Jane.

Well, the funeral was over. She could go find Bill now. He'd been asleep in his room at the Grand Central Hotel earlier. At least, he hadn't come down yet, and Calamity assumed he was asleep. But the day was half gone now, and Bill ought to be up and about.

She put her hands on her knees and pushed herself to her feet. She was a fairly short, stocky woman who wore a battered old hat on her short-cropped hair and dressed like a man in greasy buckskins and carried a gun like a man, too. But within her beat the heart of a romantic, or at least she liked to think so. She had spent a couple of weeks on the trail with Wild Bill, and during that time he hadn't been anything more than polite to her. Polite, and a little distant.

Just you wait, Bill Hickok, she thought as she shuffled off toward Deadwood's business district. You'll see the light sooner or later. Just you wait.

BELLAMY Bridges might have collapsed if it hadn't been for Laurette Parkhurst standing beside him, her hand on his arm, sharing her strength with him. Miss Laurette, as she called herself, had been Carla's employer at the Academy for Young Ladies, and now Bellamy worked for her, too. She was more than an employer, though. Miss Laurette was the only friend Bellamy had left in Deadwood.

That hadn't always been the case, of course. Bellamy had left his parents' farm in Illinois to search for gold in the Black Hills of Dakota Territory, and during the journey he had become friends with Dan Ryan, a former Army sergeant who had guided Bellamy and the other gold-seekers up here. He and Dan had been more than friends: They had been partners, going in together on a gold claim up Deadwood Gulch.

All that was over now. Bellamy had given Dan his share of the claim, although Dan had insisted he would pay him back for it someday. And it was Dan's stubborn interference in the affairs of others that had ultimately resulted in Carla's death. It was almost beyond Bellamy's comprehension now that he had ever been friends with the man.

"Come on," Laurette said as her fingers tightened on Bellamy's arm through the sleeve of his buckskin jacket. Reverend Smith had put aside his Bible and picked up his shovel. The time for prayer and words of comfort was over. All that remained now as the shoveling of dirt back into the hole. The covering up for all time of the girl that Bellamy had loved.

With a shudder, he forced himself to turn away. He and Laurette walked along the street, trailed by the other girls from the Academy.

Behind them, dirt clattered down on the coffin. Something deep inside Bellamy twitched and gibbered with each burst of sound.

* * *

Dan Ryan stood in the shadows under a tree and watched Bellamy walk away from the grave, accompanied by Miss Laurette and the rest of the women from the Academy. Young ladies, they called themselves, but while some of them were young, almost scandalously so, there wasn't much ladylike about them. They were whores, plain and simple, and recognizing that fact didn't mean he was passing judgment on them, Dan told himself. He didn't want to pass judgment on anybody.

Things sure had gotten messed up in the short time since he and his fellow prospectors had arrived in Deadwood Gulch. First, there had been his falling-out with Bellamy Bridges, the youngster who had been his friend and partner; then, his abortive romance with Aunt Lou Marchbanks, the former slave who was the cook at the Grand Central Hotel; and then, the trouble with Ord and Clate Galloway and the brothers' murder of old Ulysses Egan, who'd had a good claim up the gulch from the one Dan was working. Dan could have let the Galloways go, but instead he had chased them to the settlement and tried to rouse the citizens of Deadwood against them. There had been some shooting. . . .

And one of the people to fall had been Carla Wilkes, the girl Bellamy had convinced himself he was in love with.

Dan wished he could have gone down there to the cemetery and shaken Bellamy's hand and stood with him during the funeral, but he knew Bellamy wouldn't want that. Hell, the kid was so torn up he might have gone for his gun in an attempt to settle what he thought of as the score against Dan.

So instead, Dan had stood up here on the hill, hidden in the shadows of the trees, and watched from a distance like a coward. There was a bad taste in Dan's mouth as he turned away. It was a bitter, sour taste.

Regret. That's what it was. Regret, and helplessness.

Because there wasn't a damned thing he could do to fix everything that had gone wrong.

* * *

ON the other side of the gulch, also watching from the shadows, Fletch Parkhurst kept his eye on his mother. Laurette was fussing over Bellamy as she led him away from the grave. She already had Bellamy wrapped around her finger, and now in his grief he would lean on her even more. She had used Carla to get Bellamy to do whatever she wanted; now that Carla was gone, Laurette would have to rely on herself.

But in the end, she would get her way. She always did.

Fletch was a tall, slender young man, a few years older than Bellamy Bridges. He wore a well-cut black suit, black boots, and a flat-crowned black hat. Under his coat, a holstered revolver was belted around his waist. His long, powerful fingers could pluck the gun from its holster with the same speed and dexterity with which they shuffled and dealt cards. He was a gambler, a gunman, a ne'er-do-well. Until recently, he had been his mother's silent partner in the Academy. He supposed he still was, although he didn't intend to take any more of the money that the whorehouse earned. Fletch's dark eyes narrowed as he watched the ungainly figure of the preacher shoveling dirt into the grave.

The Reverend H. W. Smith didn't know it, but he had enemies in Deadwood. At least one of them wanted him dead, so that he would no longer interfere with business. Laurette had approached Fletch about getting rid of the preacher and making it look like the Indians were responsible.

And with that, for the first time in his life, he had been forced to ask himself if there were lines he would not cross. To his surprise, he had discovered that the answer was yes.

He hadn't been particularly surprised when he'd drifted into Deadwood a few months earlier, just as the mining camp was getting started good, and discovered that one of the local madams was the woman who had abandoned him years earlier. He had strolled into the Academy one night thinking that he might find someone there interested in playing poker, and there she was, big as life and twice as bold and brassy. For years, he had carried a watch with her picture in it, though he had been tempted to burn it many times. He had known her, but she didn't have any idea who he was.

That had opened up all sorts of intriguing possibilities.

Had he been more interested in revenge, he might have indulged himself in some of them. Instead, he had told her who he was, not asking her for anything, just informing her of the facts.

At first she hadn't believed him, or at least she had claimed not to, although he saw the doubt in her eyes. But when he told her things about her life, and his, that only her son could know, she had given in and admitted their relationship. Then she had asked him if he wanted money to go away and leave her alone. In a way, that had been a mistake on her part, assuming that everyone was as venal as she was.

So he had cut himself in for a piece of the Academy's profits, and in return he had kept the peace when the place threatened to turn unruly. He had a reputation with a gun, and not many men wanted to cross him.

Now there was a real pistoleer in Deadwood, Fletch thought as he watched Reverend Smith filling in the grave. A Prince of Pistoleers, in fact, at least according to the dime novels about him. Wild Bill Hickok himself.

Fletch had no desire to test his speed and skill and nerve against a man like Hickok. And yet he couldn't help but wonder, if only for a second. . . . How fast was Hickok, really? Fast enough to beat him? Probably, but there was only one way to find out.

With a faint smile, Fletch shook his head and left his observation post on the hill. He started working his way back down toward town. He couldn't see Laurette and Bellamy anymore. They had gone into the Academy. There would be work to do before tonight, when the miners would come in from their claims and pay their visits to the house. Grief was one thing, business was another. Life had to go on . . . until it didn't anymore.

There would be a game in the Bella Union or the Gem or the No. Ten. There was always a game.

He'd heard that Wild Bill was a poker-playing man. Fletch wanted no part of a shooting match with the famous Hickok, but he wouldn't mind facing him across a poker table. *That* was a game he would take a hand in, any day.

Chapter Two

❧❧

WERE his fingers shaking? His eyes narrowed as he watched himself in the flyspecked mirror, standing there in the hotel room tying a string tie around his neck. His fingers *were* shaking. Only a little, true enough, but that was the reason he was having trouble with the tie. With a curse under his breath, he tore the tie off and threw it down on the dressing table that had a chunk of a book torn off and shoved under one of the legs so that it wouldn't wobble.

He lifted his hands and searched intently for any sign of trembling. Nothing. They were rock steady now. They were the same hands that had served him so well for so long, that had swooped down with blinding speed to the butts of the revolvers he carried either thrust into a sash around his waist or holstered on his hips, depending on how fancy he felt like being that day.

But even though they were steady now, they had been shaking a moment earlier. He was sure of it. He had seen it with his own eyes.

"And we all know how dependable *those* are," he said

aloud, his deep voice edged with bitterness. "Just ask Mike Williams."

The thought of his friend back in Abilene, now dead and buried because one night he had come running up out of the shadows with a gun in his hand at just the wrong place and just the wrong time, did nothing to make him feel better. He took a deep breath, steadying his nerves, and picked up the tie again. This time, he looped it around his neck and tied it flawlessly. Beautifully, even.

With that done, he picked up a plain buckskin jacket from the bed and put it on over his butternut shirt. The jacket had no fringe or elaborate beadwork decoration. It was just functional, like the high-topped brown boots, the corduroy trousers, and the double-holstered gun belt that held his .45s. He had once been a gaudy dresser, to be sure, but he had just about given up wearing flashy clothes. His friend Charley Utter was the dandy now. Let Charley wear the frilly shirts and the silk vests and the velvet jackets. Let Charley be the celebrated frontiersman.

Bill Hickok had come to Deadwood to find gold, that was all. Just plain ol' Bill Hickok, that was him.

He picked up his flat-crowned, wide-brimmed brown hat and settled it on his head. One last glance at his hands before he went downstairs.

Steady as can be.

LUCRETIA Marchbanks set the best table in the Black Hills. That was the plain and simple truth of it. Everybody who could afford it came to the dining room of the Grand Central Hotel to eat as often as possible, whether they were staying in the hotel or not. At busy times, men stood in line for the food prepared by the handsome, middle-aged black woman who had begun her life as a slave. The line had been known to stretch onto the boardwalk outside the hotel.

In late morning, after the breakfast crowd had cleared out and before the lunch rush began, it wasn't so crowded in the dining room. Only three or four of the tables were occupied. But the man Charley Utter was looking for sat at one of them, so Charley made a beeline across the room toward him.

"Mornin', Mr. Merrick," Charley said to the editor and publisher of the *Black Hills Pioneer*. They had met the day before, after the wagon train pulled in to the cheers of the crowd that had gathered to greet the new whores. With the business plans that Charley had in mind, it was vital that he be well acquainted with the local representative of the Fourth Estate.

Beefy, sharp-eyed A. W. Merrick looked up from the pad of paper on which he had been scribbling notes and story ideas. His empty breakfast plate and coffee cup had been shoved aside to make room for his journalistic efforts.

"Mr. Utter, isn't it?"

Charley shoved out his hand and shook with the newspaperman. "Call me Charley," he said. "Or Colorado Charley, if you like. That's what a lot of folks call me."

Merrick smiled thinly. "Mr. Utter is fine. I mean no offense by that, sir. It's a matter of professionalism. I may be writing about you, so I tend to keep a bit of distance. Helps my objectivity, you know."

"You sure will be writin' about me," Charley said as he pulled out a chair and sat down uninvited at the table. Merrick didn't seem to mind. Charley went on. "Once you hear about my plans, you'll realize they're the biggest thing to hit the Black Hills since General Custer and his boys found gold up here a couple o' years ago."

"And I'm sure you intend to tell me all about these plans of yours, don't you?"

"Yes, sir, I do." Charley looked around. "Where's a waiter gal? I'll buy us some coffee."

Merrick wasn't going to refuse that offer. He crooked a finger, and a Scandinavian girl in an apron came over and took his order for a pot of coffee.

Charley watched the girl go into the kitchen and said, "Gal looks like she came right off the farm back in Minnesota. I like a Scandahoovian girl. They're big-boned, built for bearin' young'uns. With the pelvis on that 'un, she wouldn't have a bit o' trouble."

"You were going to tell me about your plans," Merrick reminded him.

"Oh, yeah. I reckon you probably know I got into town yesterday with that wagon train—"

"The one Wild Bill Hickok was accompanying."

"Yeah, that's right." Sooner or later, when he was talking to anybody, they had to bring up Wild Bill. Folks knew that Colorado Charley and Wild Bill were friends, and they all wanted to hear about the famous lawman and shootist. Charley had never begrudged Bill his fame, but right now, it was his own ambitions he wanted to talk about. "I brought those wagons up here to Deadwood so that—"

"Do you think it might be possible for you to persuade Mr. Hickok to do an interview with me?"

Charley gritted his teeth and held back the angry response that tried to escape from his mouth. It wouldn't do to call Merrick a dumb shit when he was counting on the newspaperman to help him publicize his new venture.

"I'll talk to Bill, but I don't think he wants to be fussed over," Charley said. "He just came to Deadwood to look for gold, like most of the other gents up here. *I* came to start a business that'll be a real boon to the town. To the whole area, really."

"You're talking about your freight line and mail delivery service?"

Charley stared in surprise. "You've already heard about it?"

"Of course. You told everyone in the Bella Union about it last night, and it's my job to keep my ear to the ground, so to speak." Merrick turned his pad of paper so that Charley could see what he had written on it. "I've already made some notes for a story."

"Oh." That took some of the wind out of Charley's sails. He recovered quickly, though. "I'll bet you don't know what I've decided to call the mail service."

"As a matter of fact, I don't." Merrick poised his pencil. "Why don't you tell me?"

"I'm goin' to call it . . ." Charley spread his hands and said dramatically, "The Pioneer Pony Express!"

Merrick looked across the table at him with a slight frown. "I thought the Pony Express was what Russell, Majors, and Waddell called their horseback mail service, back before the war."

"Well, I reckon it was," Charley said as he struggled again to keep his composure. "But this is entirely different. This is the *Pioneer* Pony Express." He leaned forward. "Like your newspaper is the *Black Hills Pioneer*."

Merrick's frown deepened. "You're not trying to imply that there's some connection between your enterprise and my newspaper, are you? Because I'm not sure that would be at all proper. . . ."

Charley thought again about calling Merrick a dumb shit, because the newspaperman seemed determined to misunderstand what Charley was trying to tell him, but again he reined in his temper.

"No, I'm not sayin' there's any connection. It just seemed to me that would be a good name, because everybody up here in Deadwood is a pioneer in one way or another. Hell, this whole country is a nation o' pioneers, ain't it? Ain't we all got the pioneerin' spirit? Why, one of the fellas who's gonna ride for my Pioneer Pony Express is none other than Dick Seymour himself."

"Who?"

"Dick Seymour. He's a famous frontiersman, used to be a buffalo hunter and an Indian trader. . . ." Charley looked over his shoulder, intending to call Dick over to the table so that he could introduce him to Merrick. He had fetched Dick from the tent Dick was sharing with the Street brothers and brought him over to the hotel for that very purpose.

But Dick was nowhere to be seen. Charley muttered, "Son of a bitch," under his breath. He would have sworn that Dick was right behind him when they came into the hotel. He should have noticed before now that the Englishman was gone.

"Well, he ain't here right now, but I'll introduce him to you later," Charley said in an attempt to recover. "He's gonna be my lead rider, and he's a fascinatin' gent. He's British, you know."

"No, I didn't know that," Merrick said.

"Really interestin' hombre." Charley hoped that was true, and hoped as well that Dick would open his goddamn mouth for a change and say a goddamn word or two when Merrick talked to him. Charley had never seen anybody who talked less about themselves than Bloody Dick Seymour.

The blond waiter gal brought their coffee then, and Charley spent several more minutes telling Merrick about how he was going to set up a freight line between Cheyenne and Deadwood in addition to having mail riders galloping back and forth between the settlements. Deadwood was an outlaw town in a way, since the Black Hills, the Paha Sapa in the Sioux language, belonged to the Indians by treaty and was regarded by them as a sacred place. But once the Utter Brothers Freight Line and the Pioneer Pony Express were established, Deadwood would become a true bastion of civilization in the wilderness, Charley enthused. Hell, it would be almost like living in a real city, like St. Louis or Chicago or Philadelphia.

Merrick was starting to look vaguely bored, but then a footstep sounded in the hotel lobby and when the newspaperman glanced over to see who was entering the dining room, he brightened right away. He stood up, practically bouncing out of his chair, and said, "Mr. Hickok, sir! Over here!" Merrick waved a hand toward Charley. "I was just having a fascinating conversation with your friend Mr. Utter."

Charley took a deep breath as Bill strolled across the room toward them, so tall and handsome even though he wasn't dressed half as nice as Charley was. Every eye in the room just naturally went right to him like iron filings to a magnet. That Scandahoovian waiter gal even clasped her hands together and pressed them against her big tits like she was so excited to see Wild Bill that she couldn't hardly stand it. Charley let his breath out in a sigh.

If he didn't like Bill so much, it would sure be easy to hate the big fucking galoot.

DICK Seymour sat down on the edge of the boardwalk, careful to keep his boots out of a puddle of horse piss. He took off his hat and held it in one hand while he used the ball of the other hand to rub his eyes as hard as he could. He hadn't slept well—his dreams had been haunted by all-too-vivid images, both good and bad, as they often were— and his eyeballs felt gritty, as if they had been taken out of their sockets, rolled around in some sand, and then popped back in his head. He yawned.

Footsteps came along the boardwalk toward him and then stopped behind him. Dick didn't look around, not really caring who was there. He didn't have any enemies who were likely to shoot him in the back, at least as far as he knew.

Whoever it was stepped to the edge of the boardwalk and then sat down beside him and said, "Mornin'."

Dick looked over and saw a slender young man several years his junior. The newcomer was fairly undistinguished except for one feature: His left eyebrow was pure white, instead of brown like the other eyebrow and the thick shock of hair under the young man's pushed-back hat. He had come to Deadwood with the wagon train from Cheyenne and his name was Jack Anderson, variously known as White-Eye Jack and the White-Eyed Kid. These Westerners displayed such stunning originality in bestowing nicknames on each other.

"Good morning," Dick said, although in his opinion it was anything but. He and Jack had become friends in Cheyenne because of their mutual acquaintance with Bill Hickok and Charley Utter. The least he could do was to be civil even though he felt like shit.

"I got drunk last night," Jack said, somewhat unnecessarily since Dick had seen him come staggering out of the

Bella Union. During the trip from Cheyenne, Jack had become smitten with one of the prostitutes bound for new jobs in Deadwood. The romance had come to a bad end, as they so often did. "It didn't do no good, though."

"It never does," Dick said. "If it did, I would have provided several small fortunes for various distilleries in my time. The best it can do is to provide a small measure of temporary forgetfulness."

"Yeah, but then it wears off and you remember again."

"And that, of course, is one of the great tragedies of this thing we call life."

The White-Eyed Kid looked over at him. "You know, Dick, sometimes you sound like you ought to be an actor. There's a theater down the street. Maybe you ought to forget about ridin' for Charley Utter and go see about gettin' a job there."

"If you're talking about the Gem, it's not a real theater. I've heard enough about it to know that it's just another saloon and brothel, despite its name."

Jack shook his head. "No, I think this place I saw is a real theater. Leastways, it had a sign in front of it sayin' that they put on plays there. It's just a big tent, but it looks like they're puttin' up a permanent building beside it. Fella name of Langrishe owns it."

For the first time in quite a while, Dick felt a tingle of real interest. "Is that so?" he murmured. "I might just investigate that."

There are more things in heaven and earth, Horatio, than are dreamt of in your philosophy. . . .

Just like that, he was trodding the boards again, the familiar words echoing in his brain. Just as quickly, he tore himself from the past to the present, reminding himself that memory was not only man's greatest blessing but also his greatest damnation as well. Memory tortured a man with the good things he no longer had, and all the bad things that could never be changed.

"What are you doin' sittin' in front of the hotel?" the Kid asked.

"Colorado Charley dragged me over here," Dick

replied. "He's inside talking to the editor of the local newspaper, no doubt trying to boost his business enterprises and finagle some free publicity out of the ink-stained wretch."

"Yeah, Mr. Utter's a big talker, all right," Jack agreed with a laugh. "I reckon he can make good on most of his boasts, though. Not everybody can say that."

That was certainly the truth. Boasts were all too often hollow, especially when a man was talking to a woman. Promises of love everlasting and security and happiness . . . They were not promises at all but rather empty lies, bound to cause disillusionment and disappointment and sometimes even death.

The Kid slapped Dick on the shoulder and said, "Well, hell, no point in us sittin' here all day and mopin'. What say we go get a drink, even if it won't do a damn bit of good?"

"Jack, that sounds like an excellent idea," Dick said with a smile that never reached his eyes.

Chapter Three

"**G**ET your ass outta bed!" A hand came down on a bare rump with a resounding crack. "I ain't payin' you to lay around and sleep the whole fuckin' day."

The girl called Jen buried her face in the pillow and moaned. She hurt all over, especially both orifices in what delicate folks would call her nether regions. Al Swearengen, the man she now worked for, had fucked her repeatedly in both the pussy and the ass, and he hadn't been gentle about it, either. She was used to fellas getting a little rough from time to time when they bedded her, but there had been something different about the way Swearengen took her. He had displayed a gleeful brutality that told her he enjoyed hurting her.

But she had been assured that she could make quite a bit of money working at the Gem Theater, and hell, that was why she was here, wasn't it? Like everybody else, she had come to Deadwood to make her fortune, only she would find hers in a nice soft bed instead of having to grub it out of the earth.

"Are you gettin' up?" Swearengen asked, his voice dangerously quiet.

Jen rolled over and swung her legs out of the bed. "Yes,

I'm gettin' up," she said as she stood up. She stood there naked and stretched her arms over her head. She felt Swearengen's eyes on her and knew she looked mighty nice. Her ass wasn't too wide, and even though her breasts were a little on the small side, they were firm and rounded like ripe apples. They looked even better when her arms were up like this. She kept her arms lifted and ran her fingers through the long brown hair that hung halfway down her back. Swearengen stepped closer to her, his eyes burning with what she took to be lust, and she smiled at him. Maybe he wanted one more go-round before the day got started good.

His hand came up so fast she could barely see it, but she sure as hell felt it as it smacked her across the face and knocked her down. She fell half on the bed and half on the floor. Her feet slipped on the boards and she slid the rest of the way to the floor to lie there huddled with her hands pressed to her face where he had hit her. It hurt like blazes.

"Don't you sass me," he said. "If you don't learn anything else, you dumb cunt, you better learn that. Understand?"

Jen was still too stunned to reply. She just lay there quivering as Swearengen stood over her in his long underwear, his black hair disheveled and his face dark with rage.

But she was alert enough to see him draw back his foot and knew he was about to kick her. She thrust up her hands in supplication and babbled, "Please don't. Please don't. I understand. I really do. I swear. I won't sass you, Mr. Swearengen."

He sniffed and said, "Better not. You're a pretty little thing. I'd hate to have to mark you up so's you won't fetch as good a price from the customers."

"I'll behave. I swear I'll behave."

Swearengen rasped his hands over his beard-stubbled cheeks and then reached down to unfasten the buttons on his long underwear. He hauled out his half-erect penis and said meaningfully, "As long as you're down there anyway . . ."

Jen scrambled to her knees in front of him, ignoring the stinging pain where he had slapped her, and leaned in to do what he wanted. He rested both hands on her head as she worked on him. His fingers twisted in her hair. It hurt, but not too bad.

That was all a girl like her could hope for out of life, wasn't it? To hurt, but not too bad?

WHEN Swearengen had had his fill of the new whore, he got dressed and went downstairs to the big main room of the Gem Theater. Despite it being the middle of the day, the place was busy. Most of the miners were out working their claims, which were scattered up and down the gulch, but there were plenty of other men in Deadwood who might want a drink and a little female companionship. Freighters, store clerks, cooks, blacksmiths, lawyers, doctors . . . It took a lot of men to keep a settlement going, and all of them got thirsty or horny at least once a day. Those natural tendencies were well on their way to making Al Swearengen a rich man.

He thought about Jen as he walked down the stairs. She was pretty, no doubt about that, and she was a good lay. A little too talkative, maybe. While he was humping away on her the night before, she had told him all about how her mama had been a whore and how she had grown up in various houses, remaining untouched until she was fourteen, when she had gone to work. That was only four years earlier, so she wasn't used up yet. Swearengen didn't give a shit about any whore's life story, so he hadn't paid much attention to what she was saying and had concentrated instead on fucking her, but damned if those details hadn't stuck in his mind for some reason.

He wasn't going to let himself get fond of her. That never worked out, he told himself sternly. The girls who worked for him were just commodities, nothing more.

When Swearengen reached the bottom of the stairs, he went over to the bar. His head bartender and second in command, Dan Dority, drifted over and gave him a nod across the hardwood. "Want a drink, Al?" Dority asked.

"Of course I want a drink," Swearengen snapped. Dority was a dumbass sometimes, but he always did what he was told. He was one of the few men on the face of the earth who could cause Swearengen to rein in his otherwise all-encompassing wrath at the sorry state of humankind. It wouldn't do to call Dan a dumbass, even if it was true.

Dority got a clean glass and a bottle from under the bar. What was in the bottle was the real thing, Scotch whiskey freighted in at considerable expense instead of the homemade rotgut that most of the Gem's customers cheerfully guzzled down even though too much of the stuff would give a man the blind staggers. Dority poured the drink and pushed it across the bar. Swearengen picked up the glass and gratefully emptied it.

"What'd you think of that new whore you took upstairs last night?" Dority asked, making conversation.

"Not bad," Swearengen replied with a nod. "She's got a bit of a mouth on her."

Dority grinned. "That ain't always a bad thing. Sort of depends on how she uses it, don't it?"

Swearengen just grunted and shoved the empty glass back across the bar. Dority refilled it.

To fill the silence, Dority went on. "I hear Carla's funeral was this mornin'."

"So?"

The bartender shrugged. "So nothin'. I was just a mite surprised you didn't go to the buryin'."

Swearengen frowned and said, "Why the hell would I do that?"

"Well, I don't know. I just recollect how you was a little sweet on her when she used to work here—"

Swearengen's mouth twisted in a grimace as his hand shot out, reaching across the bar to grab hold of Dority's shirt. He jerked the man hard against the bar and leaned in close to him to say in a breathy snarl, "I don't get sweet on whores. You understand?"

Dority's normally florid face paled as he swallowed nervously. "S-sure, Al, I understand. I didn't mean nothin' by it—"

"Carla made her own choice to leave here and go to work for that redheaded bitch across the street. I don't give a fuck that she's dead. I hope she's burnin' in hell right now." Swearengen's voice dropped even more as he went on. "And if you ever bring up her name again, I'll cut your balls off and feed them to you. You got that, Dan?"

"Yeah. Yeah, Al, I got it. I'm sorry."

Swearengen let go of the shirtfront he had crumpled in his fist. He smoothed down the shirt and gave it a little pat. Maybe he had reacted a little too strongly to Dority's comments. But he wasn't going to apologize. Damned if he would. Apologizing was for weaklings, and nobody could ever accuse Al Swearengen of being weak.

He picked up the drink and turned to stroll over to the window that looked out on Deadwood's Main Street. Almost directly across the way was that particularly irritating thorn in Swearengen's side, Miss Laurette's Academy for Young Ladies. The whorehouse sat between Nuttall and Mann's No. Ten Saloon on the west and the Bella Union Saloon, also owned by Billy Nuttall, to the east. Wall Street, which crossed Main one block west, was a dividing line of sorts. East of Wall were the Badlands, the saloons and gambling dens and houses of prostitution. West of Wall Street was the more respectable part of Deadwood, where the so-called legitimate businesses were located.

The men who lived and worked on the good side of town never hesitated to cross that invisible boundary, however. Some of them who had families had to be a little more discreet about it, but still they came and spent their money, and Al Swearengen and the other entrepreneurs of the Badlands gladly took it.

Swearengen's eyes narrowed as he stared across the street at the Parkhurst woman's place. He hated that redheaded bitch with a passion, even though she hadn't really tried to lure Carla away. It was more a case of Carla growing tired of how she was being treated at the Gem and leaving on her own. She had wound up at the Academy, and in the end it had gotten her killed.

Good riddance, Swearengen thought. Good riddance to

bad rubbish, as the old saying went. His fingers tightened on the glass they held until he realized that if he squeezed it any harder, it might break and cut his hand. A little shiver went through him. He tossed back the drink and then turned away from the window.

He noticed a stranger standing at the bar. Strangers were nothing unusual in Deadwood, which not long before had literally been a city of strangers. This one wore a decent suit and a gray hat. He had dark hair and a mustache like Swearengen, but he was slender as a reed while the saloon-keeper was stocky. Giving in to his curiosity, Swearengen went over to him and said, "Howdy."

The man turned his head and gave Swearengen a brief nod. There was a scar on his jaw, not too prominent but still hard to miss seeing. He turned his attention back to the drink in his hand.

That fleeting glance had been enough. Swearengen had seen the stranger's eyes, and he had seen madness in them.

More than once in his life, Swearengen had wondered if he might be a little mad himself. Surely, it wasn't completely normal for a man to be so angered and disillusioned and thoroughly disgusted by everyone and everything that went on around him. Swearengen knew he could be ruthless and, yes, even evil, if such a thing really existed.

But he had never seen anything in the mirror that was quite so cold and soulless as what he had seen peering out of this stranger's pale blue eyes. Swearengen liked to think that he was a man who felt no fear, yet for an instant the urge was strong in him to go upstairs to his office, lock the door, sit behind the desk, and hold a gun in his hand.

With a tightening of his jaw, Swearengen tried to banish that reaction. He wasn't afraid of anybody, he told himself. And to prove it, he said to the stranger, "My name is Al Swearengen. This is my place."

"Not a bad place," the stranger murmured. He had a half-empty drink in front of him. He toyed with it, moving the glass around so that its wet bottom left interlocking rings on the hardwood. He used his left hand to do it. The right hung at his side, motionless. Swearengen knew it would be within easy reach of the gun holstered on the stranger's hip.

"What's your name?" Swearengen demanded. If he had to bluster, then by God, he'd bluster.

For a second, he thought the stranger wasn't going to answer. That would force the issue. Whether the man was insane or not, Swearengen couldn't allow anybody to defy him in his own place.

But then the stranger tossed back his drink and said quietly, "Levy. Jim Levy."

Swearengen blinked and said, "Oh."

He had heard of Jim Levy, of course. The man was a gambler and gunman, and rumor had it that no one was faster on the draw, not even that bastard Hickok. A few years earlier at Pioche, a mining camp down in Nevada, Jim Levy had killed a man named Casey in a gunfight. One of Casey's enemies had put a bounty on his head, and Levy had set out to collect it. His first shot in the fracas had put Casey down on the ground, but instead of shooting him again, Levy had walked up to the man and started beating his brains out with a pistol. Somebody in the inevitable crowd had taken offense at such barbaric behavior and shot Levy in the jaw. That gesture had come too late to save Casey's life, though.

A man had to be a little crazy to start whaling on somebody with a pistol in the middle of the street. Getting wounded in the jaw like that must have made Levy even more unbalanced. He took offense easily and went for his gun with little or no provocation. Swearengen had no idea how many men Levy had killed. Several, that was for sure.

And now he was here in the Gem Theater, having a drink just as pretty as you please.

All those thoughts rushed through Swearengen's head in the momentary pause after Levy introduced himself. Then, to show he wasn't intimidated, Swearengen said brusquely, "I don't allow any trouble in my place."

"I don't intend to start any," Levy said.

"Well . . . good." Swearengen snapped his fingers to get

Dan Dority's attention, pointed to the empty glass in front of Levy, and nodded. "Have a drink," he said to Levy. "On the house."

Levy didn't look at him, just said, "Obliged."

Swearengen was trying to figure out what to say next, if anything, when he heard a commotion in the street. The doors of the Gem were open because of the summer heat, so it was easy to hear what went on outside. Someone was yelling about dens of iniquity and smiting the wicked.

Only one person that could be, thought Swearengen as he swung around and strode toward the doors. That fuckin' preacher.

Sure enough, the tall, skinny Reverend H. W. Smith had plopped a box down in the mud and shit and piss of the street, right in front of the Gem, and climbed on top of it. He waved around a Bible as he exhorted the citizens of Deadwood to run the evildoers out of town, just as Our Lord and Savior had driven the moneylenders from the temple back yonder in Jerusalem. Not many people paid any attention to him.

But a few did. Instead of ignoring him and hurrying on past to go about their business, a few men actually stopped and looked up at the preacher and *listened* to him.

That was a few too many. Those bastards might have been on their way to the Gem for a drink and some pussy. Now they were being delayed. Worse yet, they might listen to the preacher for a while and decide not to come in at all.

Swearengen stepped onto the boardwalk and yelled, "Hey! Preacher!"

Smith paused in his harangue and looked over at Swearengen. A big smile creased his face. To the preacher, there was nothing personal about his sin-shouting. He always had a friendly smile for everyone, even the idolaters and fornicators and whoremongers.

"Do you have to do that right there?" Swearengen demanded.

"I have to go where the Lord's work leads me, Brother Swearengen," Smith answered.

"Why don't you go across the street and badger the poor

bastards going into the Bella Union, or that Parkhurst woman's place?"

"There's plenty of sin to go around, Brother Swearengen. All in good time, my friend, all in good time."

Swearengen clenched his fists and rolled his eyes to Heaven, not that anybody who lived Up There would ever have any answers for the likes of him. If he'd had a gun on him at that moment, he might have hauled it out and shot the damn fool preacher right off that box.

All he had was a knife, though, and he didn't think he could get away with stomping out there into the street and cutting the son of a bitch into little pieces, not in broad daylight, not even in Deadwood.

Maybe there was another approach that would work. . . . "Preacher, I'd be glad to make a donation to your cause. Would that get you to move on?"

"Your donation would be gratefully accepted, Brother. The Lord can always find a good use for funds, no matter what the source."

Swearengen drew a deep breath. Now the bastard was insulting him. *"No matter what the source"!* Jesus!

"But I have to do the work I'm led to do," the preacher went on, his voice gentle despite its depth and carrying power. "I'm sure you understand."

"I understand, all right," Swearengen said, and added silently, *you bastard!* He turned away and stalked back into the saloon before he lost his temper.

And then he stopped short as his angry gaze fell on the slender stranger standing at the bar.

Jim Levy was in Deadwood, and maybe he was the answer to at least one of Al Swearengen's problems. Swearengen nodded slowly. He would have to do some thinking on this.

Chapter Four

"**I** hear that Calamity Jane has also arrived in our midst," A. W. Merrick said as he sat at the table in the Grand Central Hotel dining room with Wild Bill Hickok and Colorado Charley Utter. Hickok had taken a chair so that his back was turned toward a corner of the room and he could see the entrance from the hotel lobby.

"That's right," Hickok replied. "She came in with the wagon train after joining our little company at Fort Laramie."

Merrick made a note on his pad. "Is she as rowdy and rambunctious as all the stories about her claim?"

"You wouldn't want me to speak ill of a lady, would you, Mr. Merrick?" Hickok answered.

"She's a character, sure enough," Charley put in. "You can write that down and put it in your paper."

"I'll do that," Merrick promised, scribbling away. He paused and looked up to fix an intent gaze on Hickok. "Now to get down to more serious business. Is it true that you've come to Deadwood to establish law and order, just as you did in Abilene and Dodge City, Mr. Hickok?"

His eyes narrowing, Hickok didn't respond to the question, but in a sharp tone asked one of his own instead. "Who told you that?"

Merrick waved a hand to encompass their surroundings and said in a surprised tone, "Why, it's all over town. Everyone is talking about it, sir."

"Well, everyone is full of shit." Hickok tapped a long, strong finger on the newspaperman's pad. "Don't write that down."

Merrick shook his head, indicating that he wouldn't.

"You don't see a badge pinned to my coat, do you, Mr. Merrick?" Hickok went on.

"No, but—"

"I didn't come to Deadwood to wear one, either. You may not be aware of this, but I'm a relative newlywed."

"Yes, of course. I read that several months ago you were married to Mrs. Agnes Lake Thatcher. She used to own a circus, is that correct?"

Hickok nodded. "Yes, but financial reverses forced her to sell it. Can I be completely truthful with you, Mr. Merrick?"

"Of course," the newspaperman said eagerly.

"I came to Deadwood for the same reason as most of the pilgrims who have journeyed here. I need money, and I hope to find gold."

"Prospecting? That's the only reason?" Merrick sounded like he couldn't believe it.

"That's right."

"But surely you're aware that the legitimate business interests in town could be persuaded to offer you a position as marshal? A well-paying position, I might add."

"I offered to let him in on my freight line and the Pioneer Pony Express," Charley put in, "but he wasn't havin' none of it."

Hickok shook his head. "I'm a simple man. No offense, but it's the newspapermen and dime novelists who make me out to be a whole heap more complicated than I really am. I never wanted any more than to just do whatever job I set out to do and to be treated with simple dignity and respect along the way. Right now, my job is to find gold, and to that end, I have to start looking around for a promising claim."

"In that case," Merrick said, "that man who just came into the dining room is someone you should talk to."

Hickok had already noted the newcomer, as he always was aware of anyone entering a room where he was. The man was dressed in a sober suit and was rather short and solidly built, with graying sandy hair and a full mustache of the same shade. Merrick raised a hand to get his attention and said, "General! Over here."

The man came to the table, and Merrick went on. "General, allow me to present Mr. Hickok and Mr. Utter. Gentlemen, this is General Dawson, the local representative of the federal government."

"The government?" Charley repeated in surprise. "I thought the folks back in Washington didn't want to admit that Deadwood even exists."

General Dawson shook hands with Hickok and Charley and then said, "I've been appointed as the collector of federal revenues for this area."

"Tax collector, eh?" said Hickok. He gestured toward the empty chair. "It figures that the politicians would want to get their share of the pie, even if it's being baked illegally."

Dawson chuckled and said, "I couldn't have phrased it better, or more accurately, myself, Mr. Hickok." He sat down.

"Mr. Hickok says that he's come to Deadwood to search for gold," Merrick said. "That sort of plays hob with your plan, General."

Dawson gave Hickok a disappointed look. "Really?"

Hickok nodded solemnly and said, "Really."

"I had it in mind that perhaps you could be persuaded to take a position as town marshal. You may not be aware of it, but we average more than one murder each and every day here in Deadwood. The lawless elements hold sway in one whole end of the settlement, and their influence is felt everywhere. There are plenty of honest, hardworking people here already, but until someone establishes some law and order, their lives and property will continue to be at risk."

"I sympathize with you, sir, but my star-packing days are over."

The General sighed. "Well, I won't try to browbeat a

man into doing something he doesn't want to do. We'll find someone else to take the job of marshal. In the meantime, if there's anything I can do for you . . ."

"I'm looking for a good gold claim," Hickok said. "Mr. Merrick here seems to think you might be able to give me a lead on one."

"Of course. It won't be the first time I've steered a newcomer to a possible claim. Let me think on it and ask around town, and I'll let you know what I find out."

"Fair enough," Hickok said with a nod. "I'm obliged."

"But if you change your mind about that lawman's job . . ."

"I won't," Hickok said.

THE preacher was really telling it. Calamity stood on the boardwalk and watched him waving his arms around like he was some kind of big-ass bird while he yelled at folks not to go into the Gem Theater. Calamity was a little drunk—she'd gotten into a poker game at one of the dives in the Badlands and won enough for a bottle of Who-Hit-John, half of which was now warming her belly—but she was still thinking clearly enough to understand that the preacher was saying folks hadn't ought to go around drinking and fucking. That was just crazy, of course. If people didn't drink and fuck, how the hell were they supposed to spend their time?

With a shake of her head that made her dizzy enough to stagger a little, Calamity started up the boardwalk. She crossed Wall Street and Gold Street, tromping heedlessly through the vile puddles that dotted the road, and walked past a half-constructed building with a sign in front that said it was going to be an opera house when it was finished. That put her on the porch of the Grand Central Hotel just as the front doors opened and four men came out, talking among themselves.

"Bill!" she exclaimed as she recognized the tallest and most handsome of the men. "There you are! I been lookin' all over for you."

Wild Bill stopped short, and for a second Calamity

thought his eyes looked a little wild, like the eyes of a horse that was about to bolt. But he controlled himself, touched a finger to the brim of his hat, and said politely, "Calamity."

When would he get it through his head that she didn't want him to be polite to her? She didn't care about all that shit. She just wanted him to pull her buckskins off and spread her and ride her. She'd give him a gallop he'd never forget, damn right she would.

She couldn't come right out and say that, though, in front of Charley Utter and the other two gents who were with him and Wild Bill. She didn't know either of them, or if she did, she had forgotten who they were. Both of them wore suits and looked like tight-ass pricks.

The taller, beefier one took a step forward and said, "Miss Martha Jane Cannary, I believe?"

"That's who I am," she said. "Who the hell are you?"

"So you're the notorious Calamity Jane?"

"That's what I just said, ain't it?" She moved a hand toward the butt of the revolver on her hip. "You want me to prove how calamitous I can be, just say the word, you stuffed-shirt son of a—"

Wild Bill moved smoothly between them and said, "No need for that, Calam. This is Mr. Merrick. He writes and publishes the local paper, the *Black Hills Pioneer.*"

"Oh, a newspaperman." That changed everything. Calamity had been written about in the newspapers before, and she liked it. "Sorry," she said to Merrick. "I didn't mean to nearly call you a stuffed-shirt son of a bitch."

"That's, ah, quite all right," he said. "I was thinking about inserting a brief notice in the next edition of the paper informing the citizens that you have arrived in Deadwood, Miss Cannary. Would you like to comment? Anything you'd like to say to the people of Deadwood?"

"Just that they got themselves a fine fuckin' town, except for the parts that are already goin' to shit. But hell, that's true anywhere, ain't it?"

"I, uh, suppose so." Merrick gave her a pained smile. "Thank you for your cooperation, Miss Cannary."

"Any fuckin' time." Since Wild Bill was standing right

beside her, she reached out and took hold of his arm before he could get away. "You ready to go look for gold, Bill?"

"I wasn't aware that we were going to be partners in prospecting, Calam."

"Well, why not? You think I can't pan for gold?"

"I'm sure you can, but I tend to work better alone."

Calamity snorted. "Hell, there's lot of things you can do alone that're a whole lot better when you do 'em with somebody else, if you know what I mean."

"I certainly do." Somehow Wild Bill got his arm loose from her grip without her quite knowing what had happened. "Right now, though, I see someone else I have to talk to."

She didn't want to let him go, but she didn't figure it would do any good to argue. Once Wild Bill Hickok made up his mind about something, he was one stubborn bastard.

"All right, but we'll talk about it later," Calamity said.

Bill tipped his hat again. "Of course." Then he said to Charley Utter, "Come on, Charley, there's White-Eye Jack and Dick Seymour. You have Pony Express matters to discuss with them, don't you?"

"Uh, yeah, I sure do, Bill," Charley said. He added to Merrick and the other fella, "So long, gents. If you want to know any more about the Utter Brothers Freight Line and the Pioneer Pony Express, Mr. Merrick, you just look me up. Be glad to talk about it, any time."

With that, Wild Bill and Colorado Charley hurried off down the street, leaving Calamity standing there with the two well-dressed ginks. She sensed their disapproval and turned away without saying another word. She pulled the half-empty bottle of whiskey from the pocket of her buckskin trousers and uncorked it to take a swig. She knew where she wasn't wanted. She would just go back down to the other end of town, where she fit in better.

Folks would look at her a lot different if she was Wild Bill Hickok's woman. A thing like that could make all the difference in the world. People would look at her with respect if they saw her on Wild Bill's arm.

One of these days, she told herself. One of these days.

* * *

DICK Seymour felt a little better. The White-Eyed Kid was a boon companion, and they had shared drinks and commiseration in the No. Ten. Now, somewhat fortified by that experience, the two young men stepped out of the saloon and looked around to see what else Deadwood might have in store for them. They had barely started to take stock of the situation, however, when Dick heard his name called.

He turned and saw Bill Hickok and Charley Utter coming toward him and Jack. The legendary frontiersman said, "Howdy, boys," as he and Charley joined them. "What are you up to today?"

"Just havin' a drink," Jack said as he inclined his head toward the door of the No. Ten. "Want to go in and have one with us?"

"Maybe later," Charley said. "Bill, I know you was just tryin' to get away from Calamity without makin' a scene, but I really do need to talk to Dick here."

"Go ahead," Bill said magnanimously, with a wave of his hand.

Charley turned to Dick and went on. "I been thinkin' that we're gonna have to *show* folks around here just how much the Pioneer Pony Express is gonna mean to them. I want to gather up a pouch of mail and have you carry it down to Cheyenne for free."

"For free?" Dick frowned. "Wait a moment, Charley—"

"I don't mean you'll have to carry it for free," Charley went on hurriedly. "I'll pay you just like we agreed when you signed on to ride for me. But if folks want to mail a letter, I won't charge 'em for it . . . this time. It'll be like advertising. I'll show 'em how fast and easy it is to send mail by the Pioneer Pony Express, so they'll use it more often in the future. And then they'll have to pay for it."

Dick rubbed his jaw as he thought over the proposition. "It does sound like it might be an effective way of introducing your service," he said, "but we're not ready to start carrying the mail yet, Charley. You don't have way stations set up, and I'd need frequent changes of horses."

"You could stop at the ranches we visited on the trip up here," Charley suggested. "Jack Hunton won't mind swappin' mounts with you, and I reckon you could do the same at Hat Creek and Fort Laramie. That'll make for longer legs between stops, so you wouldn't be able to push your horse quite as fast, but you can still make the trip in good time."

"Well, it might work."

Charley clapped a hand on Dick's shoulder. "Of course it'll work! We'll show 'em, boy! The Pioneer Pony Express is gonna be the biggest thing in the Black Hills."

"I imagine the search for gold will still be the biggest thing around here, Charley," Bill suggested dryly.

"Well, yeah, but other than that, I mean." Charley took off his broad-brimmed hat, pulled a monogrammed handkerchief from the pocket of his fringed buckskin jacket, and mopped the sweat of excitement off his forehead. "I'll start spreadin' the word around town that anybody who wants to send a letter needs to come and see me. Soon as I get a pouch full of mail, off you'll go to Cheyenne, Dick."

"All right," Dick agreed with a nod. He had come up here to be part of Colorado Charley's mail enterprise, and there was no point in delaying the start of the operation. They would just set everything up as they went along, he supposed.

Anyway, work was a good thing, especially hard, dangerous work. Nothing crowded out the bad memories like long, grueling hours in the saddle and the ever-present threat of having his hair lifted by a band of bloodthirsty savages. As he thought about it, Dick realized that a smile was spreading across his face.

God help him, he was actually looking forward to it!

Chapter Five

❦

"COME on, you damn jughead! You ain't got the sense God give a dung beetle!"

Something about the voice struck Bill Hickok as familiar. Charley Utter had scurried off to drum up business for his Pony Express, leaving Hickok alone. He'd found a chair on the boardwalk and sat down to watch life in Deadwood go by. He knew he ought to be busy doing something himself, but it was so much more pleasant just to sit there and drink in the panorama of a summer day in a hurly-burly mining camp.

For another thing, folks were leaving him alone for a change. They were intent on their own business and spared only an occasional glance for the man leaning back in his chair with the ankle of one long leg cocked on the knee of the other leg. That inattention was pleasant, too.

Usually, all eyes were on him. Voices buzzed and whispered. *"Is that him?" "I think it is." "Can't be." "It sure looks like him." "Well, why don't you go up and ask?" "Why don't you, if you want to know so much!"* Hickok heard it all. His eyes might be going back on him a mite, but there was nothing wrong with his ears.

After a while, somebody would edge up to him and ask tentatively if he was Mr. Hickok, and he always nodded solemnly and admitted that he was. Some of them would come right out and ask to shake his hand. Others would try to touch his sleeve or the tail of his coat for luck without him noticing. He always noticed, of course, but he never said anything about it. Let them have their little superstitions. It didn't hurt anything. He had his own eccentricities, after all, such as not sitting where his back was to the door. That had a basis in cautious logic, of course—a man with enemies had to be careful—but it was as much a superstitious habit now as anything else.

Maybe later he wouldn't like it if the novelty of his presence in Deadwood had well and truly worn off, but this momentary respite was welcome.

And then somebody started yelling at a stubborn, balky mule he was trying to lead along the street, and Hickok sat up straight in his chair and looked at the man who'd begun to heap obscene abuse on the animal.

The man was tall, almost as tall as Hickok himself. He had long hair, too, but his was dark and streaked with gray where Hickok's was light brown. He had a mustache and beard and a weathered, strong-featured face dominated by a hawklike nose. His broad-brimmed hat was black, and he wore cavalry trousers tucked into high-topped black boots, a black vest, and a homespun shirt. A heavy revolver was holstered on his right hip, and the handle of a bowie knife jutted up from a sheath on his left hip.

A grin of recognition spread across Hickok's face as he stood up. "Joe!" he called. "California Joe!"

The man stopped berating his mule and turned sharply toward Hickok, who noted that California Joe's hand had dropped close to the butt of his gun. "Who the hell wants to know?" he demanded harshly.

Hickok chuckled. "You won't need that hogleg, Joe. Anyway, I could ventilate you half-a-dozen times before you dragged out that cannon."

"Yeah, but one shot's all it'd take to splatter you all over that boardwalk, mister," Joe called back with a fierce glare on his face. Then the glare dissolved into a grin, and he went on. "Well, I'll be hornswoggled! Bill Hickok, as I live and breathe!"

Hickok stepped down off the boardwalk, and the two frontiersmen embraced, slapping each other on the back with such force that smaller, weaker men probably would have been knocked off their feet. With them standing together like that, their similarities were more pronounced than their differences.

One similarity that wasn't visible was that both men had worked as scouts for General George Armstrong Custer. California Joe, in fact, had been Custer's chief of scouts and had led Colonel Dodge's expedition into the Black Hills a year earlier. Hickok remembered that and said, "Let me guess. You quit working for the Army and decided to get rich hunting for gold."

"Damn right!" California Joe said. "Either that, or start some sort o' business. Like I told Colonel Dodge when we was up here before, there's gold from the grassroots down, but there's *more* gold from the grassroots up!"

Hickok threw back his head and laughed. "Say what you will, Joe, I just can't picture you wearing an apron and standing behind the counter of a store."

Joe scratched his beard. "No, to tell you the truth, Bill, I can't hardly see that, neither."

After the adventurous life California Joe had led, just the thought of him clerking in a store was indeed laughable. He had gone west from his home in Kentucky when gold was discovered in California and had been part of every gold rush since then, so Hickok wasn't surprised to see him here in Deadwood. In between hunting for gold, Joe, who had been born Moses Milner but who had long since stopped using that name, had worked as a fur trapper and teamster, had fought Blackfoot and Sioux, had scouted for the Army and partnered up for a while with Kit Carson. He was colorful enough, and had lived through so many dangerous exploits, that Hickok thought the dime novelists ought to be churning out yarns about California Joe rather than Wild Bill. They would probably get around to Joe as the subject matter for some lurid, yellow-backed tales sooner or later.

"What are you doin' here, Bill?" the lanky frontiersman asked. "You come to establish law an' order in Deadwood?"

Hickok tried not to sigh. Joe couldn't be blamed for thinking such a thing.

"No, I came here for the same reason you did," he said. "I plan to look for gold."

"Wild Bill Hickok, prospectin'?" Joe shook his head. "That don't hardly seem right, neither."

"The days of Bill being wild have come and gone, old friend."

Joe snorted in disbelief. "That'll be the day!" He frowned in thought. "But if you're serious about prospectin', I'm lookin' for a claim myself. Maybe we ought to go in together. No thievin' scoundrel would ever try to jump a claim bein' worked by Bill Hickok, that's for damn sure!"

The idea was intriguing. Hickok liked and respected California Joe. He didn't know how well they would get along working side by side, though. Joe was stubborn and opinionated—sort of like Hickok himself.

"Let me think about it," he said. "I'll tell you my decision in a day or so."

"Fair enough," Joe agreed with a nod. "In the meantime, what say we go have ourselves a drink?"

Hickok smiled. "That sounds like a mighty fine idea."

"Just one thing." Joe turned toward his mule and reached for the gun on his hip. "Let me shoot this rock-headed son of a bitch first."

"No point in killing a perfectly good mule." Hickok reached for the reins. "Let me try."

"All right, but you're in for a trial. I never saw such a stubborn four-legged critter."

Hickok tugged on the reins, and the mule came with him without hesitation. California Joe stared for a second and then burst out laughing again.

"That's Wild Bill Hickok for you," he said. "Even the dumb brutes don't want to cross you, Bill!"

*   *   *

THE man who had come out of Nuttall and Mann's No. Ten Saloon a few minutes earlier stood there and watched Hickok and the stranger called Joe walk away with Hickok leading the mule. Taking out a thin black cigarillo, the man struck a match and lit it, puffing out a cloud of smoke. He was tall and thin, almost cadaverous, and wore a gray suit and a black silk hat. A pointed black beard adorned his chin, giving him a vaguely satanic look that he in fact cultivated. The fingers that shook out the match and then dropped it in the street were long, slender, and supple. A gambler's fingers. That was appropriate, since the man made his living with the pasteboards. His name, or at least the name he currently went by, was Johnny Varnes.

And he didn't believe Wild Bill Hickok, not at all.

It was too much to expect that a living legend like Hickok would settle down and be satisfied to toil with his hands like a common man, seeking to wrest riches from the hard, rocky ground of Deadwood Gulch. Even if Hickok was sincere when he professed that aim, Varnes knew that sooner or later such mundane labor would wear on him to the point that he would give it up.

When he did, the so-called respectable folks of Deadwood would be right there waiting for him, holding out a badge and offering him money and power. And he would accept the offer, as he had in Abilene. Varnes was certain of that, and he had learned never to disregard his hunches.

Once Hickok was the marshal, it was inevitable that he would try to clean up the settlement. Given his record as a lawman, it was highly likely that he would be successful in this effort. Varnes's teeth clamped down hard on the cigarillo as he thought about what it would be like to be run out of Deadwood by Wild Bill Hickok. He had plied his trade as a gambler in many towns and settlements throughout the West; nowhere, though, had he cleaned up as much as he had here in Deadwood. A man with the slightest amount of skill with cards had a virtual license to print money here. And Johnny Varnes's skill was much more than slight.

Something had to be done. Deadwood was a fucking golden goose, and he was damned if he was going to let Wild Bill Hickok ruin it.

He turned and started to go back into the No. Ten, but then he stopped and frowned. Billy Nuttall and Carl Mann, the owners of the saloon, prided themselves on being straight shooters. Their bartender, Harry Sam Young, was the same way. Likely, none of them would want anything to do with Johnny Varnes, other than being willing to take his money when he bought a drink.

Next door, though, was Miss Laurette's Academy for Young Ladies, and from what Varnes had seen of Miss Laurette, she struck him as the sort of woman who would do just about anything to get what she wanted.

He went into the whorehouse and was greeted by a Chinese girl. The Celestial was slim and elegant in a shift that was unlaced most of the way down the front, so that her nipples peeked out coyly from it whenever she moved and then ducked back into hiding. She was very pretty, with long, straight black hair, but the paint on her face failed to completely conceal the bruises there. Varnes recalled that there had been some sort of brawl in here a few days earlier. The place had gotten busted up, and so had some of the girls.

The Chinese girl was the only one in the parlor. She smiled at Varnes and asked, "You want fuckee Ling? T'ree dolla'."

He reached out, pushed aside the shift, and filled his hand with one of her firm breasts. He rubbed the nipple with his thumb and made it hard. "I would very much like to fuckee Ling," he said, "but right now I have more urgent business."

"You want Ling suckee? Fi' dolla'."

Varnes sighed. Why, oh, why did Fate always place such temptation in his path? Telling himself to be strong, he said, "I need to talk to your employer."

"Fuckee Ling ass?"

He held up a hand to stop her before she could quote the going rate for that particular service. It was possible that the girl didn't know how to speak any English except how to list the things she was available to do with the customers. "Miss Laurette," he said firmly. "I need to speak with Miss Laurette."

Ling looked at him but didn't say anything. Varnes sighed in frustration. He was about to repeat what he wanted in a louder tone of voice, even though he knew logically that wouldn't make the Celestial understand him a bit better, when a new voice said, "I'm right here, mister. What can I do for you?"

Varnes turned and saw an attractive, middle-aged redhead he recognized as the owner of the brothel. He took off his hat and said, "Miss Laurette, it's a pleasure and an honor to meet you. My name is John Varnes, and I need to speak to you on a subject of mutual interest."

"If you're looking for pussy, you won't do any better than Ling there. She's nice and tight, and she won't talk your ear off. Unless you happen to speak Chinese, that is, and then she won't shut the fuck up."

Varnes shook his head. "No, I really need to speak with you—"

"I don't go with the customers myself, if that's what you've got in mind."

Varnes finally lost his patience. "Damn it, madam, I want to talk about Wild Bill Hickok!"

Laurette's eyes widened in surprise. "Well, why didn't you say so? Come on back to my office."

She led to the way to a room furnished with a desk and a small bar. Varnes nodded when she asked him if he wanted a drink.

"Now, what's this about Wild Bill Hickok?" Laurette asked when they were seated on opposite sides of the desk, her behind it and him before it, each with a glass of whiskey in hand.

Varnes sipped his drink before replying, and he smiled in appreciation. "Very good, madam, and I say that as a Virginian who knows a thing or two about fine spirits."

Laurette knocked back all the booze in her glass and said, "I don't have time to listen to a bunch of snake oil from some tinhorn. Tell me why you're here, Varnes."

He hung onto his temper with an effort. He wasn't accustomed to being spoken to in such a high-handed manner by anyone, let alone the madam of a frontier whorehouse. Tightly, he said, "I'm certain you're aware that the notorious Wild Bill Hickok is in town."

"How could I miss him? He was standing right there in the street in front of the place yesterday when one of my girls got shot."

"Yes, I witnessed that tragedy myself." Varnes took another sip of the whiskey. "Regrettable, to be sure. But it's also regrettable that your livelihood, as well as mine and that of everyone else in the Badlands, is threatened."

"What the hell are you talking about, gambler?"

Reining in his impatience, Varnes leaned forward and said, "It's only a matter of time until Hickok pins on a badge and tries to run us all out of town. The respectable elements in Deadwood will insist on it."

Laurette frowned and shook her head. "Even when he was the marshal in Abilene, he didn't close down all the saloons and run out all the whores and gamblers," she said. "He just kept order."

Varnes snorted. "You might want to ask Phil Coe about that. You can't, though. He's dead. Hickok shot him down like a dog. I was there that night, too."

"You really think he might try to clean up Deadwood?" Laurette asked, her frown deepening.

"I think there's too great a likelihood for us to take a chance on it."

Now her green eyes narrowed in suspicion. "Just what the hell are you gettin' at? What can we do about Hickok?"

Varnes took a deep breath and said, "He can't be hired as marshal if he's dead."

There it was, out in the open. Varnes was a little surprised at himself for stating the idea so boldly. He was aware that he was taking a chance. He knew this woman only by reputation. Al Swearengen, the owner of the Gem Theater where Varnes often played poker, hated her, and more than once Varnes had heard Swearengen refer to her as "that redheaded cunt."

But the gambler was a shrewd judge of human nature—

he had to be, in his line of work—and he sensed that Swearengen wouldn't have hated Laurette so much unless he also respected and perhaps even feared her. Any woman who could provoke such a reaction in a hard case like Swearengen had the potential to make a good ally. While it was possible that Laurette might go running to Wild Bill Hickok and tell him that Varnes was plotting against him, the gambler was willing to run the risk that she wouldn't.

After a moment of silence, Laurette finally said, "You ain't suggesting that I go out and challenge ol' Wild Bill to a gunfight, are you?"

"Of course not."

"And somehow I figure that you're not the type to slap leather against him, either."

Varnes smiled thinly. "I prefer to avoid personal involvement in gunplay whenever possible."

"Yeah, that's what I figured. So what *are* you getting at?"

Varnes stroked the pointed beard on his chin, knowing that the gesture made him look even more Mephistophelean. "If Hickok is to be hired as marshal, the businessmen at the other end of town will go in together to pay his salary and make the arrangement come about. My thought is that the businessmen on *this* end of town might want to form a similar alliance in order to prevent such an occurrence."

"You mean we ought to find somebody and pay him to kill Hickok?"

"That's what I had in mind, yes," Varnes said.

"Who the hell would we find to do a thing like that?"

And as if in answer to Laurette's questions, gunshots suddenly rang out nearby, rolling like thunder from behind the Academy.

Chapter Six

BELLAMY Bridges had found a place in his mind where he could go at times like this, a far-off place where everything was quiet and still and time seemed to be moving slowly. At such moments, he could reach for his gun and take it out in a leisurely fashion that was still much faster than anything going on around him. He seemed to have all the time he needed to raise the gun, cocking the hammer as he did so, and aim it. When he fired, he was sure that the bullet would go where he wanted it to go. The whole thing was simple, and while to an observer the action occurred in the blink of an eye or less, to Bellamy it was more like a peaceful Sunday afternoon stroll. He cocked and fired again, and another empty tin can leaped off the log where he had placed it. Three more times he fired, and the remaining three tin cans all leaped into the air, punctured by the bullets. This was the second time he had emptied the gun, and he was out of empty cans to use as targets.

Bellamy opened the revolver's cylinder, shook out the empty cartridges, and began reloading.

"My God," a voice said behind him. "Can he do that all the time?"

"Just about."

Bellamy turned and saw Laurette and a stranger standing in the Academy's rear door. Laurette smiled proudly at him. At another time he would have been glad to see that he had pleased her, but right now he was still too overwhelmed by grief to care much about anything except the pain he felt. Carla was gone, Carla who had been his world, his life, and there was nothing he could do to bring her back.

Laurette stepped out of the building. "Bellamy, this is Johnny Varnes," she said, inclining her head toward the man with her. He looked a little like pictures of the Devil that Bellamy had seen in the Bible and other old books.

Bellamy nodded and said, "Hello." Even to his own ears, his voice sounded dull and disinterested.

"Hello, my boy," Varnes said. "That was mighty fine shooting."

"Thanks."

"He's been practicing a lot," Laurette said. "When he came to Deadwood he couldn't even use a handgun."

"Is that so?"

Bellamy holstered the reloaded Colt and said, "A lot of things were different then."

That was certainly the truth. Even though only a few weeks had passed, everything had changed. He had abandoned his goal of prospecting and finding his fortune that way. He had learned what it was like to know the love of a woman. And he had learned the pain of loss and of betrayal. He had come to Deadwood as a boy, but now he was a man.

Varnes came closer to him and said, "Do you know Wild Bill Hickok?"

"I know who he is. I reckon I know him when I see him. He just got into town yesterday."

"I'm aware of that," Varnes said. "People claim that he's the fastest man with a gun west of the Mississippi. Do you believe that, Bellamy?"

With a shrug, Bellamy said, "I don't know. I never really saw him enough to say."

"Do you think he's faster on the draw than you are?"

"I don't know."

"You're really fast, Bellamy," Laurette put in. "I've seen you practicing."

He shrugged again. He didn't know why Laurette and this fellow Varnes were talking to him about how fast with a gun he was. He didn't particularly care, either. He didn't care about much of anything anymore.

Varnes stepped up to him, shook his hand, and clapped a hand on his shoulder. "It's good to meet you, boy," he said heartily. "I'm sure I'll be seeing you around."

Bellamy nodded. "Fine." He wondered idly if he could shoot that fancy silk hat off Varnes's head without putting a bullet through his brain. Might be interesting to try.

"Better go on up to the parlor, Bellamy," Laurette said gently. "Customers will be coming in soon. Ling's already there waiting, and the other girls will be too before much longer."

"All right," he said. It was his job to keep the peace in the Academy. That meant sitting around the parlor nursing a drink while the men came in and picked out which of the girls they wanted to go with. Most of them knew he was a dangerous man, so they behaved themselves. It was only rarely that he had to step in and calm somebody down.

As he went by her into the building, Laurette surprised him a little by putting a hand on his arm to stop him for a moment. She came up on her toes and brushed a kiss across his cheek. As she did so, he was reminded of how his mama had used to kiss him, back in Illinois. Laurette patted him on the shoulder, and he halfway expected her to tell him to run along and play.

But playtime was over, and it would never come again.

"**HE'S** just a kid," Varnes said after Bellamy had gone inside. "Hickok would eat him for breakfast and spit him out."

"You don't know that. You saw how fast and accurate he can shoot," Laurette argued.

"He was fast," Varnes admitted grudgingly, "but there's more to it than speed. How do we know he wouldn't freeze up at the wrong time?" He shook his head. "No, we need someone with more experience. Someone who's been in a gunfight or two and knows what it's like to face a man with a gun who wants to kill you as bad as you want to kill him."

"Did you have somebody in mind?"

"I've heard that Jim Levy is in town. I knew him a little, down in Pioche. He's as cold-blooded and icy-nerved a shootist as you'll ever find. I could try approaching him, if he's really here in Deadwood."

"How much do you expect me to kick in?"

"I don't know yet," Varnes said. "That would depend on how much money he wanted, and on whether or not I can persuade some of the other business owners here in the Badlands to join in our little alliance."

Laurette snapped, "Better not try to bring Al Swearengen in on this. I don't trust that son of a bitch."

"I'll keep that in mind," Varnes said, although Al Swearengen was exactly who he planned to approach next. Swearengen had a reputation for ruthlessness, and he was probably the most successful saloon owner in town, which meant that he also had the most to lose. Swearengen would go along with the plan; Varnes was sure of it. Of course, he would probably insist that Laurette not be involved, since they were such bitter rivals.

It would be a delicate balancing act, keeping them from finding out about each other, but Varnes was confident in his ability to bring it off.

"So we'll hold your young Mr. Bridges in reserve," Varnes went on, "while I try to find someone more suitable and more likely to carry out the task of eliminating Hickok."

Laurette nodded and said, "Sounds good to me."

"I don't suppose you'd care to seal our arrangement with a, ah, physical encounter. . . ."

Her face hardened. "I told you, I don't go with customers."

"But I wouldn't be a customer," Varnes pointed out. "We're partners, remember?"

"Mister," Laurette said, "when it comes to fucking, there's nobody in the world *except* customers, as far as I'm concerned."

NEXT door in the Bella Union, Hickok and California Joe had heard the shooting somewhere nearby, but neither man paid much heed to it. Gunshots were common in Deadwood, and the evenly spaced nature of the reports told the two vastly experienced old campaigners that someone was merely taking target practice.

Joe stared down into his mug of beer and sighed. "Hard to believe ol' Custer's dead."

On the other side of the table, Hickok stretched out his long legs and took a sip of his own beer. "That's true," he agreed. "It seemed like he had his own personal lucky angel perched on his shoulder, protecting him from all misfortune."

"Well, if he did, that angel flew away as fast as it could when it saw all them fuckin' Sioux."

Hickok nodded slowly. To every man, there came a day when his guardian angel was missing at just the wrong moment. Over the past few weeks, he had started to think that his own had already taken wing.

He had said as much to Charley Utter before they reached Deadwood, but of course his dandified little friend had scoffed at such foreboding. In Charley's eyes, Bill Hickok could do no wrong, and he was well nigh indestructible as well.

Hickok could only hope that Charley was right.

"Funny thing," Joe said. "I missed the Battle of the Washita, when Custer really made a name for himself, and then I missed the fracas on the Little Big Horn, where he made himself immortal."

"You believe he's achieved immortality in death?" Hickok asked, his interest perking up.

"Well, sure. Ain't nothin' like a tragic death to make

sure folks remember you. Some of the scribblers who work for the newspapers and the illustrated weeklies are already callin' it Custer's Last Stand." Joe paused and then repeated slowly, "Custer's Last Stand . . . Don't it have a nice ring to it?"

Hickok grunted. "Not so nice for all the poor troopers who were there on that hill with him."

Joe took a gulp of his beer and nodded. "That's sure as shit true."

"How come you to miss the Battle of the Washita?"

A sheepish grin stole over Joe's rugged, bearded face. "Well, the truth of it is, Custer had just appointed me his chief of scouts, so I went out and got drunk to celebrate. I was so drunk I was sick, and the Seventh left me behind when they moved out. By the time I got to feelin' good enough to ride after 'em and catch up, Custer had already whipped ol' Black Kettle's Cheyennes. He never let me forget it, neither. But at least he didn't run me off because of it. I scouted for him for a good number o' years after that."

Hickok laughed and then drained the rest of the beer from his mug. "It really is good to see you again, Joe," he said as he set the empty mug on the table.

"Damn right. You and me always made a good team, Bill. That's why I think we ought to go in together on a claim. I got my eye on a piece o' ground. You want to ride out and take a look at it with me?"

Hickok thought about the suggestion for only a moment before he nodded. "Yes," he said. "I believe I would like to do that."

HICKOK'S horse was in a corral behind the Grand Central Hotel. Keeping a weather eye out for Calamity Jane, he walked down to fetch the mount and then met California Joe at the head of Main Street, near where Deadwood Creek and Whitewood Creek came together. Joe was atop his balky mule, which surprisingly seemed more agreeable to being ridden than to being led. The two frontiersmen headed up

Deadwood Gulch, the bulky shoulders of ground rising on either side of them. While the timber on the slopes was coming back nicely, there were still many dead, burned trees mixed in with the live ones, the legacy of a fierce forest fire that had swept through the gulch sometime in the recent past.

Many trees had also been cut down to make room for the settlement. Deadwood's Main Street itself was dotted with stumps. So was the floor of the gulch, the trees having been felled for lumber and so that riders could move more easily along the banks of the creek. The slopes themselves had quite a few tents pitched on them. Mining claims ran from rimrock to rimrock, in three-hundred-yard stretches. It was rare for a prospector to be out of sight of his neighbors up and down the gulch. Some of the gold-seekers had joined together to form smaller camps such as Gayville, Central City, and Anchor, though it seemed doubtful that any of these hamlets would ever grow to eclipse Deadwood as the area's leading settlement.

When Hickok and California Joe had ridden a couple of miles up the gulch, Joe reined in and swept a big hand around them. "This is the claim I been lookin' at," he said. "Fella who owns it is lookin' to sell because his ticker is goin' bad on him. Can't stand to do the work no more, so he wants to get out with something. I'd be honored to work the claim with you, Bill."

"Are there any diggings?" Hickok asked.

"Yep, up the slope yonder." Joe swung down from his saddle. "Come on and I'll show you."

Hickok dismounted, too, and followed his old friend up the northern slope of the gulch. It was a bright, sunny day, but as usual, the light seemed to penetrate badly into the giant folds of earth and stone and timber. Perpetual gloom hung over the gulch. What the place needed was some lantern light, the music of a hurdy-gurdy, the laughter of women and the clink of coins and the seductive whisper of the cards. . . .

"Here we go," California Joe said. He stopped and pointed to a raw wound in the hillside where someone had gouged out the beginnings of a tunnel. He hunkered on his heels and reached out to pick up a fist-sized piece of rock that had been tossed out of the hole during the digging. With a frown on his face, he studied it intently.

"Do you know what you're looking for?" Hickok asked with a touch of amusement in his voice. "It seems doubtful you'll find a nugget that way."

"You never know," Joe said. "Anyway, there's certain kinds o' rock that you look for, and if you find 'em, that's a sign there might be gold nearby. I been studyin' up on the whole deal."

"What about panning for gold?"

"We can do that, too. Lots of folks do." Joe scratched his beard. "Tell you the truth, though, I ain't overly fond of the idea o' squattin' in a cold creek all day whilst I swish water and sand around in a pan. Seems to me like a good way for a man to freeze his balls off."

"It does sound less appealing," Hickok agreed. He forced himself to bend over and pick up a rock from the tailings below the rudimentary tunnel. He looked at it closely, turning it this way and that for about half a minute before he abruptly tossed it down and said, "This is foolishness."

Joe looked up at him in surprise. "What? What's wrong, Bill?"

Hickok waved a hand at the diggings. "This. The whole thing. I'm not cut out for this sort of work, Joe."

"Looking for gold, you mean? Prospecting?"

"That's right." Suddenly, Hickok felt as if a vast weight had been lifted off his shoulders. Expressing in words the thoughts and feelings that had been lurking inside him ever since he had reached Deadwood made them real, gave them weight and validity. Ever since Colorado Charley had asked him to come along on the journey into the Black Hills, Hickok had given lip service to the idea that he planned to search for gold along with the thousands of other men who had swarmed to the area.

But Bill Hickok had never been one of the herd. He was not a common man, and he didn't believe there was anything immodest about admitting that fact. It wasn't like he was proclaiming himself better than the gold-seekers. He wasn't saying he was too good to dig for color or pan for it in the streams. He was simply acknowledging that he wasn't comfortable with the idea of such work. The zeal that a man needed to be successful in such efforts was missing in him. Really, when you came right down to it, he told himself, he was saying that he was somehow *less* than those other men, the ones willing to stake their lives on their capacity for hard work and a little luck.

Those thoughts went through Hickok's mind as California Joe stared up at him and said, "Well, shit. I thought we was gonna be partners."

Hickok spread his hands. "All I can say, Joe, is that I didn't lead you on intentionally. I really meant to search for gold, and I can't think of a finer man to be partners with than you. But right now, it's just not meant to be. Perhaps another day I'll feel differently."

Joe straightened to his full, lean height and brushed his hands off. "Another day it's liable to be too late," he said resentfully. "I'll already be a rich man and won't have no interest in sharin' my claim."

"I sincerely hope that's true, Joe," Hickok told him. "The part about you being rich, I mean. Such good fortune couldn't happen to a more deserving soul."

Joe glared at him for a moment longer, then suddenly broke into a grin. "Aw, hell," he said. "I can't stay mad at Wild Bill Hickok." He thrust out his hand. "Put 'er there, Bill. I'm glad you rode out here with me, anyway."

"I enjoyed the camaraderie as well," Hickok said as he shook hands with the former chief of scouts. "Right now, though, I think I want to get back to Deadwood. I hear the voices of the sirens, Joe, and they're singing a song of smoke and whiskey."

Chapter Seven

CHARLEY Utter walked into the unfinished building that housed Ayres Hardware and announced in a loud voice, "If there's anybody who wants to send mail to Cheyenne and points north, south, east, or west, the first run of the Pioneer Pony Express will be leavin' tomorrow! Delivery to Cheyenne free for all outbound mail! Come see me, Charley Utter, if you've got mail to send!"

Steve Utter, Charley's brother, followed him into the hardware store and started passing out fliers that Charley had paid A. W. Merrick to run off on the printing press of the *Black Hills Pioneer*. The paper was rather poor quality and the printing job was a little muddy, but the message was clear: Anyone who wanted to take advantage of the new, fast, dependable mail service between Deadwood and Cheyenne could do so for free simply by giving their letters to one of the Utter brothers.

George Ayres came out from behind the counter at the rear of the store, his mustache bristling. "Here, now!" he said. "What's all this commotion?"

Steve pressed one of the still-damp fliers into the storekeeper's hand while Charley said, "Just lettin' folks know about the inaugural run of the Pioneer Pony Express. Tomorrow my rider, the famous frontiersman Dick Seymour, will be leavin' Deadwood bound for Cheyenne, carryin' a pouch full of mail. And the best part is, the initial delivery of that mail will be absolutely free!"

Ayres frowned at the flier, grimaced at the ink that smeared his fingers, and said, "That's all well and good, Mr. Utter, but you can't come in here a-hollerin' and carryin' on like this."

Charley clapped a hand on Ayres's shoulder. "You can't blame me for being enthusiastic," he said. "Why, this is going to transform Deadwood forever. No longer will the settlement be cut off from the outside world. From now on there'll be regular communication. You can write to your loved ones and hear back from them perhaps as quickly as a matter of weeks, rather than months. Think of it!"

"Yeah, I reckon that's pretty good," Ayres admitted. He set the flier aside and wiped his fingers on his already stained apron. "I wouldn't mind sendin' a letter or two myself."

"That's the spirit! You write your letters, Mr. Ayres, and get them to me as soon as possible. I'll add them to the pouch that Dick Seymour will deliver to Cheyenne."

"And there's no charge?" Ayres asked with a dubious frown.

"None at all!"

"This time, eh? What about next time?"

"Well, a business has to operate at a profit if it's to operate at all," Charley said without missing a beat. "But I can assure you that the rates of the Pioneer Pony Express will be most reasonable and affordable by all." He leaned closer to Ayres and added quietly, "And once the Utter Brothers Freight Line is runnin', I hope you'll consider makin' use of that service as well, Mr. Ayres. Again, the rates will be most reasonable."

"Yeah, well, we'll see. When's your rider leavin'?"

"Probably around midday tomorrow."

"I'll get those letters to you first thing in the morning."

Charley nodded. "You do that, pard." He looked around

at the store's customers, who had listened to the conversation with great interest. "Same goes for the rest of you folks. Get your letters to me by noon tomorrow, and I guarantee delivery to Cheyenne!"

"How fast?" a man asked.

"How fast will the mail reach Cheyenne, you mean?"

"That's right."

"As fast as good strong horses can carry Dick Seymour. I estimate approximately four days."

The man who had asked the question let out a whistle. "That's mighty fast, all right."

"You understand," Charley said, "conditions could delay the rider a mite. We don't know what he'll run into."

"Like Indians," another man said.

"Hell, if I was to see any Sioux, I'd ride even faster!" a third man said with a laugh. Some of the others joined in.

That joviality was good. Happy folks were more likely to spend money than those who were upset or angry.

Four days was a mighty optimistic estimate, of course. Dick Seymour might be able to achieve it with luck and many long hours in the saddle, but it was more likely the trip would require five or six days. That was still pretty speedy, and if the Pioneer Pony Express could keep to that schedule, its customers would be satisfied.

A woman in a big sun bonnet asked worriedly, "What *about* the Indians? Won't your riders be takin' a mighty big chance travelin' by themselves that way?"

"That's why we'll use only the best mounts, ma'am," Charley told her. "Those Injun ponies won't be able to keep up with our horses. If they give us any trouble, we'll just outrun 'em!"

"If you can't, though, your boys will lose their hair."

Charley wished she would shut up. She was casting a pall over the gathering and forcing people to think too much. He said, "You just let us worry about that, ma'am. You've got my word that the mail will go through, come hell, high water, or redskins!"

Several men brushed past the woman to ask more questions, and Charley was glad that her pessimistic comments were soon forgotten. Hell, if folks kept dwelling on what *might* go wrong, nothing would ever get done in this world!

"There he is now!" one man said suddenly, pointing toward the front door of the hardware store. "There's Bloody Dick!"

"A cheer for the valiant Pony Expressman!" another citizen cried.

Charley swung around and saw Dick Seymour standing there, looking surprised. Worse than that, he looked like a deer caught with lantern light shining in its eyes.

He looked, Charley thought, like he was suddenly scared shitless and wanted to bolt. That wouldn't do. That wouldn't do at all.

DICK Seymour already wished he hadn't stepped into the hardware store. He had been looking for Charley Utter. He had found Charley, all right, but he had also found an eager crowd gathered around the entrepreneur. As the people surged toward him, Dick wondered if it was too late to turn and run. He didn't like crowds. He had spent too much time alone in the past year to be comfortable around a lot of people.

It hadn't always been that way, of course.

Once a crowd had been the best thing in Dick Seymour's life. The sound of hundreds of people laughing and applauding had been a balm to his senses. Night after night he had reveled in the attention. That had been before everything in his life changed, of course.

Before he knew who he really was.

Charley Utter somehow made it to his side before the citizens of Deadwood who were converging on him. Charley took hold of his arm, slapped him on the back with his other hand, and hissed in Dick's ear, "For God's sake, don't look at the folks like they're a horde of damn Sioux Indians!"

Dick forced his spine to stiffen and dragged a grin onto his lean, tanned face. Charley turned toward the townspeople and went on. "That's right, here he is, the fella who's gonna carry your mail for you! Bloody Dick Seymour, the mad Englishman!"

Dick felt the grin waver a little, but he carried on as best he could. A woman stepped up to him and asked, "Ain't you afraid of the Indians?"

"Afraid?" Charley repeated in a half-bellow. "Of course he ain't afraid—"

"I asked him, not you," the woman cut in acidly.

"No, madam, I'm not afraid," Dick said. "I believe in treating the savages with the proper amount of caution, but I lived with the Kansa tribe and I've traded with the Sioux themselves. I know how to get along with the Indians."

He wasn't sure where the words came from. Some repository of patter buried deep inside him, he supposed. Glibness had once come naturally to him. That ability had withered during the long, lonely days and nights on the prairie after the deaths of his wife and children. Even when Carries Water and Becky Finds a Flower and little Thomas Badger were still alive, Dick had fallen out of the habit of talking much. There had been no need. The family had been so close that often they seemed to communicate without words.

But now he discovered that the talent had not deserted him entirely. He kept up the spiel for several minutes, repeating and embellishing the things he had heard Charley Utter say about the Pioneer Pony Express. Charley was beaming with pleasure and pride now. Dick concluded, "It will be my honor and privilege to carry the mail for you, ladies and gentlemen, and I assure you I will do everything in my power to deliver it in a safe, expeditious fashion."

"Does that mean fast?" a man asked.

"Yes, sir," Dick said. "I plan to ride like the wind."

That bold declaration brought a fresh round of approbation from the crowd. While everybody was in such a good mood, Steve Utter moved in on Dick's other side, and together the brothers steered him toward the door, with Charley still heartily greeting everybody as he went. When they came out onto the street, Charley was still grinning as he took hold of Dick's arm and said, "Damn it, boy, I thought you was gonna freeze up on me in there. I never saw nobody look so scared of a bunch o' fuckin' prospectors and townies and women."

"My apologies, Charley," Dick muttered. "I'm not accustomed to such acclaim."

"Well, you'd better get used to it. If you're carryin' a bag of mail when you get back from Cheyenne, you'll be the biggest damned hero this here burg has seen so far."

Dick tried not to sigh. "I suppose you're right."

"What were you doin' in there, anyway?"

"Looking for you, actually. I was walking past the hotel when the proprietor came out and asked me if I thought you would mind if he put up a sign about collecting mail from his guests to give to you for the Pony Express."

"Mind?" Charley blurted out. "Goddamn, I think it's a great idea! Come on, Steve, let's go over there and talk to the fella right now!"

Charley bustled off, full of boosterism, and with a wave his brother followed him.

As Dick stood there, Bill Hickok rode past with another man Dick recognized as California Joe. He hadn't known that Joe was in Deadwood. When they reined to a halt in front of the Bella Union, Dick strolled along the street to join them. California Joe was an old acquaintance, and Dick always felt better being around Hickok. He had never known a man as full of confidence and at peace with himself as Wild Bill. He was glad he had gotten to know the legendary frontiersman.

Hickok and California Joe paused on the porch of the Bella Union to talk to Jack Anderson, who stood there with a shoulder leaning against one of the posts holding up the awning over the porch. As Dick walked up, California Joe recognized him and burst out, "Well, stick my head in the dirt and call me a prairie dog! It's the Englisher! How ya doin', Bloody Dick?"

Dick shook the calloused hand Joe thrust at him and said, "I'm fine, Joe. How are you?"

"Be better when I'm rich." He slammed an open hand between Dick's shoulder blades. "Come on in the saloon and have a drink with me an' Bill. Hell, I'll even buy the first one!"

"I don't mind if I do." Dick turned to Jack Anderson. "Are you coming, White-Eye?"

The Kid shook his head. "No, not right now. You fellas go on. Maybe I'll be along later."

"Suit yourself."

Dick went into the Bella Union with Hickok and California Joe. His spirits were already higher than they had been only a short time earlier. He knew that he needed to stop dwelling on the past. Reminding himself of what he had lost served no purpose. The past was dead and buried.

Just like his family.

THE White-Eyed Kid stood there staring across the street toward the Gem Theater. Other than the fact that it had a second story, something that only a few other buildings in Deadwood could boast, it wasn't a particularly impressive structure. He had seen a lot fancier in Denver and Cheyenne. Made of roughly planed lumber, the Gem sported a narrow balcony in front of the second-floor windows. Jack lifted his eyes up to those windows and wondered if Jen was in one of those rooms.

It took a damned fool to fall in love with a whore, he told himself. A mighty big damned fool. But there it was. Ever since he and Jen had had their falling out during the trip up here, he hadn't been able to think about much of anything except her. He missed her something fierce. He missed her smile, and the smell of her long brown hair, and the totally unself-conscious way she had taken her tits out and showed them to him the very first time they talked to each other. He knew that a lot of what he was feeling right now was just lust—he had never even gotten to bed her, for God's sake!—but there was more to it than that. He was sure of it.

Taking a deep breath, he stepped out into the street and

angled across it toward the Gem, stepping around puddles of mud and piles of horse shit as he did so. It was late in the afternoon now and the street was getting busier as the miners drifted in from their claims, ready for a night of carousing, so he had to dodge some horses and wagons, too.

The noise inside the Gem was loud and raucous when he stepped inside. The bar to his left was nearly full, and many of the tables scattered around the big room to his right were occupied as well. Laughter drew his eyes to the balcony overlooking the main room. Several women were up there, among them the whores known as Smooth Bore and Tit Bit, whom he recognized from the wagon train. They were naked from the waist up and wore only bloomers from the waist down. As Jack watched, the women leaned over the railing along the edge of the balcony, dangling their bare breasts and shaking them back and forth to the cheers of the men watching below. Some of them shook more than others.

He didn't see Jen up there with the whores. If she had been, her tits wouldn't be wobbling around so much. They were too firm for that.

"Hey! You want a drink, or did you just come in for the show?"

The sharply voiced question made him look toward the bar. A burly man with long dark hair and a beard stood behind the hardwood, a glare on his face. He wore a gray apron over his leather vest and homespun shirt. His sleeves were rolled up a couple of turns, revealing muscular forearms.

The Kid glanced once more at the whores parading on the second floor. Still no Jen. As he walked over to the bar, he looked around the rest of the room, searching for any sign of her. Nothing. She had to be upstairs somewhere.

"Want a drink?" the bartender asked again when Jack stood across from him.

"Sure. Whiskey." Jack slid a coin across the bar.

The man poured the liquor from a bottle with no label, so Jack wasn't expecting much. It was pure rotgut, and he grimaced as he downed it. The stuff had a nice warm kick in his belly, though.

The bartender was a little friendlier now that he'd raked Jack's coin into a cash drawer. "Ain't seen you around Deadwood before," he said.

"I came in with the wagons yesterday."

The bartender arched his bushy eyebrows. "With Hickok?"

"That's right."

"You know Wild Bill?"

Jack nodded. "Sure. We're pards." From a lot of people, a claim like that would be mere boasting. Jack was confident that in his case, it was the truth. Bill's closest friend seemed to be Charley Utter, but he got along all right with Jack, too.

"Al! Come over here a minute, Al." The bartender motioned to someone as he called across the crowded, noisy room.

A stocky, dark-featured man in a sober black suit came over to the bar. "What is it, Dan?" he asked.

The bartender pointed at Jack with his thumb. "Fella here says him and Wild Bill Hickok are pards."

"Is that so?" the man called Al said. His tone was slightly bored, and he sounded like he didn't particularly believe what he was hearing.

"That's right," Jack said, a little annoyed by the man's attitude.

"Where'd you get that fuckin' white eyebrow?"

"In a prairie fire. It got burned off, and it grew back in white."

"I know you," Al said. "You're the White-Eyed Kid."

"That's right," Jack said, slightly mollified.

To the bartender, Al said, "Dan, the Kid here is telling the truth. He and Hickok really are friends, from what I've heard."

"Never doubted it," Dan said.

Al stuck out his hands. "I'm Al Swearengen, the owner of this place. Any friend of Wild Bill Hickok is a friend of mine. Dan, give the Kid a drink, on the house."

"Sure, Al."

Jack shook hands with Al Swearengen. Even though he

had been in Deadwood only a little over a day, he had already heard about what an unsavory reputation the man had. Swearengen didn't seem too bad, though. A mite rough around the edges, sure, but on the frontier, a man sometimes had to be like that.

As Jack tossed back the free drink, Swearengen said, "You interested in a woman? Got plenty of good-looking girls upstairs. I can't let you fuck for free, you understand, since whores ain't the same thing as whiskey, but I can guarantee any of my girls will be worth the price you pay."

"Well . . ." Jack thought quickly. "That sounds pretty good to me, Mr. Swearengen."

Swearengen slapped him on the back and motioned to someone. "You talk to Johnny Burnes. He runs the whores for me. Tell him what kind you want, and he'll fix you right up."

Jack nodded. "I'm much obliged."

"Think nothing of it. Hope you'll come back to the Gem often. And tell your friend Wild Bill he's welcome here, too."

So that was why Swearengen was being so nice all of a sudden. He wanted Wild Bill Hickok as a customer, thinking that the presence of such a famous man might draw even more trade. Jack felt a brief flush of anger that Swearengen would try to use him that way, but he suppressed it. There was no use in getting mad, he told himself.

Hell, sooner or later, everybody got used, didn't they?

As Swearengen walked off, he paused and spoke to a tall, bearded man who came over and introduced himself to the Kid as Johnny Burnes. "Al says to fix you up, mister, so what would you like? We got mostly good old American girls, but if you'd rather have a nigger or a chink, I reckon we can handle that, too. Got 'em fat, got 'em skinny, got 'em young, got 'em old. Whatever sort o' gal you like to fuck, we got 'em."

"Well, I was thinking . . . There was a girl who came in on the wagon train yesterday . . . young, about eighteen, pretty and sort of slender, with this really long, silky brown hair that reaches halfway down her back . . ."

Johnny Burnes's face changed abruptly. "We ain't got nobody like that," he said curtly. "Come up with something else."

Jack frowned and asked, "Are you sure? I thought certain she said she was supposed to work at the Gem Theater—"

"I told you," Burnes grated, "there's nobody here like that. You want a whore or not?"

For a moment, Jack didn't answer. Then he shook his head and said, "No. No, I don't reckon I do. Thanks, anyway."

He turned and started toward the front door. Dan the bartender called after him, "You come back to see us, hear?"

"Sure," Jack flung over his shoulder without looking back.

He would return to the Gem, all right, because he knew from the look on Johnny Burnes's face and the way the man reacted that Jen *was* here. Burnes had lied to him.

And the only thing that could mean was that something was wrong in the Gem Theater. Bad wrong.

Chapter Eight

THE girl turned quickly away from the window as Swearengen came into the room. Her eyes darted toward the bed, as if she were thinking about throwing herself on it, but it was too late for that. He had told her to stay away from the window, and yet there she was, holding the curtain back with one hand and looking out. As he stared coldly at her, he noted that she was trembling. She didn't know what he was going to do to her, how he was going to punish her for disobeying him.

Hell, he didn't know, either. Lifting his hand to her just seemed like too much trouble. He didn't feel like it right now.

It might be better just to let her stay scared, he reflected. If she didn't know when it was coming, the sheer possibility of what *might* happen would weigh on her mind. Yes, he decided without letting any of his thoughts show on his face, that would be better.

"Step away from the window," he said quietly.

She did what he told her, letting the curtain drop and moving back from the window toward the bed. She wore only a thin white shift. Her face was mottled with bruises, and the way she walked told how stiff and sore she was.

"I'm s-sorry, Mr. Swearengen," she said quickly.

"So you know you did wrong?"

"I'm sorry," she said again. "I just got bored, after I woke up. I . . . I didn't think it would do any harm to look out the window just for a minute. I swear that's all it was, just a minute. Just long enough to see what's goin' on outside—"

"You don't need to know what's going on outside," he told her. "Your only concern is what happens in this room. Your only concern is keeping me happy."

"I know, and I'm sorry—"

"That's enough."

She blinked and said, "Wh-what?"

"That's enough," Swearengen said again. "Stop apologizing. Saying you're sorry doesn't mean anything. It doesn't change anything. You still did what I told you not to do."

She sank slowly on the edge of the bed. Her bottom lip trembled a little as she asked, "What are you gonna do?"

"To you?" Swearengen shrugged, and then began to take off his coat. "I haven't decided yet. Beatin' you just seems like too much trouble."

She started to look relieved as he tossed his coat on a chair and reached for the buttons of his vest. He was taking off his clothes, and he had said that he wasn't going to beat her. To her mind, that had to mean that all he was going to do right now was fuck her again. Hell, that was nothing.

"But I'll think of something," he said. He enjoyed the way her look of relief instantly vanished and was replaced again by fear and anxiety. You had to keep a whore on her toes. You couldn't let her get too complacent, or else she would start thinking that she had rights and feelings like a normal human being. He said again, "I'll think of something. Just give me a little time."

He had his vest unbuttoned and was about to tell her to take the shift off and get on her hands and knees, when a knock sounded on the door. Swearengen turned sharply in that direction and rasped, "What the hell is it?" He should have given orders downstairs that he didn't want to be disturbed, but he had forgotten to do so.

"Sorry to bother you, Al," came the voice of Dan Dority in reply, "but there's a fella downstairs who wants to talk to you. Says it's important."

Swearengen jerked the door open, and the violence of it made Dority take a step back and wipe a hand on his apron. "I'll decide whether it's important," Swearengen said. "Who the fuck is it?"

"Gambler who's been around here for a while. His name's Varnes."

Johnny Varnes . . . Swearengen knew the man, all right. Didn't think much of him, either.

Dority's gaze suddenly flicked past his boss's shoulder. Swearengen saw that and glanced behind him. Jen had stood up and lifted her shift over her hips. She tugged it on up and over her head, then shook out her long brown hair as she dropped the shift on the bed. When Swearengen looked back at Dority, the bartender was still staring.

Without worrying about his coat, Swearengen stepped out into the hall and pulled the door closed behind him. Dority began to babble, "Sorry, Al, I didn't mean to start gawkin' like that, it's just that—"

"Forget it," Swearengen cut in. "You're not to blame, Dan. Any man would have looked."

That bitch. It was like she knew that he had given orders placing her off-limits. Johnny Burnes wouldn't send any customers up to her or even admit that she was here. And Burnes and Dority and the rest of the men who worked for him knew that they wouldn't be getting any pussy off her. They could fuck the other whores whenever they wanted to, but not this one. Not yet.

Not until he was through with her.

She had acted thoroughly cowed, like he had already broken her spirit the way he intended, but he realized now that it wasn't the case. There was still some defiance in her, and it took sly ways of peeking out. So he still had work to do on her.

Right now, though, he was content to let her think she had won her tiny victory by making Dan Dority look at her. Let her have a bit of hope. It would just be that much sweeter when he ripped the last shreds of it away from her.

"I'll talk to Varnes," he said as he started toward the stairs. Whatever the gambler wanted, Swearengen didn't figure it would be very important.

The tall, gaunt figure in the gray suit sat at one of the tables, idly dealing himself a hand of solitaire. Swearengen walked over to him and said, "All right, Varnes, I'm here. What is it?"

Varnes's long, supple fingers gathered up the cards. "Why don't you sit down, Al?" he asked. "I have a business proposition for you."

Swearengen looked around the crowded, noisy barroom. "I don't do business down here." He jerked his head toward the stairs. "Come on up to my office."

Varnes rose, his movements a little like those of a disjointed scarecrow. "I appreciate that. Lead the way."

As Swearengen walked toward the stairs, he glanced around again, this time looking for Jim Levy. He didn't see the notorious gunman anywhere in the Gem. That was good, he thought with a grunt. When the hair-trigger son of a bitch finally exploded, as he was bound to do sooner or later, let him shoot up some other saloon.

Swearengen wasn't quite sure why he was being so accommodating to a tinhorn gambler like Varnes. His type was common in Deadwood, sort of like lice. But Varnes paid a cut to the house every time he played a game in the Gem, and the men who came in to play poker with him bought plenty of drinks. Usually, if they were lucky, they bought some time with one of the whores before they left. It was all part of the river of money that flowed through here, and each tributary was important.

"Drink?" Swearengen asked when he and Varnes were alone in the second-floor office, just down the hall from the room where Jen waited for him.

"Don't mind if I do."

Swearengen poured for both of them, handed Varnes a glass, and then clinked his own against it. "To vice," he said.

"To human nature," Varnes responded.

"Same fuckin' thing, ain't it?" Swearengen swallowed the fiery liquor.

They sat down, Swearengen behind the desk, Varnes in front of it. Swearengen took out a cigar and lit it. He didn't offer one to Varnes. His hospitality extended only so far.

"Now, what's this business proposition you mentioned?"

Varnes leaned forward. "You know that Wild Bill Hickok is in town?"

Swearengen grunted. "Who doesn't know? One of his pards, the White-Eyed Kid, was here in the Gem a while ago. I told him to come back any time he wanted, and to bring Hickok with him."

"You want Hickok in your saloon?" Varnes sounded surprised.

"Why the hell not? Those dumb shits flock around him like he's something special. The more people who come in, the more money I make."

"For now," Varnes said heavily.

Swearengen's teeth clamped down on the cigar. "What the fuck does that mean?"

"What about when Hickok waltzes in wearing a badge and announces that he's come to shut you down?"

Swearengen shook his head and said, "That ain't gonna happen."

"How do you know it won't?"

"Because Hickok came to Deadwood to look for gold, just like all the other suckers."

"That's what he says, anyway."

Swearengen took the cigar out of his mouth, leaned it in a glass ashtray, and put his hands flat on the desk. "He hasn't packed a badge since he was the marshal of Abilene, and that was nearly five years ago. What makes you think he'd take up lawing again?"

"He needs money," Varnes said. "He must, or he wouldn't even be thinking about prospecting for gold. And he's recently married, which means he probably needs money even more than he did before. What better way for him to get it than by hiring out to the locals who want to clean up this end of town?"

"I ain't noticed anybody wanting to clean up the Badlands," Swearengen noted dryly, "except for that crazy preacher, of course. The so-called respectable gents like poker and booze and pussy just as much as anybody else. They're just not as honest about it."

"Right now that may be true, but Deadwood is still young," Varnes argued. "More people move in all the time. More buildings go up every day. This isn't going to be a rough-and-tumble mining camp much longer, Al. It's going to turn into a city. You know what'll happen then."

Swearengen frowned. "Folks will start worrying about how things look."

"Damn right they will. And they'll want a man like Hickok to make things look better."

Varnes might have a point, but the scenario presented by the gambler still seemed unlikely to Swearengen. "People say that Hickok's eyes aren't as good as they used to be. He's spent the past five years drifting and gambling and going back East to appear in some fucking play with Bill Cody. He's past his prime, Varnes. He's no threat to men like us."

Varnes looked irritated, as if he found Swearengen's resistance annoying, but he kept his temper under control. "Not everyone feels the same way you do, Al," he said.

"What do you mean by that?" Swearengen snapped.

"I've already talked to some of the other business owners on this end of town. They agree with me that Hickok could present a problem."

"Who have you talked to?"

Varnes shook his head. "I think under the circumstances that should be confidential, don't you? I mean, you wouldn't want me going around town telling everyone about our conversation, would you?"

"This ain't much of a conversation. More of a fuckin' fairy tale, seems to me like." Swearengen shrugged. "But suit yourself. What are you and these mysterious friends of yours going to do?"

Varnes turned coy. "I don't know that I should tell you. You might decide it was in your best interest to expose our plans—"

"Goddamn it, expose them to who? There's no law in Deadwood! Hell, it's a fuckin' outlaw town, you know that!"

"You might go to Hickok himself," Varnes said grimly.

Swearengen leaned back in his chair as the realization hit him. "Well, I'll be goddamned," he said softly. "You're going to kill Wild Bill Hickok."

"Not me personally," Varnes said. "I'm not a shootist. But I'm hoping that I can convince enough of the Badlanders to go in with me so that we can offer a good price to someone more suitable for the job—"

"Jim Levy," Swearengen said.

Varnes nodded enthusiastically. "Yes, I know he's in town. And he seems to be perfect for the job. He has a reputation as a fast man with a gun, and he doesn't seem the sort who would be afraid of Hickok—"

"Levy's too fuckin' crazy to be afraid of anybody," Swearengen said. "But there's no way of knowing if he'd go along with it. A man like that, you can't ever tell what he's liable to do."

"That's why somebody needs to approach him."

Swearengen chuckled humorlessly. "Better you than me, Varnes. Better you than me."

Varnes flushed. "I'll do it. I don't mind. As long as I know that I'm not alone—"

"I thought you said you'd already talked to some of the others down here."

"Yes, but none of them have the influence that you do. The Gem is the biggest and best saloon in Deadwood."

Swearengen picked up his cigar and rolled it between his fingers. He liked hearing things like that, even from a snake like Varnes. Billy Nuttall owned an interest in two saloons, the Bella Union and the No. Ten, but Swearengen liked to think that even added together, those places didn't amount to as much as the Gem.

"All right," he said abruptly, making his decision. "I still think maybe you're borrowin' trouble, but if you want to try to get rid of Hickok, have at it. I'll chip in on hiring Levy or some other gunman." He pointed the cigar at

Varnes. "But you'd better be mighty fuckin' discreet about it, and whoever you pick for the job better get it done right. I don't want any shit comin' back on me from this job."

"It won't, Al. You have my word on that."

Swearengen put the cigar in his mouth again and said around it, "You'd better be right. Because if you're not, I'll kill you. I won't hire it done, either. I'll do it myself . . . and I'll enjoy every fucking minute of it."

Chapter Nine

PRACTICALLY everyone in Deadwood turned out to watch the launching of the Pioneer Pony Express, even the whores and gamblers who normally slept well past noon. The sun was directly overhead when Dick Seymour led his horse through the crowd gathered on Main Street. With that many people around, some of them had to be standing in shit, but nobody seemed to mind. They had come to witness something important, something that would have some meaning to them when they looked back on it in years to come. They were there, they could tell their children and grandchildren. They were there when the first line of regular communication was opened between Deadwood and the rest of the world.

Dick stopped in front of the Grand Central Hotel. Colorado Charley Utter was waiting for him there, a pair of saddlebags stuffed full of letters hanging over his arm. Charley was dressed even fancier than usual for this momentous occasion, with a frilly shirt, silk cravat with diamond stickpin, fringed and beaded buckskin shirt, and fawn-skin trousers tucked into high, brightly polished boots. He wore a huge, creamy hat, and his hair hung in ringlets to his shoulders. Dick knew one of Charley's secrets: He kept a curling iron in his tent and heated it in a fire to make his hair look like that. Charley looked like most folks expected Wild Bill Hickok to look.

In contrast, Bill stood at the end of the porch, leaning against one of the posts, dressed in a plain coat and trousers, an amused smile on his face. The only thing fancy about him were the ivory butts of the twin .38-caliber Colt revolvers holstered on his hips.

Also on the porch were Steve Utter, Colorado Charley's brother; White-Eye Jack Anderson and his brother Charlie; Dick and Brant Street, who had agreed to ride for the Pioneer Pony Express on later runs; and various Deadwood dignitaries including Charles Wagner, the owner of the hotel, Billy Nuttall, the comedian and theater owner Jack Langrishe, General Dawson, Doc Peirce, A. W. Merrick, merchant E. B. Farnum, who it was said had political ambitions, and banker James Wood. Standing in the doorway of the hotel was Lucretia Marchbanks, and no one would dare tell Aunt Lou she shouldn't be there; nobody wanted to risk being banned from the hotel dining room. It was a big crowd, and Dick found himself hoping that there wouldn't be any speeches.

That proved to be a forlorn hope. E. B. Farnum had to make a few remarks, and so did Charles Wagner. A. W. Merrick scribbled notes on a pad as they talked about what a momentous day this was not only for Deadwood but also for the entire Black Hills region. General Dawson was called on to explain that he was drafting a letter to certain high officials in Washington with the intent that the treaty with the Sioux be rescinded so that Deadwood's legal standing and right to exist could finally be established. The general had been working on this effort for quite a while, Dick presumed, judging by the somewhat impatient reaction of some in the crowd.

Finally, Charley Utter motioned for Dick to come up onto the porch. Dick handed the reins of his horse to one of the men standing near him and climbed the steps to the porch. Charley held out the saddlebags to him.

"Dick, I hereby charge you with the swift, safe delivery of this mail to Cheyenne," Charley intoned dramatically. In all his years on the stage in England, Dick had never seen an actor with more of a natural flair for the dramatic than Colorado Charley. He really knew how to play to the crowd. "This is an awesome responsibility," Charley went on. "You're not just carrying the mail, Dick. You're carrying the hopes and dreams of all these fine folks. You're the lifeline that connects them to their friends and families back home. Without you, they would be cut off, lost in an untrammeled wilderness."

Dick hefted the saddlebags and said simply, "I'll do my best."

"He'll do his best!" Charley said, his booming voice carrying out over the crowd. "Let's hear it for Dick Seymour! Three cheers! Hip! Hip! Hurrah!"

The cheers went up and washed over Dick like a tide of approval. He couldn't deny that the sensation was a pleasant one. A man became accustomed to the acclaim, and when it was gone he missed it, at least a little.

But it was time to get moving. There was a job to do. He went down the steps, threw the saddlebags over the back of his horse, and lashed them securely in place. He took back the reins from the man who had been holding them, placed his foot in the stirrup, and swung up into the saddle. Mounting was a bit more awkward than usual because of the press of people around him, but he managed without looking too bad.

Charley came down the hotel steps, waving his arms in the air and shouting, "Make way! Make way! Clear a path for the Pioneer Pony Express!"

As more cheers filled the air, the crowd divided and surged toward the buildings on either side of the street, creating a lane for Dick's horse. Charley had told him to rear the animal on its hind legs, just for a little added flair, but Dick thought that was a bad idea. He was a good rider, an excellent rider, actually, but he didn't have confidence that his horsemanship was up to such grandstanding. Instead, he just took his hat off, waved it in circles over his head, and let out a whoop as he jammed his heels into the horse's flanks. The horse leaped forward into a gallop as Dick continued waving his hat and whooping. A few stragglers had to leap out of the way of the running horse. Dick had ridden twenty yards before he shoved his hat back down on his head.

The cheers followed him as he raced out of Deadwood, and Dick felt his heart thudding hard with excitement. The Pioneer Pony Express was on its way.

ALL during the wagon train trip from Cheyenne, Dick had studied their route closely, making mental note of all the landmarks, charting in his brain the obstacles to be avoided and memorizing the easiest path. He had known that he was going to be riding this trail again, this time alone and at the best speed he could muster. He hadn't expected to be making the return trip quite so soon, however. He had thought it might take Charley Utter a week or so to set up the Pony Express operation. Charley wasn't the sort of man to let grass grow under his feet, though. Why take a week for something when a day and a half would suffice?

And so Dick found himself galloping along the twisting valley of Whitewood Creek as the stream curved southwestward away from Deadwood. The thickly wooded hills loomed darkly on either side of him. He passed miners' tents and occasional small camps, and as he did so the men came out to cheer him on. Word had spread all through the Black Hills about this initial run of the Pioneer Pony Express. It was a mystifying process, the way news was passed along from claim to claim and camp to camp, but there was no denying that it happened. The excited reactions of the prospectors were proof of that.

Dick kept a sharp eye out for less friendly denizens of these hills. Indians had ambushed and killed men only eight or nine miles from Deadwood. The Sioux seemed to have no fear of approaching the settlements, and they had been known to attack even well-armed groups of men. They would certainly not hesitate to set upon a lone rider if they happened to spy him galloping through the hills.

Dick was well armed himself, with a Colt revolver on his hip, another cached with his supplies, and a fully loaded Winchester repeater in a sheath strapped under the fender of his saddle. Colorado Charley had worried a little about the extra weight of the rifle slowing him down, but as far as Dick was concerned, the weapon was a necessity. He wasn't going to make the ride without it. He hoped, though, that he wouldn't need the Winchester. He didn't want to have a skirmish with the Sioux or anyone else.

He had already fought enough battles in his life. Already killed enough.

Today, however, no battles loomed on the horizon. Dick saw no Indians, only miners and the occasional pilgrim or group of pilgrims on their way to Deadwood or one of the other camps. Most of the time he rode alone, and he preferred it that way.

As the sun dipped toward the rounded tops of the hills, he began to look for a good place to spend the night. Darkness fell with a surprising suddenness in the Black Hills. Once the sun had set, any lingering light departed quickly.

He veered off the trail into some trees and found a small clearing. Tending to his horse came first, and then, before it was completely dark, he built a tiny fire and heated water for coffee. He had brought a pack of provisions, including some biscuits provided by Lou Marchbanks, and he made a satisfying supper on them and some salt pork, washed down by strong black coffee. He made sure the fire was out before nightfall. Even somewhat hidden in the clearing, he didn't want any chance of the flames serving as a beacon to announce his presence.

Though it was cool up here at night, even during the middle of summer, he didn't need the fire for heat. His bedroll would keep him warm enough. As darkness settled down over the rugged landscape, he spread his blankets under the pines and crawled into them. He had been in the saddle only half the day today, but he was tired enough anyway so that he fell asleep almost immediately.

As always, his last conscious thought was the hope that exhaustion would keep any dreams away.

I⊤ was the best of times, it was the worst of times, or so Mr. Charles Dickens put it, but of course Dickens was writing about the French Revolution, not the moment before the actors took the stage and the curtain went up. Still, when Dick Seymour had first read that line in *A Tale of Two Cities,* he had immediately thought of that moment and the many times he had experienced that exact sensation, a mixture of feverish anticipation and sick dread.

Richard Seymour he was then, the sobriquet Bloody Dick being still some years in the future. A young man, perhaps worldly wise beyond his years from his association with the theater and those who populated that milieu. He was filled with ambition, and when he looked up from the stages of London's theaters and saw the beautiful, the wealthy, the impeccably dressed people who populated the expensive private boxes, he vowed that someday he would be one of them.

In earlier eras that would have been impossible, of course. Actors had been thought of as belonging to the lower classes, little better than gypsies. A woman who took up a life in the theater was considered only slightly more respectable than a prostitute. That had changed over time. It was no longer unheard of for thespians to mingle with the rich and powerful. Some actors had even grown wealthy in their own right, especially those who owned theaters.

His time was coming, Richard Seymour believed. As a boy, he had known grinding poverty and a life on the edge of crime in London's slums. Then one evening, he had seen a man being attacked by thieves, and for some reason unknown to him, instead of joining in and trying to snatch some of the loot for himself, he had leapt into the fray and rescued the gentleman, who turned out to be Edwin Abbott, an actor and the owner of quite a successful theater.

Abbott had taken his young rescuer under his wing, and in the next few years Richard Seymour had gone from performing odd jobs around the theater to performing on its stage. His life was a whirlwind of exciting activity. Abbott retired from performing and concentrated on supervising the company in its productions. In the past, there had been no one individual in charge of staging the plays the company put on. Everything was worked out by the entire group. These days, however, with productions becoming more complicated all the time, a single steady hand was needed, and Abbott furnished that. Since he directed all the action on stage, he began to be called the director.

With Abbott's retirement, that left Dick to step into the roles that the older man had always played. Despite his youth, he quickly became the company's leading man. It was a heady time, filled with the excitement of the performances themselves, the parties afterward that lasted sometimes until dawn of the next day, the laughter, the champagne, the women. . . . Ah, the women! Not only the actresses, so skilled in playing roles even when they were not on the stage, but also the wives and daughters of the rich men who attended the performances. They found handsome young actors quite appealing as well, and Richard Seymour could have happily remained in that life for the foreseeable future . . . if things had not changed.

"Mr. Seymour, you were quite wonderful! I genuinely believed that you were Sidney Carton!"

Best of times, worst of times, he thought with a smile. The stage adaptation of Dickens's novel had gone well, and now as he was leaving the theater, he found a carriage waiting for him outside the building's rear door, with a beautiful young woman looking at him from the vehicle's window and a well-dressed older man standing beside the open door.

"Would you care to join us, Mr. Seymour?" the man invited. "I'm Clive Drummond, and there's going to be a bit of a soiree at my house this evening."

Richard knew the name. Clive Drummond was a shipping magnate, and there was talk that he was being considered for an O.B.E. Soon he might be Sir Clive. Refusing an invitation from him would be decidedly unwise.

"Of course, sir," he said. "It would be my honor, and my pleasure."

He climbed into the carriage, followed by Drummond, and sat across from the couple. Drummond introduced his wife as Fiona. She had thrown her cloak back so that her bare shoulders were revealed by the low neckline of the gown she wore. Masses of thick golden curls fell to those enticing shoulders. Gemstones sparkled in her hair. She was one of the most breathtaking women Richard had ever seen . . . and he had seen his share of beautiful women.

The Drummonds lived in an impressive pile of stone and masonry in an exclusive section of London. They also had a country estate, Fiona explained rather breathlessly to Richard, and she hoped that he would come to visit them there. He agreed that he would, as soon as he could take the time away from the theater. "I can't let the company down, you know," he said.

"Of course not," Drummond said.

The big house was filled with music and talk and laughter. Richard could practically smell the aristocracy. He blessed his good fortune. These were the sort of people with whom he wanted to mingle. He wanted to be included among them, to be one of them himself. He had come so far from his less-than-humble beginnings. More than once as a child, he'd had to stay awake all night to keep the rats off him. Now he stood in an opulent ballroom with a glass of fine champagne in his hand, surrounded by wealthy admirers, one of whom, Fiona Drummond, stood so close to him that from time to time the softness of her breast brushed against his arm.

Life could not get any better than this, and then he amended, yes, it could. It most certainly could.

In time he visited the Drummond estate, as he had promised, and went riding and shooting with Clive and his friends. Since he had grown up in the teeming, crowded city, Richard had never had the chance to ride until now. He found that after a few moments of initial discomfort at being on the back of a horse, he was a natural at it. By the end of the afternoon he was galloping across the English countryside with ease. Skill at handling a gun came equally naturally to him. He was a fine shot with rifle and pistol and fowling piece. As they went back into the mansion at the center of the sprawling estate that evening, Drummond clapped a familiar hand on Richard's shoulder and proclaimed, "You have the makings of a true gentleman, my boy."

The makings of a gentleman? As far as Richard was concerned, he had already achieved that end.

That night, after a late evening of cigars and brandy with Drummond and some of the other male guests, Richard had climbed the broad, curving staircase and gone to the bedroom he was using that weekend. As he stepped inside, motion against the flames of the small fire burning in the room's fireplace caught his eye and made him stop on the threshold.

Fiona Drummond, wearing a silk wrapper, stood in front of the fireplace with a smile on her face and a glass of champagne in her hand. There were no gems in her hair tonight, but it fell loosely down her back and sparkled with highlights of its own in the glow from the flames.

"Come in, Richard," she said, "and close the door."

He stepped on into the room and quietly closed the door behind him. She was beautiful, so lovely and vital that she took his breath away and made his heart pound madly in his chest. Still, his brain was working well enough to urge caution on him.

"I'm not sure this is a good idea, Mrs. Drummond," he heard himself saying. "If your husband found out you were here—"

"Clive *knows* I'm here," she said. "It was his idea . . . well, not entirely, I had something to do with it . . . but he thoroughly approves."

Richard Seymour gave a little shake of his head. If pressed, he would have said that he was a rather jaded young man, well versed in the pleasures of the flesh and the almost infinite variations thereof, including quite a few that he had not experienced himself. And yet, he had never come across this particular situation before or even heard about such a thing.

"Your husband . . . wants you to be here . . . with me?"

"That's right." Fiona came closer to him. "You see, when Clive came back from the Crimea, he . . . was not the man he once was, if you understand what I mean. So, as his wife, I have to seek certain pleasures elsewhere, and he's very understanding, even helpful, about that."

Richard swallowed. "Were you married to him when he came back from the war?"

"No, we were married only five years ago."

"Then he didn't tell you about . . . about . . ."

"Of course he did. Clive was very forthcoming with me."

"Then why did you marry him?"

She lifted her free hand, touched his cheek, and then slid that arm around his neck as she leaned against him. The yielding warmth of her body told him that she wore nothing underneath the silk wrapper.

"Don't be foolish," she said. She sipped from the glass of champagne and added, "He's *rich*."

There was nothing Richard could say to that. He couldn't have spoken anyway, because at that moment she lifted her mouth to his and kissed him, and she tasted of champagne and lust. He didn't know if money had a taste or not, but if it did, she tasted of it, too.

If this was what both of his hosts wanted, it would be rude of him as a guest to deny them. . . .

They were naked together in the big four-poster bed, with him on top of her and thrusting deeply within her, before he realized that he felt eyes on him, watching him. Abruptly, he stopped what he was doing, causing her to open her eyes and look up at him in confusion. "What is it?" she asked.

"I . . . I don't know. Something's wrong. . . . There's someone. . . ."

"Oh, that's just Clive. Don't mind him." Her hands reached around him and her fingers dug hard into his buttocks. "Keep going. You can't stop now."

And she was right. He couldn't stop. . . .

HE woke up six years and thousands of miles away in the Dakota Territory, drenched in sweat despite the coolness of the night. He had hoped for a dreamless sleep, but that had been denied him.

He would be in the saddle for twice as long tomorrow, he told himself as he looked up through the branches of the pine trees and saw stars peeking through here and there. Maybe that would do it. Maybe then he would be tired enough for oblivion to claim him.

Chapter Ten

FLETCH Parkhurst raked in the pot in the center of the table as the man seated across from him said in disgust, "I'm out. You've cleaned me."

"Come back when you've got more money," Fletch said with a friendly grin that took any sting out of the words. "I'd be glad to give you a chance to get even with me."

Chair legs scraped on the floor as the man stood up and grunted. "I'll just bet you would be," he said. He seemed more disappointed by his losses than angry because of them, however, and Fletch sensed that there wouldn't be any trouble. The man was a miner, accustomed to scraping a little gold out of the ground and then coming to town and spending all his hard-earned money on whiskey and women and cards. He'd just go back out to his claim and in the morning resume his likely futile quest to become rich.

The prospector's departure left an open chair in the game, but it didn't stay that way for long. A tall figure moved in, and a deep voice asked, "Mind if I sit in?"

Fletch looked up and recognized the long hair and drooping mustache of Wild Bill Hickok. He gathered the scattered cards with one hand while he used the other to gesture toward the empty chair. "Please join us, Mr. Hickok," he said. "It's an honor to sit at the same table with you."

"Hope you still feel the same way when the game's done, son," Hickok said dryly. "There's just one thing . . ."

"What's that?"

"You reckon you'd mind swapping chairs?"

Fletch frowned. "You want me to sit over there?"

"That's right. You've got the wall behind you, and I sort of like that arrangement myself."

Fletch thought about it for a second and then shrugged. As he stood up and started around the table, he said, "It doesn't matter to me. If you want that seat, you're welcome to it."

"I'm obliged," Hickok said.

Fletch had heard of the famous gunman's eccentricity about where he sat. Hickok didn't want anyone being able to sneak up behind him. Given his checkered career and the number of enemies he had made, such caution was probably a good idea . . . although Fletch thought it was highly unlikely that anyone would waltz into the Bella Union in broad daylight and try to gun down Wild Bill Hickok. Nobody in Deadwood was that foolish, surely.

Even though he had moved, Fletch still had the deal. He shuffled the cards, let the man on his right cut the deck, and then began passing them out.

Midday games were usually rather slow and good-natured. For some reason most men didn't get cutthroat about winning and losing until after the sun had gone down. A poker session like this one was more about companionship and finding a pleasant way to pass the time. So quite a bit of idle conversation went on, and as the hands ebbed and flowed, Fletch found himself growing to like Wild Bill. For someone who was so famous, Hickok was more unassuming than Fletch would have expected, and he had a sly, self-deprecating wit. Most of his amusing stories drew chuckles at his own expense.

"So there I was, trapped in that cabin by the very outlaw gang I'd been chasing," Bill said as he studied his cards. "To make matters worse, they set the place on fire, so I had my choice of staying in there and burning to death or busting out and getting shot to ribbons by thirty owlhoots."

"What did you do?" one of the other players asked eagerly, caught up in the yarn Bill was spinning.

"Why, I just waited until I was on fire real good and *then* ran out. Those old boys were so shocked to see me blazing like that they didn't think to shoot."

The men around the table stared at him for a long moment before one of them asked tentatively, "But didn't you burn up?"

"That was the drawback in my plan," Bill drawled.

Fletch grinned as he folded. He tossed his cards in and said, "Mr. Hickok, you are a caution."

"I find it's often easier to tell lies," Bill said. "People are more inclined to believe them than they are the truth."

Fletch chuckled, knowing that Hickok was right about that. He played a few more hands, losing more than he won, and that was confirmation of the hunch that had been building. His luck was gone for now, and since he was still well ahead in the game, that meant it was time for him to quit for a while.

"That'll do me, gentlemen," he said as he began to gather up his winnings. "I believe I'm out."

One of the other players, a miner with a jutting red beard, hadn't said much during the game, but now he frowned and asked, "Kind of early to be quittin', ain't it?"

"Don't think of it as quitting," Fletch said. "Just think of it as me taking a hiatus."

"What you're takin' is most of my money." The man's tone was taut with anger.

He was one of the last players Fletch would have expected to show such a reaction. During the game, the miner had been quiet, stolid, even dull. He hadn't seemed to care whether he won or lost. Obviously, he *did* care, and now he was showing it.

"I'm always around town, friend," Fletch told him, "and I'm never away from the gaming tables for very long at a time. Just be patient, and I'm sure you'll have a chance to win back everything you've lost."

"I want to win it back *now*."

Fletch shook his head. His instincts told him it was time to quit, and he never went against his instincts. "Sorry. I'm out." He stacked the bills he had won, folded them, and slipped them into an inner jacket pocket as he stood up.

"You son of a—"

Bill Hickok's hands both lay flat on the table. As the miner started to curse, Hickok lifted his left hand, pointed his index finger, and moved it back and forth in a gently admonishing gesture. "There's no need for that," Hickok said quietly.

The miner glanced angrily at him. "I know who you are, mister, but this ain't none o' your business. My beef is with this fancy-dressed tinhorn here."

"Are you trying to insult me or compliment my sartorial sense?" Fletch asked.

The miner started to growl a curse, but Hickok's deep voice overrode him. "You're not accusing Mr. Parkhurst of cheating, are you? Because I can assure you, he wasn't. He played the game entirely square. I ought to know. I've seen enough cardsharps in my life to populate an entire small town."

The miner raked his fingers through his beard and then shook his head. "No, I ain't sayin' he cheated. But he still can't just walk off with my money like that. I won't allow it."

"You don't have any real choice in the matter," Hickok pointed out.

"The hell I don't. He'll play, even if it has to be at gunpoint!"

With that, the man reached for the butt of the revolver tucked behind his broad leather belt.

He was slow, of course. Fletch would have been embarrassed to try a fast draw if he wasn't any better at it than the red-bearded miner. The man's calloused fingers had barely closed around the butt of his gun before he found himself staring down the short barrel of the Colt that had appeared in Fletch's hand as if by magic.

"My friend," Fletch said, "since you tried to draw first, I'd be completely justified in pulling the trigger now. But I have no interest in killing you, so I'd appreciate it if you'd let go of your gun, turn around, and walk out of here."

The miner's eyes were wide with fear. From where he stood, the mouth of the gun barrel must have looked like a cannon. He licked suddenly dry lips.

"I . . . I never said you was cheatin'," he choked out.

"I know that. That's why I don't want to kill you. You just let your disappointment at losing get the better of you. That's understandable. It could happen to anyone."

"I reckon I'm sorry—"

"There's no need to apologize. I just think you should leave and not come back until you're in a better frame of mind."

"Y-yeah. I'll do that."

The miner let go of his gun like it was the head of a snake. He took an unsteady step back away from the table. Looking around at the other players, he muttered, "Sorry, gents." Then he turned and shuffled toward the front door of the Bella Union, his eyes on the floor.

Over at the bar, Harry Sam Young put the sawed-off shotgun he was holding back on the shelf underneath the hardwood.

Fletch waited until the miner was gone before holstering his gun. He sighed and shook his head. "I regret the unpleasantness, gentlemen," he said to the other men around the table.

"Not your fault," Bill Hickok said. "That's a pretty slick draw you've got."

"Thanks. Coming from someone like you, that means something."

"Of course, I've seen faster. Wes Hardin, Ben Thompson, fellows like that."

"I never set out to be the fastest," Fletch said. "Just fast enough to stay alive."

"The goal of us all," Hickok murmured. "I'll see you around, Mr. Parkhurst."

Fletch nodded and left the saloon. He paused in the street outside and glanced toward the Academy for Young Ladies next door. He hadn't been there in a while, and he couldn't help but wonder how his mother was doing.

He wasn't curious enough to step into the place and find out, however.

BELLAMY Bridges stirred restlessly in the tangled, sweated sheets. He hadn't slept well. He never slept well anymore, not since Carla had been killed.

His bunk was in a small room just down the hall from Laurette's office. He never turned in until nearly dawn, when the last of the customers staggered out of the Academy. Then Bellamy took a bottle with him to his room and drank until he fell into an agitated slumber. He usually awoke almost as exhausted as when he had gone to bed.

It had only been a few days, he told himself. He had to give it time. Sooner or later he would get over what had happened.

But somehow he doubted it. He feared that nothing would ever be the same again.

The straw mattress shifted slightly, but he hadn't moved. Instantly, Bellamy's eyes flicked open, and his hand darted toward the butt of the gun under his thin pillow. He jerked it out and swept it up, earing back the hammer as he brought the barrel to bear on the figure crouched next to him, indistinct in the shadows of the room. The only light came through a tiny, filthy window.

"No shoot!" a woman's voice gasped.

Bellamy's finger held off on the trigger just in time. He lowered the gun, carefully eased the hammer off cock, and said, "Shit, Ling, I almost blew your head off!"

"Sorry, sorry, Bellamy." Not all the letters came out exactly right, but he knew what she was trying to say. "Miss Laurette send me."

He put the Colt in the holster that hung along with the

coiled shell belt on a nail in the wall. Then he swung his legs out of the bunk, sat up, and groaned. His eyes felt gritty and his skull throbbed. He held his face in his hands for a moment and said, his voice muffled, "What does she want?"

"Not want."

He looked up, puzzled. "I thought you said she sent you to get me."

Ling shook her head. "No. Send me *to* you."

With that, she slipped the straps of the simple gown she wore off her shoulders and let it slide down her body to crumple at her feet.

Even in the dim light, Ling's bare skin seemed to have a golden glow to it. She was slim-hipped and firm-breasted. The triangle of hair between her legs was thick and luxurious. In the shadows, the fading bruises were no longer visible on her face. Even to Bellamy's bleary eyes, she was lovely.

He lowered his gaze to the floor and shook his head. "You're wasting your time," he said. "I'm not interested."

Moving gracefully, she came over to the bunk and sat down beside him, nude. He wore only a pair of long underwear, and he could feel the heat from her body as her hip pressed against his. She put an arm around him. He wanted to pull away from her, but he lacked the energy.

She leaned against him and rested her head on his shoulder. "No fuck," she said. "Just sit."

Bellamy closed his eyes. It felt good to sit there with someone close to him again. His breathing was ragged from the pounding ache in his head, but as the minutes passed slowly, the pain lessened and his chest began to rise and fall in a more regular rhythm. He felt almost like he could go to sleep again, only it would be a natural slumber this time, not one forced onto whiskey-dulled senses.

After so long a time, Ling reached over with her other hand and rested it on his groin.

Bellamy jerked away, but she was insistent. Old habits were hard to break. She grasped his hardening penis through his underwear and pumped up and down on it. He wouldn't have thought it was possible anymore for him to become aroused, but there was no denying what was happening.

And as his erection rose, so did the bitter taste of revulsion and self-loathing until it filled his throat and almost choked him. Carla was barely cold in the ground, God damn it. The girl he loved had been struck down viciously, mercilessly, and yet here he was getting hard just because a whore was playing with his cock. He burned with shame.

Ling's deft fingers unfastened the buttons on the underwear and freed his erection. She said, "Bellamy feel better now," and leaned over to take him in her mouth.

He wanted to tell her to get the hell away from him, but the words froze in his throat. He couldn't say anything, couldn't even whimper. His shoulders tilted back against the wall behind him as her head bobbed up and down above his groin. He closed his eyes and tangled his fingers in her long, thick, black hair.

It was only a few moments before she skillfully brought him to a climax. Gasping, he spent in her mouth. When she lifted her head, she was smiling.

"Bellamy feel *better* now," she repeated.

He couldn't argue with that. His headache was completely gone, and instead of flowing sluggishly in his veins, his blood now raced again, coursing along with the vitality of youth that was rightfully his.

She snuggled against him again and murmured, "Bellamy fuck Ling any time."

"Yes," he said, still breathless. "Yes, I'll do that."

"Not be sad."

He didn't say anything. A whore's mouth could accomplish a lot of things, but it couldn't make him forget. Not completely. He still mourned Carla's death. He thought that he might for the rest of his life.

The door of his room opened and Laurette stepped inside. Bellamy sat up sharply and tried to push his now-limp penis back through the opening in his underwear. Laurette laughed.

"Honey, you think I haven't already seen thousands of those things? You don't have to worry about hidin' it from me."

Bellamy awkwardly fastened the buttons anyway. Beside him, Ling stood and picked up her gown from the floor. Unself-consciously, she put it on and then started for the door.

"Thanks, Ling," Laurette said. She patted Ling on the shoulder as the Chinese girl went by and left the room. She turned to Bellamy and went on. "Now, then. Welcome back. You ready to get to work?"

"I've been working," he said hoarsely. "Haven't missed a night."

"That's not what I'm talking about."

He frowned. "You mean practicing with my guns? I've been doing that, too."

"I know, and you're mighty good with them. But all that skill don't mean a damn thing unless it's put to use in a good cause."

"A good cause?" he repeated. "What do you mean?"

"I'm talkin' about how before we're done, Bellamy, you and me are gonna run this whole end of town, and we're gonna be richer than you ever dreamed of." A smile lit up her face. "I don't reckon you'll find a much better cause than that."

Chapter Eleven

THINGS might have been much different if Ena Raymonde had shown any interest in him other than friendship. Ena with her long, dark, curly hair, her quick intelligence, her sharp wit. Her brother, Paddy Miles, had come west from Georgia after the war and fallen in with the buffalo hunters who had started a primitive settlement along the twisting bends of Medicine Creek in southwestern Nebraska. Paddy had fallen in love with the area and sent for his parents and sister to come join him there. Dick Seymour had told the quick-tempered Irishman that perhaps it wasn't a good idea to bring a couple of ladies into a land that was barely one step removed from an untamed wilderness, but Paddy had insisted that it would be all right. His sister, who had been widowed after a very brief marriage, would especially love it along Medicine Creek, he insisted.

And he had been right. Ena Raymonde had taken to life on the prairie right away.

Dick was a single man, and Ena was young and pretty and vivacious. It was natural that he would be attracted to her. He had put the bitter memories of his life in England behind him and was ready to make a new start in America. He wanted Ena to be part of his new, American life.

At first he had thought that she returned his interest. She had even made a beautiful buckskin shirt with her own hands and given it to him as a gift. They could sit for hours discussing things of which the other hunters had little or no knowledge: art and literature and music, life in London and the other capitals of Europe, the sort of culture that was so foreign to the American West it might as well have been on another planet rather than merely across the sea on a distant continent.

But even though she was friendly and enjoyed his company, Ena always drew back just enough whenever Dick tried to take things farther. Just enough for him to know that any romantic future for the two of them simply wasn't in the cards. It was another bitter pill for him to swallow, the latest of many he had choked down in his life, but he managed. He even stayed friendly with her, though he made a point of being away from Medicine Creek more often than he had been in the past.

Shortly after that, he had met Carries Water, and his life had changed yet again, this time for the better. Occasionally, on dark nights when he couldn't sleep, he asked himself if he had turned to the Indian woman simply because Ena Raymonde had rejected him. He didn't believe that was the case—Carries Water was a wonderful woman in her own right—but still the possibility haunted him. He had never been able to put it completely from his mind.

Even now, as he galloped through the rugged Dakota Territory, memories of those days with Ena along Medicine Creek strayed into his thoughts. He shoved them aside forcefully in order to concentrate on what he was doing. If his horse stepped in a prairie-dog hole and snapped a leg, it would be ruination for both of them. If he allowed himself to be distracted and rode right into a war party of Sioux, that would be the end of him. Staying alive on the frontier meant being alert, not dwelling on the past and all of Fate's painful twists and turns.

He wasn't far from Jack Bowman's Hat Creek Ranch, where the wagon train had met up briefly with a party of scouts led by Buffalo Bill Cody during the journey to Deadwood. Dick had crossed paths several times over the years with Cody and with the famous frontiersman's crony Texas Jack Omohundro. In fact, Dick had taken part in a roundup of buffalo led by Texas Jack, and once the great shaggy beasts had been corralled, they were shipped back East to appear in one of the extravaganzas that Cody staged. Dick could have taken part in those productions along with Buffalo Bill and Texas Jack; more than once Cody had told him there was room for Bloody Dick Seymour in his show. But that would have smacked too much of Dick's previous life in England. He was through with performing.

Dick reined in as he realized that his thoughts were drifting once again. He let his horse blow as he took off his hat and wearily rubbed a hand over his face. He had been in the saddle since before dawn, and now the sun was hovering over the hills to the west. He had hoped to make Hat Creek before dark, but he might not reach the ranch.

Suddenly, he stiffened as he caught sight of movement at the crest of the hills. Several riders were skylighted as they topped the slopes and came toward him. Although they were quite a way off, Dick's eyesight was keen and he recognized the distinctive headdresses the riders wore.

Sioux warriors—and they were headed in his direction.

TALKING Bear was a war chief, a leader of the Dog Soldiers of the Lakota people. As a young man, he had gone into the wilderness to seek his true name and his destiny, and a bear had spoken to him, promising him that he would be a great leader of his people.

So far, that had not happened.

He was a respected warrior, there was no doubt of that, and had counted coup on many enemies and stolen many horses. He had led raids on the other tribes that were not real human beings and had killed many of them and taken many more as slaves. When the council fires burned, he was listened to, and the elders weighed his opinion carefully.

But as long as there were chiefs such as Crazy Horse and Sitting Bull and Gall, Talking Bear would never achieve his true destiny, but would always be overshadowed by those other warriors. This was his belief, and at times it burned bitterly in his belly.

He pulled back on the rope hackamore and brought his pony to a halt a moment after riding over the top of the hill. He knew he and his companions were visible up here against the setting sun, but he cared little. Were the Sioux warriors not the lords of the plains? The white interlopers were here only temporarily. The day would come when they were all gone and the People still remained, and Talking Bear prayed it would be soon. In the meantime, he would show no fear of the white men.

Feeds His Horses came up alongside him and pointed. "One rider," he said in the language of the People. "A white man."

Talking Bear nodded. He had seen the same thing as Feeds His Horses. He looked to the south, where the hills ended and the prairie began. There was a ranch nearby, run by a man named Bowman. It was on a stream called Hat Creek by some of the whites and Sage Creek by others. That was just like the white men, who were easily confused and too stupid to know where they really were.

The lone white man on horseback was riding hard and probably hoped to reach the ranch before nightfall, thinking that he would be safe there. Less than a bowshot behind Talking Bear, twenty warriors waited, and if he gave the order, they would give chase and overtake the white man before he could make it to the ranch. But the rider probably had a gun and would fire at the Sioux if they pursued him, and the whites who worked at the ranch might hear and come out to fight. While Talking Bear was not afraid of the white men, no, never afraid of them, he was not foolish, either. It was said that back East there were as many white men as there were blades of grass and that more and more of them would come west, but there were only a limited number of the warriors of his people and a good leader would not spend their lives needlessly. He was a good leader. The bear had said so. Sometimes, he wondered if it had been a real bear or a spirit bear, but either way it had spoken the truth.

"Do you want the white man's hair?" Feeds His Horses asked.

"Another day," Talking Bear said solemnly. "We will kill him another day."

"How will you know it is him?"

Talking Bear frowned. The question asked by Feeds His Horses showed a bit of defiance, a hint of challenge. Feeds His Horses was a proud, able warrior, too, and might believe that he was better suited to lead this band of warriors than Talking Bear was. He failed to understand that even if this particular white man was not around to be killed, another one would be. One white man or another, it mattered not. All were the same.

But Talking Bear could not allow even a hint of challenge to go unanswered. He said, "We will watch the ranch, and if the man leaves in the morning, we will follow him."

"How do you know he will leave?"

"See how he rides," Talking Bear said with scorn edging into his voice. "Even a child can see that he is on his way somewhere."

Feeds His Horses scowled at the rebuke, but evidently he was not ready to escalate from defiance to outright rebellion. He nodded and said, "If he leaves the ranch, we will take his hair."

Talking Bear nodded. It was settled.

But in the future he would keep a close eye on Feeds His Horses.

HAVING lived with the Indians, Dick Seymour knew that not all of them were the bloody-handed savages many people believed them to be. Although the warriors were implacable enemies in battle, some of them could be reasoned with. Some chiefs counseled peace and knew that the key to the future would be the ability of the Indians to get along with the white men, rather than defeating them in battle. Victory was never going to happen except on a limited basis. What was perhaps the largest Indian army in history had annihilated Custer and the Seventh Cavalry less than a month earlier; no one could deny that. But in reality, this magnificent triumph for the Indians had eliminated only a tiny fraction of the force that opposed them. The Seventh would be rebuilt, and the Army would carry on as if nothing had happened.

No, that wasn't entirely true, Dick mused as he rode toward Hat Creek. The soldiers would remember what had happened to Custer, and in the future, if they found themselves looking over their gunsights at Indian faces, they would not hesitate to pull the trigger.

The Sioux didn't care, didn't see that waging war on the whites would be futile in the end. Superior numbers and armament meant nothing to them. They trusted in their fierce pride and their skill in battle and their belief that the spirits were on their side. So they fought, and would continue to fight.

That was why Dick Seymour rode hell-bent-for-leather toward the Hat Creek Ranch. He didn't believe for a second that the few Indians he had seen skylighted against the sunset were alone. There was a war party up there, and they might not be able to resist the temptation of a lone white man riding across their land.

All he could do was to urge as much speed as possible from his tired horse and hope it would be enough. If the Indians closed in on him, he would rein his mount to a halt, force the horse to lie down, and use the animal as a shield while he tried to drive them off with his rifle. He didn't hold out any real hope that such tactics would prove successful, though.

But as he looked back over his shoulder, he didn't see any signs of pursuit. If the Indians were back there, they weren't trying to catch him. He reached the edge of the hills and galloped out onto the prairie. Still nothing behind him. He slowed slightly, not wanting the horse to give out and collapse under him.

The sun was down and the shadows of dusk were thick by the time Dick rode up to the cluster of crude cabins and corrals on Hat Creek. Jack Bowman and his men must have heard him coming, because as Dick slowed his horse to a walk, a voice called, "Sing out, friend! There's a rifle on you!"

Dick would have been willing to bet that more than one rifle was trained on him at the moment. He took his hat off, waved it over his head, and replied, "It's Dick Seymour, carrying the mail from Deadwood to Cheyenne!"

"Come ahead!"

Dick heeled his horse forward. Just as he thought, several men emerged from the cabins, each of them carrying a rifle. He recognized the strapping, mustachioed figure of Jack Bowman, the owner of the ranch.

"Howdy, Dick!" Bowman boomed. "Carryin' the mail, you said?"

"That's right," Dick said as he swung down from the saddle. "For Charley Utter's Pioneer Pony Express."

Bowman grinned in the shadows. "That feisty little popinjay! I remember him talkin' about that when y'all came through with those wagons a while back, but I didn't think he'd get it up and runnin' this soon. Up and ridin', I should say, since it's all horseback." The rancher rested his hand on the flank of Dick's horse. "Been ridin' hard, haven't you?"

Dick turned and pointed to the north. "I saw several Sioux warriors back that way a couple of miles."

"Damn it!" one of the other men burst out. Like his companions, he was a cowboy who worked for Bowman. "I told you them redskins was lurkin' around, Boss. We're lucky we ain't all been scalped in our bunks!"

"Take it easy, Marsh," Bowman said. "We've knowed all along there were Indians around here. That's why nobody ever rides the range alone. They're lookin' for one man by himself, so's they can pick him off easylike."

Dick wasn't sure if that assessment was completely accurate, but it was true that the Indians were more likely to jump a lone man. That meant anyone who rode for the Pioneer Pony Express would be running quite a risk. They would be well paid, though, according to Colorado Charley, and it would certainly be a life not lacking in adventure.

"Boys, take care o' Bloody Dick's horse," Bowman went on. He clapped a hand on Dick's shoulder. "Come on in. There's stew and coffee on the stove, and you look like you could use a bunk to stretch out in for a while."

"All of that sounds wonderful, Jack. Thank you."

When he was seated at a rough table inside Bowman's cabin, with a bowl of stew and a cup of coffee in front of him, both of them steaming aromatically, Bowman sat down opposite him and several of the ranch hands gathered around. "Tell us about Deadwood," Bowman said. "And about ol' Wild Bill."

All the young cowboys listened eagerly as Dick described life in Deadwood. Of course, he had spent only a few days there before starting on this ride for Charley Utter, so he was far from an expert on the subject. And Bill Hickok hadn't really done anything since reaching the mining camp, as far as Dick knew, so that part of the story wasn't very exciting. The ranch hands didn't seem to care. They were just glad to hear anything about any place that wasn't this isolated spread on Hat Creek. Ranching was a lonely life.

But of course, that was true of many occupations on the frontier. . . .

After eating, he turned in hoping once again for dreamless sleep, but as usual, he was disappointed. Vivid images haunted his slumber, images of himself and Carries Water and their children, in a happier time when they had gone out with their wagons to trade with the Sioux, before there was so much war and bloodshed on the plains. The two wagons had been full of barrels and crates of sugar, flour, beans, coffee, cloth, buttons, knives, and anything else that might attract the attention of the Indians. The Sioux traded fine buffalo robes for these staples, and the robes fetched a higher price back in the civilized world than the raw hides did. Dick and his family had made several of these trips, each of them more profitable than the ones before it. He planned to continue as long as it wasn't too dangerous. In those days, before gold had been discovered in the Black Hills, the Sioux were less hostile. Some actually regarded the white men as friends.

But some of the warriors had already come to resent the white interlopers, and as Dick began to toss and turn on the rope bunk, the face of the man who had nearly destroyed his life seemed to be burned into his brain. It was a hard face, all planes and sharp angles, framed by thick black hair pulled into two braids and dominated by a pair of dark eyes that radiated hatred when they looked at the white man. While the wagons were parked in front of the lodges of the Sioux village where Dick had stopped, the warrior stood off to one side, arms folded, and watched with a scowl on his face as the women of the tribe chattered and laughed and pawed through the wares that Dick had brought to trade. Carries Water spoke to them in their own tongue. Dick could speak a little of the Sioux language, but his wife was much more fluent. He noticed that some of the women glanced toward the angry warrior as they talked to Carries Water, and later he asked her if they had said anything about the man.

"He hates the whites," she explained. "He says that the Sioux should not be trading with the whites but should be killing them instead. The elders of the tribe do not agree with him . . . yet."

Dick nodded. He sensed that there was something else, and when he prodded Carries Water about it, she said uncomfortably, "He does not like me."

"You?" Dick said in surprise. "What does he have against you?"

"I am married to a white man," she said. "To him, I have turned my back on my people. I have betrayed who I am."

"The man's daft," Dick muttered. "Anyway, it's none of his business. Who does he think he is, anyway?"

So Carries Water had told him the name of the angry warrior who hated all whites and hated her for marrying one of them, and the words echoed in Dick Seymour's dream as he tossed restlessly in the bunk at Hat Creek Ranch.

He is called Talking Bear . . . Talking Bear . . . Talking Bear . . .

Chapter Twelve

CALAMITY Jane came out of the Senate Saloon, wiped the back of her hand across her mouth, and looked up and down Deadwood's Main Street. She was only a little drunk, but she was tired of the Senate and figured she'd find some other place to do her howling tonight. She wondered where Wild Bill was. Playing cards, most likely. He claimed he'd come to Deadwood to look for gold, but from everything Calamity had seen and heard, the only prospecting he'd done had been across the green felt.

She turned toward the Bella Union. That was the most likely place for Bill to be, she had decided. But she'd only gone a few steps when she ran smack-dab into somebody. She grunted as she rebounded from the collision.

"Watch your fuckin' step!" she growled at the man. If he took offense, that would be just too damn bad. She moved her hand toward the butt of the gun on her hip.

"I'm sorry, sister," came the gentle tones of the man's reply.

"Sister? I ain't your sister." Calamity tried to focus her bleary eyes on the man. She made out that he was tall and skinny and had a black beard. . . . "Oh!" she exclaimed. "Sorry, Preacher."

"That's quite all right, Miss Cannary. It *is* Miss Cannary, isn't it?"

"Yeah, but everybody calls me Calamity Jane, or just Calam. Or hey, you fuckin' whore, if they're mad at me." She lifted a hand to her mouth. "Oh, shit. I cussed again, didn't I?"

"It's all right," the preacher said. He sighed and went on. "I hear a great deal of indelicate language every day in Deadwood. It seems that some men are incapable of expressing themselves without being either coarse or blasphemous or both. If you've ever spoken with Mr. Swearengen, you know what I mean."

"Yeah, that cocksuck—I mean, that son of a—that fu—that da—" Calamity clenched her fists and said, "Aaarrgh!" With an effort, she went on. "That *fellow* sure enough does have a mouth on him, you got that right, Preacher."

In the faint light that came through the windows of the nearby buildings, a smile spread across Smith's face. "The Lord says we are to hate the sin but love the sinner. I shall endeavor to persevere in doing so. And I can't think of a better place to practice that particular teaching than right here in Deadwood."

Calamity slapped him on the shoulder and laughed. "You got that right, Preacher! The whole dang place is full o' sinners!"

"Yes," he murmured as she stumbled on past him. "Just like the rest of the world."

Calamity heard the comment but didn't pay any attention to it. She was bent once more upon reaching the Bella Union and looking inside to see if Wild Bill Hickok was there.

She stepped up onto the saloon's porch and saw a man leaning on the railing. Recognizing him, she said, "Howdy, White-Eye."

Jack Anderson turned his head and nodded to her. "Calam. Been drinkin'?"

That was a stupid question. She laughed and poked him

in the chest with a finger. "You think I'm three sheets to the wind, don't you? Well, I ain't. I'm only two sheets. Maybe just one." She wiped her nose. "Is Wild Bill inside?"

"I haven't seen him." Jack was staring across the street again, as he had been when Calamity first came up onto the porch.

"What the hell you lookin' at?" She turned her head and squinted at Al Swearengen's place. After a moment her whiskey-muddled brain figured out the reason for the White-Eyed Kid's fascination. "That whore's over there, ain't she? The one you fancied, the one called Silky Jen?"

Jack looked at her again, his head jerking toward her. "Have you seen her in there?"

Calamity was a little surprised by his vehemence. "Fuck, no," she said. "But I ain't been lookin' for her, neither. I never was one to get dirty with other gals, like some whores do."

"But you *have* been in the Gem since we got to Deadwood?"

"Well, sure." She cackled. "They sell whiskey there, don't they?"

"But you didn't see Jen any time you were in there?"

"I told you I ain't seen her." The young man's concern got through to Calamity, and she stepped closer to him. "What's wrong?"

"I went in there yesterday and I . . . I asked for her. Not by name, but I described her. Nobody could ever mistake her for anybody else." He shook his head. "But one of the men who works for Swearengen said that she doesn't work there, that there's nobody there who looks like that."

"Maybe she went to work somewheres else," Calamity suggested. "Whores ain't the most dependable sort o' folks in the world."

Jack nodded slowly. "Maybe . . . but I'm sure she told me the Gem Theater was where she planned to work. She was hoping maybe she'd get to sing and dance some, since it's a theater, too, and not just a saloon." He gave a hollow laugh. "Besides, I've been to every other saloon and gambling den and brothel in Deadwood today, and she's not at any of them." His eyes fastened on the Gem again. "No, she's over there. I'm sure of it."

An idea percolated its way through Calamity's brain. "Tell you what," she said to Jack. "I'll go and have a look around myself. I recollect what that Jen gal looks like. If I spot her, I'll come right back over here and tell you. How'd that be?"

"You really think you can find her?" Jack sounded doubtful.

Calamity drew herself up straight, somewhat offended by the question. "Hell, I scouted for General Crook, didn't I? If that gal you're sweet on is over there, I'll find her, by Godfrey!"

"Thanks, Calam," the Kid said. "I really appreciate it. You'd better be careful, though. I hear Swearengen's a bad man to cross, and he might not like you snoopin' around."

Calamity snorted contemptuously. "I ain't a-scared o' that cocksucker. If he's got any sense, he'll know better'n to tangle with Calamity Jane!"

Leaving Jack on the front porch of the Bella Union, she ventured out into the street. Since it was dark, it was harder to avoid the mud puddles and the shit piles, but since she thought it was foolish to worry too much about being clean, she just tromped straight across to the Gem and didn't pay any attention to what she was stepping in. A pungent aroma rose around her and followed her into the saloon.

Several men turned to makes faces and frown after her when she went past them, but Calamity ignored them. She headed for the bar, where a stocky gent with a beard was working behind the hardwood.

"Whiskey, barkeep!" she demanded.

The man looked at her with narrowed eyes. "You're Calamity Jane, ain't you?"

"That's what they call me!"

"You got money?"

She glared at him. "O' course I got money! What kind o' cheap fucker you think I am?"

"The kind who's got to pay up before I pour any

drinks," the bartender said. "There's no fightin' in here, either, so don't go startin' a ruckus."

Calamity sneered at him. "Mighty high-class son of a bitch, ain't you?"

"You got money or not?"

Grumbling, she dug around in the pockets of her buckskins until she found a coin. Saying, "Ah-hah!" she slapped it on the bar. "Now gimme that drink."

The bartender poured a shot of booze in a glass that wasn't too smeared with fingerprints and shoved it across the hardwood. Calamity picked it up and swallowed the whiskey in one slug. It was raw, vile stuff, more suitable for peeling paint off boards than drinking. She licked her lips and decided that she'd had worse.

The bartender picked up the coin. "Want another?"

"Don't mind if I do."

She took her time with this one, turning so that her back was to the bar as she sipped the Who-Hit-John. Her gaze roved over the room. She knew she probably looked a little owl-eyed . . . hell, she *was* a little owl-eyed . . . but she wasn't as muddled as she appeared to be.

The Gem offered plenty of gambling: Several poker games were going on, half-a-dozen miners were gathered in front of a faro bank, and more were clustered around a roulette wheel. A slick-haired professor was banging on an out-of-tune piano, and several couples whirled around in time to the music on an open area that served as a dance floor. At more than one table, a miner had drunk himself into a stupor and then collapsed face down. Their snores blended with the tinny music, the stomping of feet, and the raucous laughter to create a distinctive melody.

There was steady traffic on the stairs as the soiled doves who worked here took their customers up to their rooms or brought them back down when they were done. Most of the whores pulled on bloomers or shifts to come downstairs, but as Calamity watched, she saw one with frizzy orange hair, enormous breasts, and a butt like a plow horse prance down the stairs stark naked, a grinning young prospector on her arm. When they reached the bottom, she reached over and gave his crotch a farewell squeeze, then patted him on the ass to send him on his way and hollered, "Who wants a shot at me next?" Several men scrambled to volunteer.

Damn fools, thought Calamity. A cow like that was a disgrace to hardworking whores everywhere. Calamity knew she was no beauty, but in her day she'd been better than that. Still, the naked woman didn't have any trouble finding somebody to go upstairs with her. There would always be plenty of men who didn't care where they stuck it, as long as it was warm.

Still nursing her drink, Calamity drifted away from the bar. She watched a hand of poker, checked out the action at the faro bank and the roulette wheel, and gradually worked her way toward the back of the room. She wanted to get up to the second floor, since that was likely where Silky Jen would be found if she was here, and Calamity figured there were some rear stairs somewhere.

Nobody was paying attention to her. The customers were all caught up in enjoying themselves, and the bartenders and the floor men and the whores were busy insuring that the money kept flowing into Al Swearengen's pockets. Calamity didn't see Swearengen himself. The stocky, dark-featured man was hard to miss when he was around.

Calamity found a hallway that led back to the kitchen. She sauntered along it, figuring that if she ran into anybody who wanted to know what she was doing back here, she could say that she was looking for the way to the privy. That is, if snarling, "What the fuck are *you* doin' back here?" didn't work.

She didn't see anybody, though, and a few minutes later she found the steep, narrow set of stairs she expected to find. The stairway was dark, but she wasn't scared. She tossed back the whiskey that was left in the glass and started up.

The boards creaked under her feet. She moved closer to the wall and kept climbing. The stairs were quieter now. She saw a smoky yellow glow at the top, and when she reached the landing she found herself in a small rear hallway lit by a single lamp with its flame turned low to save oil.

She looked both ways along the hall, trying to figure out what to do next. There were doors on one side of the hall, but not the other since that was the rear wall of the building. Calamity went to the nearest door and pressed her ear to it. She didn't hear any sounds coming from inside, and when she tried the knob, it was unlocked. Carefully, she eased the door open and looked inside.

The room was dark except for the dim light that came from the hall. It revealed a stack of chairs and a couple of tables. This was just a storage room; that was all. Calamity pulled the door closed and moved to the next door.

Somebody was in this room, and the grunting noises she heard made it clear what they were doing. She had heard plenty of men make those same sounds as they humped away on top of her. She listened until she heard a long "Ahhhhh!" that indicated the gent had finished what he was doing. Calamity gave it a few seconds longer, and then, knowing that the soiled dove would be getting up to wash herself, she opened the door a crack and peeked inside.

The whore didn't notice, and the customer was still lying on the bunk, satisfied and worn out by his efforts. The lamp on the bedside table revealed the whore to be short and dumpy and blond, nothing at all like Silky Jen. Calamity closed the door, being careful not to let it click.

She knew the customer in this room would be leaving soon, so she retreated to the stairwell and stayed there until she heard the customer and the whore leaving to go back down the main staircase. This was going to take longer than she had anticipated. Calamity hoped the White-Eyed Kid wouldn't get impatient and bust into the Gem demanding to see his gal.

There were four more rooms back here. Two of them were also used for storage, Calamity discovered over the next half hour, and the whores in the other two weren't the one she was looking for. She found a narrow side corridor that led to the rooms along the front of the building, the ones that overlooked the barroom, and she slipped along it until she reached the end. When she stepped out of its protection, she would be on the balcony and would be visible from downstairs, if anybody happened to be looking up here.

She wasn't doing anything wrong, she told herself. And if she was caught, she could always claim to be so drunk she didn't know what she was doing. Hell, it wasn't that far from the truth, now, was it?

She got lucky and saw two whores lead their current customers into a couple of the rooms, so she could eliminate those. Two more whores came out of a couple of different rooms, so again she could cross those off the list. That left only three doors, and she knew that Swearengen's office was behind one of them. She had seen him going in and out of it several times over the past few days.

It was likely that the room where Swearengen slept would be next to his office. She stepped out and risked a glance over the balcony railing. Swearengen was down below, standing at the bar talking to the bearded bartender. It was hard to miss the man. He seemed to dominate any room he was in. Bill Hickok had sort of the same quality, but with Swearengen it was different. Swearengen held the same sort of fascination that a big ugly snake did.

Knowing that it was safe for the moment, Calamity stepped quickly to the door of the room she had pegged as Swearengen's bedchamber. She tried the knob. It wasn't locked. That made sense in a way. Swearengen knew he had all his employees so buffaloed and afraid of him that he figured none of them would dare bother anything of his.

Calamity Jane didn't work for the son of a bitch, though, and she sure as hell wasn't afraid of him. She twisted the knob, swung the door open, stepped into the room, and pulled the door shut behind her.

A single lamp burned in the room, and its wick was turned very low. The weak yellow glow from the flame fell over a small table with a chair in front of it, a big, heavy wardrobe, and a bed with a thick mattress on it. Sprawled facedown on the bed was a naked young woman. Her wrists and ankles were tied with short lengths of rope to the posts at the head and foot of the bed. Calamity's breath caught in her throat as she saw that the young woman's buttocks were covered with bruises in various stages of mottling, as if somebody had been beating her ass for several days.

Thick brown hair reached halfway down the woman's back. Calamity recognized the hair and the slender body. She knew she had found Silky Jen.

She didn't have much time. Swearengen might come up here without any warning. So far, Jen hadn't responded to Calamity's entrance into the room. She was either asleep or unconscious. Calamity stepped to her side, reached down with a calloused hand, and lightly touched her shoulder.

Jen moaned and stirred. The bonds on her wrists and ankles were long enough to give her a little slack. She pulled her legs up and raised her butt. In an oddly thick voice, she muttered, "Please don't fuck me in the ass again, Mr. Swearengen. It's too sore. Use my pussy. Please."

Lord, thought Calamity Jane, and as Jen turned her head on the pillow so that Calamity could see her face, she thought again, *Lord!*

Jen's face was as bruised as her ass. Her lips were swollen, which explained why her voice had sounded that way. There was dried blood on them, too. Her eyes were closed, so she didn't know that it wasn't Al Swearengen standing over her. Calamity's eyes drifted down to the side of the one breast she could see.

Were those fuckin' *bite marks* on it?

Jen still hadn't opened her eyes. She said, "Mr. Swearengen? Are you gonna fuck me?"

Calamity backed away. The shock of what she had seen in this room had leeched all the drunkenness out of her. She was filled with rage. Sure, whores had a hard life, and they had to expect to get knocked around some, from time to time. But this . . . this went beyond that. Even a whore shouldn't be treated like this.

At the same time, although she would have been loath to admit it, she was a little afraid. Al Swearengen was a hard, ruthless man without any warmth in him. Calamity could tell that just by looking at the man. But she hadn't known that he was a monster, and that was truly what he had to be in order to treat Jen this way.

Calamity Jane wasn't afraid of any man. She wasn't so sure about monsters. . . .

And he might come back at any minute.

Calamity turned and reached for the doorknob. She froze as Jen murmured, "Who . . . ?"

Turning, Calamity saw the whore looking at her.

Jen's bloody, swollen lips moved, and she whispered, "H-help me . . ."

"Don't you say anything about me bein' here!" Calamity hissed. "I'll do what I can for you, but don't you say anything!"

Jen shook her head slightly. Calamity didn't know what she meant by that, whether she was agreeing or disagreeing, but there was no time to stand there and argue. She opened the door an inch and looked out. The hall was empty, so Calamity got while the getting was good. She stepped out into the hall, pulled the door shut behind her, and lowered her head as she strode swiftly toward the corridor leading to the rear stairs.

She tried not to think about the small sound of despair she had heard come from behind the door of Swearengen's room.

Nobody had seen her, nobody bothered her as she went downstairs and out a back door. In the alley behind the Gem, she stopped and pressed her back against the wall of the building, steadying herself. Her pulse pounded wildly in her brain. She wished she could forget what she had seen up there, just forget it.

By the time she got back to the Bella Union, she was composed and knew what she had to do. Jack Anderson was waiting for her. As she came up onto the porch, he stepped toward her eagerly and asked, "Well? Did you find her? Did you see her anywhere in there?"

Calamity Jane looked him straight in the eye and said, "Sorry, Kid. I didn't see her nowheres. I reckon that gal Jen just ain't over there."

Chapter Thirteen

⤙∽⤚

DICK Seymour was up well before dawn the next morning and had a good breakfast in Jack Bowman's cabin. Even though his horse had had a night's rest, Dick knew the animal had to be fagged out after the past two days of hard riding. The night before, he had reached an agreement with Bowman to exchange horses, and when Dick went out to the corral he found that some of Bowman's ranch hands had already put his saddle on a rangy, long-legged dun with a dark stripe down its otherwise mouse-colored back.

"That lineback may not look like much," said Bowman, who had followed Dick out of the cabin, "but he'll run all day like the very Devil himself is after him. You just want to watch yourself about turnin' your back to him when you're around his head. If he thinks he can get away with it, he'll sure take a bite out of your hide."

"I'll bear that in mind," Dick promised. "He's well rested?"

Bowman nodded. "Ain't been ridden in nearly a week. I noticed yesterday he was gettin' a mite skittish in the corral, so I reckon he's ready to run, all right."

"Thanks, Jack. I appreciate you making the swap like this."

"Don't think anything about it. I'm glad to help." Bowman hesitated for a second and then went on. "But if you think Colorado Charley wouldn't mind, there is one thing you could do for me." He slipped a hand inside the canvas jacket he wore against the early morning chill.

"Of course, Jack," Dick said. "What is it?"

Bowman brought out several sheets of paper that had been folded and sealed with wax. "I got a letter I'd like to mail to the folks back home."

Dick reached out to take it. "I'd be glad to slip it in the pouch, no charge." Even if Charley Utter had been making folks pay for mailing privileges on this inaugural run, Dick wouldn't have charged Bowman under these circumstances.

"I'm much obliged, Dick. You want some of the boys to ride with you for a ways, sort of keep you company?"

Dick remembered the Indians he had seen the day before and knew that Bowman was offering him protection. The idea was appealing, but Dick knew he couldn't accept. If he was going to ride for the Pioneer Pony Express, he had to be able to go it alone.

"I appreciate it, but I'm sure I'll be fine. You lads have plenty of work to do around here without nursemaiding me."

"Aw, now, that ain't it, Dick—"

He raised a hand to forestall Bowman's protest. "Really, it's all right." He patted the lineback dun's rump. "You've already provided me with this excellent mount, which I'm sure can outrun any danger in which we might find ourselves."

The horse turned his head and gave Dick a dubious look, as if he had understood every word.

"Well, all right," Bowman said grudgingly. "You got plenty of supplies?"

"More than adequate, thanks." Dick stowed Bowman's letter in the saddlebags with the rest of the mail and then turned to the rancher with his hand extended. "So long, Jack. I'll see you on my way back to Deadwood."

Bowman pumped his hand. "Damn well better. There'll be hot food and coffee and a fresh horse waitin' for you."

With that, Dick swung up into the saddle. He waved to Bowman and the ranch hands and then heeled the dun into a trot that carried him away from the cabins and the corrals. When he was about fifty yards away he urged the horse into a gallop. The early morning air was cold in his face as he rode south.

There was enough gray, predawn light in the sky for Dick to be able to see where he was going, but details at a distance were vague. He watched his surroundings as closely as possible anyway, just in case there was any sign of trouble. He wanted to believe that the Indians he had seen the day before had moved on and were now miles from here and represented no threat. But there was no way of knowing that for certain, and the lingering doubt kept Dick alert and watchful, especially before the sun came up.

But once the great blazing orb was above the eastern horizon, he relaxed a bit. He could see better now, and here on the prairie, it would be more difficult for any enemies to approach without him noticing them while they were still a good distance away. Not only that, but the dun was running easily, and Dick could tell from the way the horse felt under him that his mount did indeed possess the speed and strength and stamina that Jack Bowman had promised. If nothing intervened, he thought he could reach the Hunton ranch by nightfall, and then tomorrow it would be on to Fort Laramie.

He was rocking along with the dun in that ground-eating gallop when trouble came at him from a direction he didn't expect.

Directly in front of him.

TALKING Bear and the rest of the Sioux were well south of the Bowman ranch by that morning. One scout, a young warrior named Round Rock, had been left close by the ranch to watch for the white man they had seen yesterday. If the white man left the ranch and continued on south,

Round Rock would race ahead and tell Talking Bear and the others. That was exactly what had happened. Talking Bear got the war party moving and they headed farther south, so that they would be well away from the ranch before they jumped the lone, foolish white man.

When Talking Bear judged they had gone far enough, he halted the warriors. They dismounted and pulled their ponies down on the ground so that they lay flat and were difficult to see. The white man would ride toward them without knowing they were there until it was too late. If all went according to plan, he would be practically on top of them before they rose up to slay him and take his hair. He would have no chance to get away.

Talking Bear lay there with his hand on his horse's neck, keeping the animal still. Faintly, he sensed the vibrations in the earth from the hoofbeats of the white man's horse as it approached. At least, he told himself that he did. Perhaps it was just anticipation he felt.

And deep within his brain, he wondered if he should not feel some shame, as well. They were many, and the white man was only one. Did it really require so many Sioux to kill one white man? Would there not be more honor if he were to face the man alone, the two of them in combat to the death?

Talking Bear shoved those thoughts out of his head. He was a war chief. There should be no room in him for doubt. His actions were just and honorable because they were his actions. And the white man would die, which in the end was all that really mattered. Soon the rider would be there, to meet his doom.

It would have happened that way, too, if a snake, eager to seek the warmth of the day, had not slithered out of its hole right in front of the nose of one of the ponies. With a shrill whinny, the pony jerked its head up and its body convulsed as it sought to leap back onto its legs and get away from the snake.

The spirits, in their sometimes perverse way, had turned on him and ruined his plan, Talking Bear thought as the pony kicked its way up and the warrior who owned it had to leap up as well to keep the animal from bolting. Talking Bear yelled for his men to attack as he surged onto his feet.

More than a bow shot away, the white man yanked his mount to a sliding stop, wheeled the horse into an almost impossibly sharp turn, and galloped away, heading back to the north.

There were no words in the Sioux tongue equivalent to the foul cursing of the white men . . . but if there had been, Talking Bear would have been using them at that moment. He leaped onto his pony and gave chase. That was all he could do. The white man had to die, no matter what it took.

Talking Bear's honor now demanded it.

DICK was shocked right down to his toes when the Indians and their ponies seemed to grow right up out of the prairie a couple of hundred yards ahead of him. He didn't stop to think about what he was seeing, however. Instinct made him haul back hard on the reins. Almost as if reading his mind, the dun skidded to a stop, turned on a dime, and lunged back in the direction they had come from. Obviously, Dick had communicated a great deal of urgency in that tug on the reins.

Now he leaned forward over the dun's neck and held his hat on with one hand as the horse stretched out and ran at even greater speeds than before. The grass-covered prairie landscape flew by and was little more than a blur to Dick. He didn't look back. If the Sioux were gaining on him, he didn't want to know about it just yet. It took all his concentration just to keep the dun under control at this breakneck speed.

He had a good lead on them, he told himself. His horse could outrun them. It wasn't that far back to Bowman's ranch, less than ten miles, in fact. All he had to do was to stay comfortably in front of the pursuit until he reached Hat Creek. He believed the Indians would turn back then. He didn't think they would attack the ranch, knowing that the cowboys were well armed and good shots and had sturdy cabins to fort up in. Everything depended, though, on actually reaching the ranch before the Sioux could catch him.

Finally, when he couldn't stand the suspense any longer, he glanced over his shoulder. The Indian ponies were swift, but so was the dun. Dick saw to his surprise that he had opened up even more of a lead on them. The Indians were at least fifty yards farther behind him than they had been when the chase started. He was out of range of their bows, and while the ones who had rifles could have stopped and tried to pick him off, they didn't seem inclined to do so. It would have been a difficult shot, anyway.

Dick's confidence grew. There were too many Indians for him to fight, probably between twenty and thirty, but he could outrun them. He kept telling himself that as he urged the dun on. The rangy horse never faltered.

When he looked back again, he saw that some of the warriors had fallen even farther back. Though he couldn't be certain, he thought that some of them had slowed and dropped out of the chase entirely. Anything that helped decrease the odds against him was a good thing.

But there was one troubling development. One of the Sioux had pulled well ahead of the others and was still coming on at a very fast pace. The man rode a sturdy black horse that was slightly bigger than the other ponies. The Indian was a bit bigger than his companions, too, Dick judged. He sensed a stubbornness about the warrior, as if the man intended to keep up the chase no matter how long it took, whether the others kept coming or not. He would fight the white man alone if he had to.

That sort of fanaticism was worrisome. It reminded Dick of stories he had heard from soldiers who had returned to England from wars in the far-flung outposts of the empire. He recalled how the *other* Indians, the ones on the far side of the world, had fought to the death during the Sepoy Rebellion, which soldiers of the British East India Company had barely been able to quell. They were civilized Englishmen and had forgotten what it was like to be barbarians. They had forgotten those long-ago days when their own ancestors had painted their faces blue and come down from the north beyond Hadrian's Wall to wage war on the Roman occupiers. The wild days faded away as civilization inevitably rose . . . but equally inevitable was the fall, since, as a wise man once said, barbarism was the natural state of mankind.

Dick Seymour had one of those barbarians behind him now, a man who had never heard of the Sepoys or the ancient Britons, but one who would fight with all the fierceness of those natural cousins of his. Dick looked back and saw that the warrior was still gaining on him. The Indian was going to ride his horse to death if he wasn't careful, but it was doubtful that meant anything to him. He would trade a horse, even a good one, for the death of a hated enemy.

Dick estimated he had covered at least half the distance back to Hat Creek. But now the Indian was only a little more than a hundred yards behind him. The dun was still running well, but Dick sensed the horse had lost a fraction of his speed. Could he keep up the pace long enough to reach safety?

Or would that lone Sioux warrior close in on him?

One man, Dick thought. They had outstripped the rest of the pursuit, and now there was only one man in sight behind him.

The odds, in other words, were now even.

As the thought flashed through his brain, Dick tried to shove it away, telling himself that he was crazy. If he turned back to meet the pursuer, he would be playing right into the hands of the Indians. He might not be able to see the rest of the war party anymore, but that didn't mean they weren't back there, and not very far back, at that. Besides, even though he had lived an adventurous life for the past half decade and knew quite well how to fight and handle a gun, there was no guarantee he could defeat the Indian in single combat. In fact, it was likely that he couldn't. So to even consider turning back and meeting the danger head-on was madness, pure madness. . . .

A bit like the madness of his forebears who had risked all to drive the Roman invaders from their land, all those centuries ago.

A shout burned its way out of Dick's throat as he pulled back on the reins. The dun broke stride, evidently shocked to be reined in, and the horse almost fell. Dick's hand was firm. He brought the dun to a halt and then turned the horse to face south again. A hundred yards away, the Indian on the black pony galloped toward them.

Dick drew his pistol. A grimace pulled his lips back from his teeth. He shouted again as he kicked the horse into a run and charged straight at his enemy.

It *was* mad. Totally insane.

And all he could think about was how damned *good* it felt now that he had stopped running. Now that he was taking the fight to the foe.

Within seconds, the dun was galloping again. The Sioux warrior had never slowed. The distance between them vanished almost in a heartbeat. Dick was in pistol range now, so he raised the Colt and tried to aim. The back of a racing horse made a terrible shooting platform, but Dick fired anyway, squeezing off a shot, cocking the revolver, and deliberately firing again. At the same time, smoke and flame geysered from the muzzle of the repeating rifle the Indian carried, stolen no doubt from some white man he had killed. Dick didn't know where the Indian's bullet went, but he was sure he wasn't hit. Unfortunately, neither of his shots seemed to have found their target, either.

They flashed past each other like knights of old in a joust. For an instant, a shaved heartbeat of time, only a few feet separated them, and in that moment Dick got a good clear look at the painted face of his enemy. Even with the colorful daubs obscuring some of the features, Dick recognized the hard, sharply planed face. He would never forget it. That recognition hit him hard, like a physical blow that threatened to topple him from the saddle. For a second, it was all he could do to stay mounted and to retain his grip on his pistol.

Then, thankfully, instinct took over again and he hauled on the reins, pulling the dun around in a tight turn. Some twenty yards away, the Indian was doing the same thing with his pony. Both men were ready to continue the fight. The warrior thrust his rifle over his head, howled a challenge, and drove his horse toward Dick.

Calmly, Dick lifted his Colt. The Indian could have tried to shoot him from a distance. At twenty yards, the rifle would be more accurate than Dick's handgun. But instead the warrior had charged him again, and Dick thought he knew why.

The Sioux wanted to count coup on him. He had no coup stick, but he could use the rifle for that, reaching out to hit Dick with the barrel when he rode past. It was the height of courage and honor for a warrior to do such a thing.

Dick cared nothing for courage or honor or any other empty concept. Ever since he had recognized his foe, the only thing that mattered to him was the rage that filled his entire being. That warrior . . . that man . . . was the one responsible for taking away his happiness, taking away everything that had meant anything in his life. He had to die.

Dick lined his sights on the screaming face and pulled the trigger.

The hammer snapped, but there was no blast of exploding powder, no recoil. The Colt had misfired. Dick's eyes widened as he tried to get his thumb on the hammer and pull it back for another shot.

But he was too late. The Sioux warrior was on him and the rifle barrel lashed out toward him, just as Dick expected. It slammed into his head as the Indian counted coup. No light tap this, but a crushing blow that slewed Dick sideways in the saddle. The dun reared and jerked away from a collision with the Indian's black pony.

That was too much. Dick tried to retain his grip on the reins, but they slipped away from him. He made a grab for the saddle horn, but missed. The grip he had with his knees wasn't enough to keep him in the saddle. He felt himself falling. . . .

But he didn't feel himself hit the ground. By that time, a black nothingness had claimed him.

Chapter Fourteen

❧

JEN had known a lot of trouble and abuse in her relatively short life. Most of it she had just witnessed as she grew up in the various houses where her mother worked. She had seen whores slapped around pretty badly by their customers. Often they were left bruised, sometimes even bloody. Once in St. Louis, a man had grown enraged for some reason and had pulled a knife and used it to cut the face of the woman he was with. She had screamed, and the bruiser who kept the peace in the house, a giant black man named Ulysses, went in the room, took the knife away from the man, and broke his arm. Jen had seen the injured woman a few minutes later as the madam and some of the other whores tried to care for her. They had held a towel to her face to try to stop the bleeding, and it had become soaked almost immediately. Jen, standing unnoticed in the room's doorway, had watched as they took the towel away, and she had seen the white of bone under the crimson. The whore's face was laid open so badly it would never heal properly. She would always have a hideous scar.

Jen had been only ten years old at the time, and she thought Ulysses had been too easy with the man who'd done the cutting. She solemnly informed her mother later on that he should have broken the bastard's neck instead of his arm.

Since then she had been inducted into the business herself, and on occasion she had been abused by her customers. Some men just liked to be rough with a woman. They enjoyed grabbing her wrists and cruelly pinning her arms above her head. They drove into her hard, not caring if it hurt. They grasped her chin, digging their fingers into her flesh, and bruised and bloodied her lips with theirs. Sometimes, they even liked to slip their fingers around her neck and pretend to be choking her. Those times always scared her. She was afraid they would go too far and actually strangle her. That was why she usually kept a small knife under her pillow. The customers never knew it, but if they got carried away and she felt that her life was actually in danger, she would have slipped that knife out and used it. She wouldn't have hesitated to plunge the blade into some violent son of a bitch's belly and rip him wide open.

Thankfully, it had never come to that. Using her other skills, she had been able to calm down even the most wild-eyed sorts of men.

But she had never met a man like Al Swearengen before.

She had been slapped plenty of times, but she had never been beaten with a closed fist until Swearengen came along. She had allowed men to use her anus before, but none of them had taken her as hard and brutally and painfully that way as Swearengen did, tearing her so that she bled. When he was through with her she felt as if she'd had a fireplace log rammed all the way into her bowels. The attacks were always accompanied by slapping and punching and even biting, and while he was at it, Swearengen kept up a stream of verbal abuse as well, heaping indignities and obscenities on her head that might have bothered her if she hadn't been so numbed by the rest of his assault. Ever since he had caught her looking out the window, he had kept her tied to the bed whenever he wasn't in the room. Often, he left her tied while he attacked her.

She had come to Deadwood to be a whore; she had no illusions about that. But she hadn't known that she would wind up the prisoner of a madman, a monster. This wasn't Deadwood at all, she caught herself thinking sometimes. . . .

It was Hell, and Al Swearengen was the Devil.

No one was going to rescue her, either. She vaguely remembered someone else coming into the room . . . a short, ugly man in buckskins and a floppy-brimmed hat . . . but Jen's vision had been blurred by pain and she hadn't gotten a good look at the man. Anyway, whoever he was, he had left without doing a thing to help her, despite her pleading.

Maybe Swearengen would tire of tormenting her and release her from her captivity before she died from the mistreatment. Then she could go on with the life she had intended to lead when she came here, that of a frontier soiled dove. Right now, even that sounded wonderful.

As she lay facedown on the bed, she heard the click of a key in the lock. A shudder ran through her. Swearengen was back, and Lord only know what he would do to her next. She whimpered in fear, but no one heard.

The door opened and then closed. Footsteps approached the bed. Jen didn't move, didn't open her eyes. Whatever was about to happen to her, she didn't want to see it coming.

The mattress shifted underneath her as someone sat down on the bed. Something cool, gloriously cool, gently touched her face. She gasped in shock at the sensation. Her eyes flew open, and she saw the narrow, bearded face of the man who leaned over her. He had a wet cloth in his hand, and he dabbed it over her bruised and swollen features, washing away the dried blood and bringing, at least for the moment, blessed relief from the aches and pains.

"Lord have mercy," the man muttered under his breath. "Lord have mercy on us all, gal. I knew Al had likely been a mite rough on you, but I didn't know it was like this."

"Wh-who . . . ?" Jen managed to gasp.

"You askin' me who I am? I reckon you don't remember. I'm Johnny Burnes. I sort of take care of the whores who work here at the Gem. You know, keep 'em in line, make sure they're doin' what they're supposed to. Bring the doc to see 'em if they get too sick to work. Things like that. Al said you might need some cleanin' up."

She remembered Burnes now from her first night at the Gem, but only vaguely. As he continued washing her face, she whispered, "Is he . . . going to . . . let me go?"

"I wouldn't know nothin' about that," Burnes answered too quickly. "He never said nothin' to me about that, either way."

She knew he was lying. She knew she wasn't going anywhere yet. Swearengen had not yet grown tired of her.

Desperation welled up inside her. She had to do something, anything, to try to get out of here. If she could get loose, she could climb out of the window and drop from the balcony to the street, stark naked if she had to. Anything to get out of the Gem.

So when Burnes left off washing her face and ran his hand down her back to the curve of her buttocks, she parted her thighs a little, invitingly.

No doubt Swearengen had given his flunky orders to just clean Jen up and leave her alone otherwise. He was a jealous man and wouldn't want his employees fucking her until he was through with her.

But Burnes was just a man, and Swearengen wasn't here to make sure he followed orders. Jen wasn't the least bit surprised when Burnes's hand strayed between her legs and began to caress her. She was dry, but after a minute he slipped a finger into her anyway.

"Don't you tell Al about this," he hissed into her ear as he leaned closer to her. "If you do, I'll tell him you're lyin', and you'll get beat worse'n ever. You understand?"

Jen nodded without looking at him. She made her hips move a little, as if what he was doing to her was arousing her.

Burnes let out a quiet moan as he pumped his finger in and out of her. He said, "Lord, that's sweet!"

"Untie me," Jen said in a deliberately throaty voice.

Even in her battered state, she had no trouble sounding as if she were getting caught up in the grip of passion. And that idiot Burnes believed it, of course. Just like a man.

"I . . . I can't. Al'd skin me alive."

"Just one hand and foot," Jen suggested. "That way I can roll over and you . . . you can get to my front."

She knew men liked her breasts. Enough of them had told her so. She twisted as much as she could and looked up at Burnes. He licked his lips and looked both extremely nervous and extremely aroused. The way she was lying now, he could see most of one breast, but Jen was counting on the hope that one beautiful tit wouldn't be enough to satisfy him.

"Just one hand and foot," she said again. "If you do that, I still can't get away, but you can do so much more with me." She played her last card. "And I could do more for you."

"You ain't gonna try to get away?"

He was weakening; she was sure of it. "I told you, I couldn't."

"Well . . . I reckon it wouldn't hurt . . . just for a few minutes."

He reached for the rope holding her left wrist to the bed, and she thought, *Thank God men think with their peckers!*

It took only a moment for Burnes to untie her left wrist and ankle. She flexed her leg and arm and winced at the stiffness of her muscles. But it felt good to be able to move around again, even on a limited basis. She rolled to her right and wound up on her back with the ropes binding her right wrist and ankle now underneath her. It was still awkward, but she had a lot more freedom of movement.

At least she did for a second, before Johnny Burnes climbed on top of her.

He didn't try to fuck her, which made her more convinced than ever that Swearengen had forbidden that. But when she spread her legs he started fingering her again, and at the same time he slobbered on her breasts, kissing and licking them and sucking the nipples into his mouth.

He dry-humped her hip. He was going to be squirting in his long underwear pretty soon.

She let her left arm drop off the bed, and her fingers touched the smooth porcelain of the heavy chamber pot she knew was there. Swearengen didn't let her use it except when he was there in the room with her. That was one more humiliation, one more mark against the bastard. She got a good grip on the pot as Burnes moved up from her tits and started trying to kiss her on the mouth. He said urgently, "Can . . . can you take my dick out and play with it?"

"Sure, honey," she told him, and then with all the strength she could muster she swung the half-full chamber pot up and over and smashed it into his head.

Waste flew everywhere as the pot shattered, filling the air with its stench. The impact knocked Burnes halfway off the bed. He slid the rest of the way, knocked senseless. Jen could tell by the way his eyes rolled up in their sockets that he wouldn't regain his senses for several minutes, at the earliest. Now, if no one had heard the crash of the chamber pot . . .

She didn't have any time to waste. She reached across her body with her free hand and tugged frantically at the knots securing the rope to her right wrist. They were maddeningly stubborn, but finally, after what seemed like an eternity, the rope fell away from her skin. She sat up, ignoring the dizziness in her head, and went to work on the last rope, the one binding her right ankle. With both hands free, untying it didn't take quite as long.

She swung her legs out of bed and stood up. The dizziness got worse. It was bad enough she thought she was going to fall down and pass out. But when Johnny Burnes groaned as he tried to come around, that stiffened Jen's spine and made her more determined than ever to get out of here. She took a deep breath, waited a second longer to let her head steady even more, and then bent over him to see if he had a gun or a knife on him.

Shit, she thought a moment later. He was unarmed. She had told herself she would climb out of that window naked if she had to, she reminded herself. It was time to do just that.

She stepped to the window, pushed the curtains aside, and flung up the sash. All she had to do now was to swing a leg over the sill and step out onto the narrow, decorative balcony.

Before she could do that, the door of the room opened behind her, and Al Swearengen burst out, "What the fuck!"

Panic exploded inside Jen and made her clumsy as she tried to clamber out the window. She heard the swift thud of Swearengen's boots on the floor, and she let out a scream as his arms went around her from behind and jerked her away from the window. He threw her across the room. She landed on the bed, bounced off the mattress, and fell to the floor on the far side of the bed. Swearengen rushed around it and launched a kick that caught her in the side. She cried out again as the kick knocked her against the wall. Pain flooded through her. As Swearengen loomed over her, images of him stomping her to death filled her frenzied brain. She held up her hands toward him, knowing how futile the gesture was, and begged softly, "No, please, no . . ."

To her surprise, he didn't kick her again. He turned his wrath instead on Johnny Burnes. Jen heard Swearengen's boot smack into Burnes's body as Swearengen cursed. She kept her eyes squeezed tightly shut. Maybe he would vent most of his insane anger on Burnes.

Somebody else came into the room. A man said, "Al! Al, stop it! You're gonna kill him!"

That was Dan Dority. Jen recognized his voice. She risked opening her eyes a slit. She saw Dority with his arms around Swearengen's waist, holding him back from behind. Swearengen's face was purple with rage. Jen found herself hoping that he'd get so mad, something would burst inside him.

That didn't happen. Dority pulled Swearengen away from the huddled shape on the floor that was Johnny Burnes. Swearengen rasped, "I'm all right. Let me go, Dan. Let me go!"

Reluctantly, Dority relinquished his grip. Swearengen raised his hands and covered his face with them. Jen was surprised to see that both of the saloon owner's hands were shaking violently. He was shaking all over, in fact. He stood there for a long moment until he had settled down somewhat. Then he lowered his hands and used one of them to point at her.

"Tie her up again," he said to Dority in a choked voice. "Then take Johnny downstairs and tend to him. Tell him I'm sorry for what I did to him."

Sorry? Al Swearengen? Jen never would have believed she would hear those words come out of the evil man's mouth.

"He had it comin', Al," Dority said. "He must've untied the girl, when you gave him orders not to do that, and to watch out for any tricks she might pull."

"Yeah, that must be what happened, all right," Swearengen agreed. "But I shouldn't have tried to bust him up. He's been with me a long time. No whore's worth that."

"Yeah. Yeah, I reckon so." Dority just wanted to agree with his boss and keep Swearengen calm, Jen could tell. "Why don't you go downstairs, Al? Have yourself a drink."

"That's what I'll do," Swearengen said, sounding a little distracted. "I'll have a drink."

He walked out of the room, stumbling a little as he went.

Dority stepped around the moaning Burnes and came over to Jen. She flinched away from him. He bent and grabbed her arms, pulling her up and then shoving her down onto the bed. He was rough, but not too rough.

"You are one lucky whore," he told her. "And a mighty stupid one, too. I'm a mite surprised Al didn't just kill you. I wouldn't care so much about that, but he might've killed Johnny, too, and Johnny's my friend. Don't you ever try nothin' like that again."

Dority picked up the pieces of rope and began using them to tie Jen to the bed again. Tears ran down her face as she sobbed, "I . . . I just want him to let me go!"

Dority jerked a knot tight. "Well, that ain't gonna happen until Al is good an' ready, and there ain't no tellin' when that's gonna be." He finished tying her, with her lying on her back this time, and stepped back. "Tell you the truth, I don't think Al'd be quite so rough on you if it wasn't for what happened with that gal Carla. She ran off on him, and he don't want that happenin' ever again."

"So he's going to keep me a prisoner the rest of my life?" Jen wailed.

"Maybe. He'll keep you as long as he wants, that's for damned sure."

With that, he stooped to pull the semiconscious Johnny Burnes onto his feet and half-carry, half-drag the man out of the room. Jen watched them go and then closed her eyes in misery.

He'll keep you as long as he wants. The words echoed in her brain. There was no escape, no hope. She told herself that she might as well admit that and try to figure out what she needed to do next.

She started trying to think of some way she could kill herself. Death was better than this.

CALAMITY Jane had pitched her tent on the edge of the settlement, and she was asleep in it when the flap was pushed aside and somebody rushed in. Even drunk, she had pretty good reflexes. When a hand grabbed her shoulder and started to shake her, she rolled over quickly, kicked the intruder's legs out from under him, and shoved the barrel of her six-shooter under his nose. She didn't pull the trigger because she saw the wide, fear-filled eyes of Jack Anderson staring up at her.

"Goddamn it, White-Eye, I almost blowed your fuckin' head off!" Calamity said as she carefully lowered the revolver's hammer. "What was you thinkin', bustin' in here like that?"

She took the gun away from his face and settled back on her cot. He sat up, still looking pale and shaken, and she realized that she wasn't entirely to blame for the state he was in.

"I saw her!" he said. "I swear, Calam, I saw her! She

was in one of the upstairs windows of Swearengen's place, and it looked like she was trying to climb out. Then somebody grabbed her and jerked her back in, and she screamed! But it was her, I swear it!"

Calamity frowned. "You're talkin' about that whore?"

"Yes. You said yesterday she wasn't in there, but I know I saw her!"

Calamity sighed and slid her revolver back in its holster. Ever since she'd lied to the boy, she had been feeling unaccountably guilty about it. She wasn't sure why she felt that way—Lord knows she had told plenty of whoppers and done plenty of mean shit in her life—but she did and there was no denying it. She hadn't decided yet, though, whether she ought to do anything about it.

Now it looked like the decision had been made for her. Now that he had caught a glimpse of the girl, the White-Eyed Kid would never let this rest. He was just the sort of young, romantic, shit-for-brains fool who'd go storming into the Gem and demand to know what was going on. He would get himself killed, that was what he would do.

"Calam?" Jack said tentatively.

She patted the tangled blankets on the cot beside her and said, "Sit down, Kid. You and me got some talkin' to do."

Chapter Fifteen

RICHARD Seymour's stage career had lasted for roughly two years, and he had enjoyed them for the most part. The productions put on by Edwin Abbott were quite successful, and as the lead in most of them, Richard came in for his fair share of the acclaim. He moved easily among the upper circles of London society. Though not rich in his own right, he enjoyed the company of the elite. Being taken under the wing of Clive Drummond had opened many doors for him.

Being taken under *Fiona* Drummond's wing had opened other doors, most of them leading to the boudoirs of wealthy older women.

The perversity of some of these relationships bothered Richard for a while, but a man could grow accustomed to almost anything, he supposed. Luckily for him, Fiona was not jealous and had no objection to sharing him with some of her friends. She even arranged some of the liaisons herself. A select few, she even participated in.

Meanwhile, Clive Drummond introduced the young man to other sorts of pleasures. Drummond was a member of a special club in London that met in secret for the purpose of administering discipline to certain young women of dubious virtue. Richard hated it. Seducing older, willing women was one thing; watching a bunch of puffing, red-faced, middle-aged English "gentlemen" taking birch canes and blacksnake whips to young women who had been paid to suffer for those peculiar "pleasures" was something else again entirely.

Richard didn't want to offend his mentor, however, so he went along with what Drummond wanted, and it was at one of those clandestine meetings that he became acquainted with Sir Cyril Blakiston. Sir Cyril was a member of the House of Lords, a wealthy, powerful, influential man. He took an immediate liking to the young actor, and soon Richard was spending time at Sir Cyril's country estate, just as he was at the Drummond estate. That was where he met Helena Blakiston, Sir Cyril's beautiful seventeen-year-old daughter. He was immediately drawn to her, and she to him.

Nature, as they say, took its course.

And everything would have been fine if Sir Cyril had not caught them one day in the stables. The old gentleman's face had become even more flushed than usual; he had gawped and opened and closed his mouth several times and harrumphed in his soup-strainer of a mustache and finally exploded, "Bloody hell, boy, don't ye know ye're fuckin' yer own sister!"

Then he had clutched at his chest, gasped some more, and fallen facedown in a pile of horse shit. He would have died there if Richard hadn't shaken off his own stunned reaction in time to roll him over. Helena had run from the stables, screaming for help, forgetting in the process to put on her clothes. She had given the help quite a shock—and quite a show. But the gardener had recovered in time to fetch a doctor, and Sir Cyril had survived what the physician referred to a coronary incident.

Richard was summoned to the bedchamber of the weak, half-conscious aristocrat. Sir Cyril had come around enough to send everyone else away, and then he had explained to Richard, "You're my son. Bastard son, mind you, but still my son. Been lookin' for you for years. Never dreamed you'd start ruttin' with Helena 'fore I had the chance to tell you who ye really are."

"How do you know this is true?" Richard demanded. It seemed impossible to him. "My mother was a back-alley whore. She had no idea who my father was."

"Not true . . . The gal worked in my house in London. When she turned up pregnant, I gave her money and sent her away. I reckon some low-life gent must've taken advantage of her, got the money away from her somehow, you know. Maybe she wound up as you say, but she didn't start out that way. She was a fine gal. Lower class, to be sure, but still fine."

The story was still too far-fetched for Richard to believe, but then Sir Cyril went on. "Tell me . . . you've got a strawberry birthmark on yer hip, don't ye? Right about . . . here?" He pointed to his own hip under the covers.

Richard stiffened. It was true that he had such a birthmark.

"Yer mother met me one time after ye were born," Blakiston rasped. "It was in Kensington Park. She had you with her, and I saw the mark. Never forgot it."

"There must be other men in London with such a mark," Richard argued.

"Aye, but ye're the right age. And just look at ye. Look at the picture . . . on the wall." Sir Cyril's eyes moved toward the wall to his right, and Richard looked in that direction. A portrait hung there, a painting of a much younger Sir Cyril, and Richard had to admit that he bore a certain resemblance to it.

"Now do ye . . . see?" Sir Cyril asked.

Slowly, Richard nodded. "How did you find out about me?"

"I have my . . . sources. Fiona Drummond spoke of you and mentioned the birthmark."

"It just came up in conversation at some dinner party?" Richard asked coldly.

"Fiona and I were . . . *in flagrante delicto* at the time."

"My God!" Richard burst out, unable to contain himself. "Does she sleep with everything in trousers?"

Sir Cyril chuckled. "Just about, my boy. Just about." He dragged in a deep breath. "At any rate, after she said that, I investigated your background and decided that you might be my son. I suggested to Clive Drummond that he invite you to one of our special little gatherings. Once I saw you for myself, I knew. I knew."

"And you invited me out here to your estate to break the news to me?"

"Perhaps . . . perhaps. I hadn't decided yet. Then I find you rompin' with my daughter . . . with yer own sister! . . . and the decision was taken out of my hands."

"I didn't know she was my sister. Neither did Helena. You can't blame her."

Sir Cyril waved a hand. "I'm not interested in blame. But the fact of who you are can't come out now. Too many people know about the two of you. If it was revealed that ye're related . . . well, the scandal would simply be too much. Ye have to go, lad."

"Go?" Richard repeated hollowly.

"Far, far from England. I'll give ye plenty of money, don't worry about that. I don't expect ye to start over somewhere else, destitute. I'll pay for you to go anywhere you want, and I'll give ye money to get started there. How about it? You'll do what yer old dad wants ye to do?"

What Richard wanted to do was to tell Sir Cyril to go to hell. But the offer was an appealing one. As a boy, he had thought that he would never travel farther than the few square blocks of warrenlike slums in London. He had already gone much farther afield than that. But with Sir Cyril's money, he could afford to travel the world.

"If I go," he said, "it'll cost you."

"Fine, fine, whatever ye want," the old man mumbled. "I've got to protect Helena, ye understand."

Richard understood, all right. And while he had grown very fond of Helena in a short period of time, he liked riches even more.

Less than a month later, he was in America, embarking on a new life paid for by Sir Cyril Blakiston. He had read all the colorful, exciting stories about the American West in the British newspapers, and he wanted to see all that color and excitement for himself. He set out for St. Louis, intending to travel from there deeper into the country.

By the time he got there, he had lost some of his money in a poker game and been robbed of most of the rest of it. He took a chance on the cards again, ran his small stake into a slightly larger one, and used it to buy a buffalo rifle and a small outfit, because he had heard that a man could get rich hunting the massive, shaggy creatures that were almost the stuff of legend to a young man from England who had never seen such great beasts.

That was how Bloody Dick Seymour the buffalo hunter was born. He had gone on to become an Indian trader, husband to Carries Water and father to their two children, friend of Wild Bill Hickok, and Pony Express rider. A lot of adventures packed into a relatively short life. He didn't want to die. He wasn't ready to die. . . .

His head hurt so badly when he woke up that he wished he *could* go ahead and die and be put out of his misery.

As he crawled up out of the black pit into which he had tumbled, he sensed heat on his face and heard voices. The fires of Hell and the imps of Satan? Given the life he had led, that was certainly the place he deserved to end up. But no, he was in too much pain to be dead, he decided. And there was no reason Lucifer's minions should possess the twang of American cowboys.

"Hey, Boss, looks like ol' Bloody Dick's comin' around."

A moment later, a hand touched Dick's shoulder and a voice he recognized as belonging to Jack Bowman asked, "Hey, Dick, you alive in there?"

Dick forced his eyes open and saw that he was lying on a bunk in Bowman's cabin at the Hat Creek Ranch headquarters. The bunk was near the fireplace, and that accounted for the warmth he felt. Bowman knelt beside him, and several of the ranch hands stood nearby, watching anxiously.

"Wha . . . what happened?" Dick asked, although his voice sounded odd to his ears.

"You like to got your head busted open by a damned redskin," Bowman told him. "When we first got to you, we were afraid your brains had leaked out along with all that blood. But you were still breathin', so we loaded you up and brung you back here to the ranch."

A damned redskin . . . Talking Bear! Dick closed his eyes as the memory of his fight with the war chief came back to him. He'd had no idea that the lone Indian who had pursued him so stubbornly would turn out to be the same man who had led the raid on his trading camp more than a year earlier. The same man responsible for the deaths of Carries Water and the two little ones. Talking Bear had come close to killing Dick Seymour on that day, and today he had come close again. Dick knew that he would never forget the warrior's face.

"He counted coup on me," Dick whispered. "Hit me with his rifle instead of a coup stick. That's . . . the last thing I remember. What happened to him? Why didn't he kill me?"

"Reckon he would have, sure enough," Bowman said, "if we hadn't come up a-gallopin' and a-shootin' right about then. The boys and me were out on the range, workin' the cattle, when we heard shots. We knew it couldn't be nothin' good, so we hurried to see what was goin' on. Rode up in time to see you take a tumble out of your saddle. We threw a bunch of lead at the Injun, made him turn tail and run. Then we collected you and carried you back here so we could wash the blood off of you and tie a bandage around your head. Didn't know if you were gonna make it or not, so I'm really glad you woke up, Dick."

"So am I," Dick murmured as he closed his eyes.

Had Talking Bear known who he was when he and the other Sioux warriors laid their ambush? There was no way of being certain, but Dick suspected the war chief hadn't been aware of his identity. It was pure coincidence that had brought the two men together again, although given the circumstances, the coincidence wasn't so far-fetched as to strain credulity. The West, despite its vastness, was a small place in many ways. Men often ran into old acquaintances they had last seen years earlier and a thousand miles away. Old enemies had a way of bumping into each other, too.

Jack Bowman squeezed his shoulder. "You're a lucky man, Dick. You want something to eat?"

Dick's stomach felt too queasy for that. "Not right now, thanks," he said. "I believe I just want to rest. I've lost a day, so I'll have to be riding quite early in the morning."

Bowman frowned. "Hell, after a wallop on the head like that, you're gonna get right back in the saddle tomorrow?"

"Colorado Charley is counting on me. The mail must go through."

"Well, all I got to say is that you are one stubborn bastard," Bowman said as he shook his head. "No offense."

"None taken," Dick said, smiling faintly.

After all, Bowman was just telling the truth, especially about the bastard part.

THE next morning, well before dawn, Dick was able to eat a little breakfast, but the strong black coffee did him more good than anything else. His head ached, and the gash under the bandage itched, but the annoyance was bearable.

He asked Jack Bowman to treat the valiant lineback dun kindly, and arranged with the rancher to pick up the horse on his way back to Deadwood. He would ride the dun for that leg of the return trip. In the meantime, the roan he had ridden here to start with was well rested now, so he took that horse and headed for John Hunton's ranch. Bowman insisted on sending several heavily armed cowboys with him part of the way.

"Just to make sure them damn Sioux ain't still lurkin' around," as Bowman put it.

There was no sign of the Indians, even after Bowman's

cowboys turned back to Hat Creek, and Dick reached the Hunton ranch without incident. He traded horses there and rode on, with Fort Laramie his next stop.

When he reached the fort, the sergeant of the guard greeted him and said, "The commanding officer wants to see you, Dick."

Dick frowned in surprise. "What about?"

"I don't know. The colonel just said that when you rode in, to bring you over to his office."

Dick shrugged in acceptance of that edict. The Pioneer Pony Express was depending to a large extent on the cooperation of the Army, so he didn't want to do anything to anger the local commander.

His head still hurt some, but in the two days since leaving Hat Creek Dick had regained most of his strength. Riding all day was tiring, of course, but he was growing accustomed to the pace. He left his horse being cared for by Army hostlers and followed the sergeant across the parade ground to Officers' Row. An adjutant in Colonel Stilwell's office took him straight in to see the commander. Dick took off his hat as he stepped into the colonel's office.

Colonel Stilwell was a wiry man with piercing eyes and a short beard shot through with gray streaks. He shook hands with Dick and motioned him into a chair in front of the desk. As they sat down, Stilwell asked, "What happened to your head?"

Gingerly, Dick touched the bandage that he thought made him look rather piratical and said, "I had a run-in with a Sioux warrior."

"What did he do, count coup on you with a rifle barrel?"

"Exactly."

Stilwell's eyes widened. "I wasn't being serious."

"Talking Bear was."

The colonel took out a cigar, offered one to Dick, and then lit it for himself when Dick shook his head. "Talking Bear, eh?" Stilwell said. "We'd had reports that he was around, but this is the first time I've heard of him actually attacking anybody. You sure it was him?"

"We've encountered each other before," Dick said

tightly. He didn't want to have to explain the circumstances, and thankfully, the colonel didn't press the issue.

"Well, I'm glad you made it through. I've got something for you."

It was Dick's turn to frown in confusion. He wasn't sure what Stilwell might have for him, other than a fresh horse.

"Brewster, bring in those pouches," Stilwell called to his adjutant.

The man carried two sets of saddlebags into the office and placed them on Stilwell's desk. They were much like the ones Dick had used to bring the mail from Deadwood, and they appeared to be stuffed full.

Stilwell slapped a hand down on the saddlebags and said, "John Ingalls brought these in a couple of days ago. They're full of mail for Deadwood."

Now it began to make sense. John James Ingalls was one of Colorado Charley Utter's associates from Cheyenne. Dick had expected to deliver the mail pouches to him when he reached that city. Evidently, though, Ingalls had come to Fort Laramie to meet him part of the way. That would speed up the return trip.

"Ingalls is still here waiting for you," Stilwell went on. "He'll take the mail on to Cheyenne so you can get started back to Deadwood with these letters. If there's anything we can do to help you, the Army will be glad to do it."

"Thanks, Colonel." Dick said. "A military escort would be nice."

Stilwell grinned around the cigar. "Can't do that, I'm afraid. Legally, all those miners and gamblers and whores aren't even supposed to be up there in the Black Hills. You know that and I know that. But at this late date, the government's not going to try to run them out. We both know that, too. So my unofficial orders are to turn a blind eye to the situation and do what I can to further the cause of progress and civilization without being too blatant about it."

"I appreciate that, Colonel. All I really need is a place to get some sleep and a fresh horse in the morning."

"We can accommodate you, Mr. Seymour." Stilwell ran his hand over the full mail pouches. "A lot of folks are counting on you to deliver these letters from their loved ones. You can be proud of what you're doing."

Dick thought about the life he had led and decided that pride was something he had not felt for quite a few years now. Each time he thought he had put his past behind him, it cropped up again, in some new and ugly way. Now it was Talking Bear who served as a reminder of all he had lost.

And the Sioux war chief was still out there somewhere, waiting for him. Dick was sure of it. They would meet again.

If there was one thing that performing in scores of poorly written melodramas had taught him, it was that destiny would not be thwarted.

Chapter Sixteen

BELLAMY Bridges sauntered into the Gem Theater and headed for the bar. He saw Dan Dority stiffen in wariness on the other side of the hardwood. Dority knew that Bellamy worked for Laurette Parkhurst, and he knew that Laurette and his own boss, Al Swearengen, were business rivals. More than that, Swearengen and Laurette just flat out didn't like each other. Bitter enemies, they were. Dority probably wondered if Bellamy was here to cause trouble.

Bellamy put a smile on his face to ease the bartender's worries. He rested his left hand on the bar and said, "Whiskey."

Dority jerked his head toward the door. "What, you can't drink across the street at the Academy?"

"Of course I can. I just thought I'd like to have a drink in here for a change. For old times' sake, I guess you could say. Remember the first time I came in here for a drink, Dan?"

Bellamy's friendly tone just confused Dority more, but he recalled the time Bellamy was talking about. Bellamy had been just a young prospector then, green as could be, and a shot of the Gem's potent bar whiskey had made him sick. Dan Ryan and Fletch Parkhurst had taken him to the

Academy to sleep it off, and that was where he had met Carla.

Hard to believe that was only a few weeks in the past. A lifetime had gone by since then.

Reminding Dority of that occasion had brought back memories for Bellamy, too. Painful memories. He shoved them aside by reminding himself why he was there and said mildly, "What about that drink?"

"Yeah, yeah, I guess it'd be all right," Dority said grudgingly. "If you can pay for it."

"I'm flush, don't worry about that." Bellamy dropped a coin on the bar.

Dority poured the drink, and Bellamy knocked it back with ease. The vile stuff didn't make him sick now. It would take something a lot worse to accomplish that.

"Al around?"

Dority's frown of suspicion came back. "What do you want with Al?"

"Nothing, I was just curious."

"Al's busy," Dority said curtly.

"Fine," Bellamy said with a shrug. "Maybe I'll play some poker or something. Or have a go at one of the whores."

Dority shook his head. "Can't do that. Al don't allow the competition to sample the goods."

"Who says I'm competition?"

"You work for that Parkhurst woman."

"I just keep the peace over there," Bellamy said. "I'm not interested in giving Miss Laurette any information about the whores you have over here."

"Still, it's a rule," Dority said stubbornly. "You can drink and play cards down here, but you don't go upstairs."

"Fine, I don't care. Give me another drink."

Dority splashed more whiskey into Bellamy's empty glass. Bellamy picked up the drink and sipped it as he walked over to one of the tables where a poker game was going on. There was an empty chair, so when the hand was over, he said, "You boys mind if I sit in?"

One of the players who had his back to Bellamy turned and looked up at him. Bellamy stiffened a little as he rec-

ognized Fletch Parkhurst. Fletch didn't object to him joining the game, though. He just gave a little half smile and
said, "It's all right by me."

Mutters of agreement came from the other players. Bellamy drew back the empty chair and sat down, placing his
drink on the table in front of him. He took a small sheaf of
greenbacks from inside his coat and peeled a bill off, toss-
ing it into the center of the table to ante up for the next hand.

Bellamy looked around the table. He didn't see anyone
he knew, although some of the faces of the other players
were familiar because they had visited the Academy in the
past. He had hoped that Wild Bill Hickok would be sitting
in on this game, but the legendary pistoleer wasn't there.
Hickok did most of his cardplaying in the Bella Union or
the No. Ten.

Several hands went by. Bellamy lost all of them, but he
was playing cautiously and didn't bet much, so he didn't
lose much. He was more interested in studying the other
players, and after a while he picked out the man he was
looking for, a professional gambler in a tweed suit and a
derby hat that made him look more like a traveling sales-
man than a cardsharp. He was no drummer, though; his
hands were much too deft for him to be anything but a professional at what he was doing.

Bellamy bet heavier on the next hand and won, then
folded for a small loss. The deal went to the gambler in the
derby. Bellamy studied his cards and plunged. Everyone
else gradually dropped out until no one was left except Bellamy and the man in the derby. Bellamy called and laid
down his three kings. The man in the derby smirked,
showed his three aces, and reached for the pot.

"Wait a minute," Bellamy said sharply. "I don't know
where that third ace came from, but it sure as hell didn't
come out of that deck."

The gambler froze and lifted an icy glare from the
money. "What are you saying, mister?"

"I'm saying you cheated," Bellamy responded bluntly.
"You slipped that third ace into your hand from somewhere
else."

"Goddamn it, I won't take that!"

"What are you going to do about it?" Bellamy asked, his voice cool.

The gambler jerked up out of his chair. The other players, with one exception, threw themselves away from the table, trying to get out of the line of fire. That lone exception was Fletch Parkhurst, who sat there calmly as Bellamy surged to his feet, too. The gambler's hand twitched as a derringer slid into it from a spring holster concealed under his sleeve. It was a fast, slick move, almost as slick as the one with which the gambler had taken the ace from his other sleeve. But it was too late, because both of Bellamy's Colts were already in his hands, appearing there as if by magic. The revolvers roared as flame licked from their barrels. Both slugs drove into the gambler's chest at close range and lifted him off his feet, so that he came down hard on his back on the sawdust-littered floor. A couple of places on his vest smoldered where sparks from Bellamy's guns threatened to set the garment on fire.

Bellamy didn't lower the weapons until he had walked around the table and kicked the gambler in the side to make sure he was dead. Then he holstered the Colts and looked at Fletch, who still hadn't budged.

"He was cheating," Bellamy said.

"I know," Fletch said. "I saw him, too."

Johnny Burnes came hurrying up with a shotgun in his hands. Dan Dority wasn't far behind him. "What the fuck's goin' on here?" Dority demanded. "Why'd you shoot him, Bridges?"

"He was cheating," Bellamy said again, as if that explained everything. In a way, it did.

"Damn it, we got only your word for that—" Dority began.

"No, you have my word, too," Fletch said. "I saw the man take a card from his sleeve. It wasn't the first time, either. If Bellamy hadn't challenged him, I probably would have in another hand or two."

Al Swearengen came up in time to hear Fletch's statement. He glowered at the dead man lying on the floor. "Get him out of here," he snapped at Burnes. "Bloodstains are damn hard to get out of those boards." Then he looked at Bellamy and went on. "That Parkhurst woman send you over here to kill one of my customers, kid? Maybe make gents think twice about comin' into the Gem because they might get shot?"

"He was cheating," Bellamy said again. "I would have killed him no matter where we were."

Swearengen just grunted skeptically. He jerked his head toward the door. "Get out. You're not welcome in here."

"Fine. I'll go. I'm going to finish my drink first, though." Deliberately, Bellamy reached down and picked up his glass, which had only a few drops of whiskey left in it. He drank them, said, "Ah," and licked his lips. Then he turned to walk out.

The skin between his shoulder blades crawled. He had seen the hatred blazing in Al Swearengen's eyes. Swearengen would have liked to kill him. But he wouldn't gun a man in the back in the middle of his own saloon. At least, that was what Bellamy was counting on to get him out of here alive.

Pick a fight, Laurette had said. Find somebody and kill him. Simple enough. But Bellamy wouldn't have done it unless the circumstances were right. Luckily, they had been, and he had been able to draw and fire with a clear conscience, knowing that if he didn't, the gambler in the derby hat would kill him. Swearengen had been right about Laurette being behind this incident. She was serving notice on him that she had a real gunman working for her now. Before the day was over, the story of the killing would be all over Deadwood. Not that a shooting over a game of cards was that unusual in the settlement. But there had been plenty of witnesses to Bellamy's uncommon speed on the draw. Folks might even start to say that he was faster than Wild Bill Hickok, whether it was true or not.

Bellamy stepped through the door onto the porch. He was alive. He had survived this baptism of fire, one of many he had already faced in his young life. Now the war was on, and he couldn't help but wonder what Swearengen would do in retaliation.

* * *

FLETCH was about to get up and follow Bellamy out of the Gem, intending to ask him what the hell that had been all about, when Swearengen stopped him by putting a hand on his shoulder.

"Come upstairs with me, Fletch," Swearengen said, in about as friendly a tone as the saloon owner ever mustered.

That came as something of a surprise. Swearengen and Laurette were bitter enemies, and Swearengen knew that Laurette was his mother. That hadn't stopped Fletch from drinking and playing cards in the Gem, and Swearengen hadn't tried to run him off, even before the estrangement between Fletch and his mother. But Swearengen had never acted friendly, either.

Fletch was just curious enough to get up and go with him.

They went into Swearengen's office and sat down. Swearengen offered him a cigar. Fletch shook his head. "What is it you want, Al?" he asked mildly.

"That kid gunfighter put on quite a show, didn't he?"

Fletch shrugged.

"I noticed you didn't move," Swearengen went on.

"I've watched Bellamy practicing when he didn't know I was around," Fletch said. "I knew he was a lot faster than that gambler. I didn't figure it would amount to much of a fight. An execution was more like it."

"Your mother put him up to it, you know. She sent him over here to pick a fight and kill one of my customers."

"That's what it looks like, all right," Fletch admitted, "but what my mother does is her business, not mine."

"The two of you used to work together."

"Not anymore. Not for a while."

"Yeah, that's what I'd heard." Swearengen looked intently across the desk at him. "How'd you like to work for me, Fletch?"

The offer took Fletch by surprise. "Doing what, swamping out the place?"

Swearengen leaned back in his chair and waved a hand casually. "I don't need another fuckin' swamper. But I know

you're good with a gun, and if your mother's going to have
a shootist working for her, maybe I ought to have one, too."

"I don't think so."

"I'll pay you a good wage, and I've got the best whores
in Deadwood. Take 'em whenever and however you like."

"No, thanks."

Swearengen frowned. "You're sure?"

"I'm positive," Fletch said.

"Well, I tried." Swearengen shrugged his shoulders.
"Can't blame a fella for trying, now can you?"

Fletch didn't answer that. Swearengen was acting odd
and he just wanted to get out of there, so he said, "Was
there anything else you wanted, Al?"

"No, I reckon not. Thanks, anyway."

Fletch got to his feet and left the office. He was puzzled
and confused by the offer and by Swearengen's uncharac-
teristic attitude. It wasn't like Swearengen to give up that
easily when he wanted something, even if what he wanted
didn't make any sense.

It might be a good idea, Fletch decided, for him to avoid
the Gem for a while. That wouldn't be any great loss.

If there was one thing Deadwood had, it was plenty of
places to drink and play cards.

WHEN Fletch was gone, Swearengen's hands clenched into
fists and his face darkened with the rush of blood as fury
swept through him. Nobody turned down Al Swearengen.
Nobody!

As if he didn't have enough trouble on his plate right
now, what with that rebellious whore Jen. She might have
broken Johnny Burnes's head open, busting a chamber pot
on it that way. Then there was the continuing threat that
Wild Bill Hickok might decide to pin on a badge and clean
up Deadwood. Swearengen didn't know if Varnes had approached Jim Levy yet about killing Hickok; obviously, it
hadn't happened so far, or Swearengen would have heard
about it already. Hell, the whole territory would hear about
a gunfight between Wild Bill Hickok and Jim Levy, who

some said was even faster on the draw than Hickok. And always, there was the annoyance of that fuckin' preacher and his passionate sermons about how folks ought to stop sinning and start walking in the paths of righteousness. Sooner or later, something was going to have to be done about *him,* too.

It was frustrating trying to deal with all those problems at once. Fletch Parkhurst's refusal to work for him was just the latest in a string of problems.

But Swearengen knew how to deal with this one. Fletch would come around.

Not before he learned that it wasn't wise to say no to Al Swearengen, though.

Chapter Seventeen

"**R**EMEMBER," Calamity Jane said, "you don't do a fuckin' thing until you hear the commotion break out. You got that?"

The White-Eyed Kid nodded. He and Calamity had gone over the plan several times, and he knew exactly what he was supposed to do. If everything worked out, Jen would soon be free from the bondage and torture she had endured at the hands of Al Swearengen.

There would be some risk, of course; there always was when you set out to cross a man like Swearengen. Jack wouldn't be running that risk alone, though. Calamity had agreed to help him, and after what she had done, it was only fair that she take some of the chances, too.

He had hardly been able to believe his ears when she'd told him what she had really seen in that upstairs room in the Gem. How could anyone be such a craven coward as to turn away from a tied, beaten young woman who was pleading for help?

When he'd said as much, Calamity had flushed with anger and reached for the gun on her hip. "Shut your fuckin' mouth!" she'd said to him. "You wasn't there. You don't know what it was like."

"I know that he's torturing Jen, and you let him get away with it." It had taken courage to defy the wrath of Calamity Jane, but Jack's outrage gave him the balls to do it.

"We ain't lettin' him get away with nothin'. I was just tryin' to figure out the best way of gettin' that gal outta there. Figured until I did there was no point in gettin' you all het up about it. And you actin' the way you are just proves I was right."

Jack hadn't believed her blustering explanation for a second. He knew that if he hadn't seen Jen with his own eyes, Calamity never would have admitted that she'd found her during the search of the saloon's upstairs rooms. She had been scared, pure and simple, and now she was ashamed of that fear.

Even though he was young, Jack Anderson knew that sometimes you just had to let folks live with the lies they told themselves, especially if you wanted them to help you. And he needed help from somebody; there was no doubt about that. He couldn't go busting into the Gem and waving a gun around. That would just get him killed.

Calamity, however, proved to be a pretty good plotter when she was sober—and when she had a guilty conscience goading her on. She had told Jack how to find his way around in the Gem, and had even drawn diagrams in the dirt to show him exactly where the back stairs and the room where Jen was being held were located.

"Thing is, that Burnes fella is up and down from the first floor to the second all the time, checkin' on the whores," Calamity had explained. "I expect he looks in on that Jen gal, too, to make sure she ain't tryin' somehow to get away. Hell, for all I know, Al's got a permanent guard posted on her room. If he does, you're liable to have to deal with that fucker yourself."

"I'll do whatever I have to do," Jack had sworn, and he'd meant every word of the vow.

Calamity had slapped the butt of the gun on Jack's hip.

"You can point this hogleg at some son of a bitch and pull the trigger?"

"If it means saving Jen, I can."

"I sure as shit hope you're right, Kid, 'cause if you hesitate at the wrong time, you'll be dead, more'n likely. Understand?"

He had swallowed hard and nodded.

"All right, here's how we'll do it. We'll wait for night, when the place is busiest. I'll go in the saloon and raise a ruckus so bad it'll take Swearengen and all his goddamn flunkies to settle it down. Whilst I'm doin' that, you slip in the back door, go up them stairs, and get the girl outta the room where she's bein' held. Got your knife?"

Jack had pulled a bowie knife with a long, heavy blade from its sheath at his waist.

"Good, you'll need that pigsticker to cut the ropes. Don't waste any time tryin' to untie 'em. You can do that later. Just cut 'em, grab the girl, and skedaddle outta there. Nice an' simple."

"Are you sure you can come up with a big enough distraction?"

She'd just glared at him. "You *do* know they call me Calamity Jane, don't you? You leave the fuckin' distraction to me, hear?"

So now it was night, after one of the longest afternoons of the White-Eyed Kid's life, and he was in the alley behind the Gem Theater, waiting. Stygian darkness surrounded him, but he had located the rear door by feel and the knob was within easy reach. It was locked, but the door itself was flimsy and Jack knew that if he put his shoulder against it a couple of times, the jamb would give way and he could get inside. He was trusting to Calamity's commotion to cover up any sounds that the forced entry would make.

His lips were dry and his heart was pounding. He had fought Indians, and he had survived the prairie fire that had turned his eyebrow white. But tonight he didn't mind admitting that he was scared.

He had to ignore that fear, though. Jen's life depended on

finding the courage he needed, and if her life depended on it, then as far as he was concerned, *everything* depended on it. Because without her, nothing else mattered. That was a hell of a way to feel about a whore, he told himself, but there it was. It was the truth, and there was no denying it.

Standing in the darkness of the alley, he took a deep breath and waited for all hell to break loose.

CALAMITY had taken a nip or two before she went into the Gem, just to oil up her joints and sharpen her senses. She wasn't drunk, no, sir, not even close. She just had a pleasant glow about her.

She went to the bar, rang a coin on it, and demanded, "Gimme a fuckin' drink!"

Dan Dority was several yards away, pouring whiskey for another customer. "Hold your horses," he said to her. "I'll be there in a minute."

Calamity took a deep breath, swelling her bosom like a pouter pigeon. "Hold your horses?" she repeated. "Did you just tell me to hold my fuckin' horses? Do you know who the hell I am?"

"Yeah, yeah," Dority said as he came along the bar with the bottle still in his hand. He snagged a glass off the back bar, set it on the hardwood in front of Calamity, and splashed liquor into it. "There's your drink."

"It's about goddamn time." Calamity practically threw the coin at him, snatched up the glass, and slugged down the whiskey. Immediately, she spewed it right back out of her mouth. Some of it went on the bar, but most of it splattered Dority's apron. "Shit! What was that? Tasted worse'n horse piss!"

Her voice was loud, but there was a lot of talk and laughter in the room and not many of the customers paid any attention to her. Calamity Jane hadn't been in Deadwood all that long, but many of the citizens had already learned to ignore her.

"Settle down," Dority told her sharply as he glared at her

and dabbed at his wet apron with a bar rag. "That's the house whiskey, and there ain't a damned thing wrong with it."

"Not a damned thing wrong with it? I'll say there is! What'd you do when you were brewin' it up, take a shit in it? Or did you and that cocksuckin' boss o' yours and all the other cocksuckers who work here stand around and jack off in it? I'll bet you did! I bet you jacked off in it!"

She was getting loud enough and vile enough so that more folks were looking around at her now. That was good. She had just started to put on the show she had planned.

"Damn it!" Dority burst out. "If you can't behave yourself, you drunken old bawd, you'd better get out of here before Al hears you carryin' on."

"You think I'm a-scared of Al fuckin' Swearengen? Gimme that!"

She lunged halfway over the bar and grabbed the bottle from Dority. He made a swipe at her with one big paw, but missed as she jerked back. Dancing unsteadily away from the bar, she tilted the bottle to her mouth and guzzled a big mouthful of the fiery liquor. Then, turning, she sprayed it out over the closest tables that were crowded with men drinking and fondling the whores who perched on their laps. A couple of the soiled doves screamed at the unexpected shower of whiskey, and men yelled angrily as they started up from their chairs.

"Come on, you limp-dick bastards!" Calamity shouted at them, brandishing the whiskey bottle. "Come and get me! If you want a fight or a fuck, I'm your huckleberry!"

Fuming with anger, Dority started around the end of the bar and motioned to some of the other men who worked in the saloon as he came toward Calamity. Angry customers were closing in on her, too. With a howl, she threw the bottle at them and then swept up a chair and flung it across the room. Another whore screamed as she ducked out of the way of the missile. Calamity grabbed a table and turned it over with a crash, then jerked her gun from its holster and blasted a couple of shots into the floor at Dority's feet. "Dance, you cocksucker, dance!" she shrieked.

From the corner of her eye, she saw Al Swearengen rushing down the stairs from the second floor. He shouted, "Get her! Stop that crazy bitch!"

Crazy? He just *thought* he'd seen crazy.

Spinning, brandishing the gun so that men leaped and ducked away from it, she took aim at one of the chandeliers and pressed the trigger. The revolver bucked against her palm as it roared again. With a crash of glass, the bullet sent the chandelier spinning madly. With her free hand she grabbed another chair and threw it. Up on the balcony overlooking the barroom, the whores' rooms had emptied as soiled doves and customers alike came out to see what all the ruckus was about. The attention of everybody in the Gem was focused on Calamity Jane, and suddenly she felt like she was at the center of a vast, angry sea.

Let it storm. She was ready.

She just hoped that the White-Eyed Kid was, too.

JACK waited for a moment after the yelling started, but when something crashed and a gun went off, he knew it was time for him to make his move. He grasped the doorknob and rammed his shoulder against the panel. Feeling the door give a little, he drew back and hit it again. This time, with a splintering of wood, it slammed open and he stumbled through into the darkened rear hall of the Gem.

He took a second to orient himself, remembering the diagrams Calamity had drawn in the dirt. Then he turned to his left and felt his way along the corridor until he came to the narrow staircase. Light trickled down it from the top. He went up fast, taking the stairs two at a time.

The trick was going to be reaching the room next to Swearengen's office where Jen was being held. To do that he would have to cross a short length of balcony in full view of everyone downstairs. He wasn't going to come back that way. He planned to wrap up Jen in the sheet from the bed and go out the window with her. They would have to climb down from the outside balcony. She might have trouble doing that, the shape she was in, but she would have to make it if she wanted to be free. He believed she could do it.

Walking quickly, he reached the main balcony. To his left, no more than twenty feet away, stood several whores. They were watching the brawl below. Evidently, their customers had gone downstairs to get in on the fun. As Jack moved swiftly toward Swearengen's office, from the corner of his eye he saw Calamity Jane at the center of the maelstrom, flailing around wildly as Swearengen, Dority, Johnny Burnes, and several other men tried to hang onto her. Not only that, but fistfights had broken out in other places in the barroom, so that nobody was paying any attention to what was going on up here on the second floor.

Best of all, there was no guard at the door of the room where Jen was being held. Jack reached it without being challenged. The knob was locked, but this time he kicked it open.

The room was dark except for a single lamp with the wick turned so low that the flame was tiny. Its faint glow showed Jack the huddled shape on the bed, hidden for the most part by a sheet thrown over it. He could see the long brown hair spread out on the pillow, though, and for an awful moment he thought she was dead, she was lying there so still. Swearengen must have beaten the life out of her, or torn her so badly inside that she had bled to death.

But then she stirred and moaned, and relief flooded through him. She was alive! No matter what she had suffered, as long as she was alive she could recover from it.

He heeled the door closed behind him, even though with the broken latch it wouldn't fasten, and bounded across the room to the bed. He swept the sheet back and tried not to waste time gasping and staring at the bruises that colored her body. Sliding the bowie knife from its sheath, he got busy sawing through the ropes that held her arms and legs to the bed. The keen blade of the knife cut through the bonds without much trouble. Hope grew inside him, hope that they would get away before anyone could stop them.

When she was loose, he rammed the knife back in its sheath and bent to lift her. She seemed to be aware that someone was with her, although she hadn't opened her eyes yet and didn't try to help him at all. She was so much deadweight, and for a slender girl she was surprisingly heavy. With a grunt of effort, he got her off the bed and onto her feet. She sagged loosely against him.

He had dreamed of holding her naked in his arms, but this wasn't the way it had been in his dreams. She was battered and bloodied and only semiconscious, and there was nothing the least bit gentle or tender or romantic about it. This moment was ugly and frightening and a little bit sickening, to tell the truth. He just wanted to get her out of here before they got caught.

Holding her up awkwardly with one arm around her, he reached down and tore the sheet off the bed. He wrapped it around her and said urgently, "Come on, Jen. We've got to go. Come on now."

"What . . . who . . . ?" she said in a hoarse voice that pained him to hear it.

"It's me, Jack Anderson," he told her. "White-Eye Jack. Come on."

"Wh-White-eye . . . ?"

"That's right. I'll help you, Jen, but we've got to get out of here first."

He turned his head toward the door and listened. The commotion from downstairs was dying away. Swearengen and his men must have gotten Calamity under control. He hoped they hadn't hurt her, at least not too badly. He was still mad at her for lying to him and for ignoring Jen's pleas for help, but he didn't want any harm to come to her.

Jen's legs wouldn't work when he tried to steer her toward the window. They were limp and went out from under her, so that he had to hold tightly to her just to keep her from falling. Well, if she couldn't walk, he would just have to drag her, he told himself. He was more worried now, though, about how they would get down from the outside balcony. If he had more time, he could tie the sheet around her in a sort of makeshift sling and lower her to the street, maybe, but he doubted if he would have the chance to do that.

A second later, he knew he wouldn't have time. They hadn't even reached the window yet when the door of the room flew open, and with a bellow of rage, Al Swearengen lunged at them.

Chapter Eighteen

꿍

SWEARENGEN swung wildly at Jack's head. The blow just grazed him, glancing off his skull above the ear, but it still landed with enough power to stagger him. Having to hold up Jen's weight made him stumble even more, and though he fought against it, he lost his grip on her and went to one knee. Jen fell loosely on the floor in front of the window.

Jack saw Swearengen draw back his leg, and twisted to try to avoid the kick that came at him. There wasn't room to get out of the way. Swearengen's booted foot crashed into Jack's side and drove him hard against the wall. The impact knocked the breath out of him. Gasping for air, he got a hand on the windowsill and levered himself up, onto his feet. He knew if he went all the way to the floor, Swearengen might kick and stomp him to death.

The saloon owner wasn't a big man, but he was strong. More than that, he was ruthless and brutal. He bored in on Jack, hooking short, wicked punches to the younger man's body. Jack tried to fend off the blows and throw a punch of his own, but it missed badly. Swearengen crowded against him and lifted a knee into Jack's groin. Pain exploded through Jack. He screamed and doubled over, trying unsuccessfully to ease the agony flooding along his nerves.

Sheer desperation sent an arm flailing out again, and this time luck guided his fist to Swearengen's face. The blow landed with enough pain-maddened strength to snap Swearengen's head back. That gave Jack a second to catch his breath. Still hunched over, he lurched forward and rammed a shoulder into Swearengen's chest. The collision knocked Swearengen back a step. He probably would have recovered quickly, but he tripped over one of Jen's outstretched legs and fell backward. His head thudded against the footboard of the bed, stunning him.

Jack knew he had only a few seconds before Swearengen recovered his wits. The swift rataplan of heavy footsteps on the balcony outside the room told him that more men were coming, and chances were they wouldn't be on his side. He bent, ignoring the pain in his groin, and got his arms around Jen's limp form. With a groan, he lifted her and turned toward the window.

Swearengen reached out, grabbed his ankle, and pulled hard. Jack fell forward, losing his grip on Jen yet again. She hit the window hard enough to break it and fell through it onto the balcony in a shower of shattering glass.

"Jen!" Her name tore from Jack's throat in a ragged scream. He scrambled up, grabbing the windowsill, cutting his hands on shards of glass. He ignored the stinging pain and reached through the broken window toward her.

Somebody took hold of him from behind and jerked him away from the window before he could touch her. Jack's feet left the floor as he was picked up and thrown across the room. He crashed into the wall, bounced off, and fell to the floor again. A figure loomed over him, dark and shadowy in the faint light from the lowered lamp. As Jack looked up, he caught a glimpse of Dan Dority's bearded face and knew that Swearengen's lieutenant had arrived to come to his boss's aid. Dority reached down, twisted a fist in Jack's shirt collar, and hauled him upright with seemingly as little effort as if Jack had been a child. Dority's other fist came at his face, and there was nowhere Jack could go to get out of the way.

The blow landed solidly and so hard that it seemed about to tear Jack's head right off his shoulders. Still holding him by the collar, Dority drew back and hit him again, this time in the belly. Jack retched, but he hadn't eaten supper so there was nothing in his stomach to come up.

"Get out of the way," Swearengen said. The saloon owner was on his feet again. He shouldered Dority aside and swung a left and a right. Both blows hit Jack in the face. He was barely aware of slamming into the wall again, driven backward by Swearengen's punches. Swearengen kicked him in his already painful balls. They hadn't stopped hurting from being kneed earlier in the fight.

That was enough. More than enough, really. Jack toppled forward and passed out from the pain. He was out cold when he hit the floor at Al Swearengen's feet.

CALAMITY Jane picked herself up out of the mud and shit of Deadwood's Main Street. This wasn't the first time she had been thrown out of a saloon, of course, and likely it wouldn't be the last. She stood there, a little unsteady on her feet, and slapped the worst of the muck off her buckskins. It had been a good tussle while it lasted.

She was proud of the fact that it had taken Swearengen, Dority, Burnes, and the rest of the Gem's bartenders and floor men to subdue her, drag her over to the door, and toss her into the street. More than half-a-dozen men, and her just a weak woman. They were pussies, the whole lot of 'em.

A sudden crash of breaking glass made her look up. To her shock, she saw a white-shrouded shape tumbling through a second-floor window. Then a man appeared in the window, reaching through it, only to be jerked back. Calamity caught a glimpse of Dan Dority's face, and she thought the first man had been the White-Eyed Kid.

Her heart sank, the fierce exultation of the brawl abruptly forgotten in the realization that the plan she had worked out with the Kid must not have worked. He had made it into the whore's room, but the fact that Dority was up there meant that he had been caught before he could get Jen out of there. Calamity wondered if that had been Jen who fell through the broken window onto the balcony.

There was one way to find out. She went over to one of the pillars that supported the Gem's front porch and started to shinny up it like it was a tree. That was harder than she expected, because her buckskins were still slippery from the mud and shit. She kept climbing stubbornly, though, determined to find out what was going on up there.

AL Swearengen's chest heaved from the exertion of the fight and the depth of the anger that filled him. That damned White-Eyed Kid just wouldn't give up. He was bound and determined to get the girl out of the Gem. But Swearengen was just as determined to keep her, and he was lord of this domain, make no fuckin' mistake about that.

When one of the whores had come running downstairs and told him somebody was up here, after he and Dority and the others had tossed that drunken Cannary woman into the street, Swearengen had guessed right away what was going on. Somebody had taken advantage of the disturbance to try to reach Jen, and there was only one person it could be. As he had bounded up the stairs, Swearengen had even wondered if Calamity Jane had been in on the whole thing, had been part of the plot to steal away the whore who was his own private property.

Now Swearengen stood over the Kid's limp body and glared at it, wondering how many times he would have to kick the Kid in the head before his skull was completely shattered. "Get the girl," he growled at Dan Dority without taking his furious gaze away from the unconscious young man.

"Sure, Al," Dan said. He was rubbing the knuckles he had barked on the Kid's face. He left off doing that and went over to the window. Carefully, he reached through and got hold of the whore called Silky Jen. Her hair wasn't so silky anymore. After days of captivity, it was rather lank and greasy, in fact. Even so, it still looked better than most women's hair.

He started to lift her, and then realized that he wouldn't be able to pull her back through the broken window without slicing her to ribbons on the broken glass still sticking out from the window frame. He was liable to cut himself, too, and he didn't want that. So he lowered her to the balcony again and straightened from his crouch. He raised the window all the way and started brushing away the broken glass on the sill.

Outside the balcony, Jen's sheet-wrapped body suddenly scooted away from the window toward the edge of the balcony. Dority didn't believe his eyes at first. He had thought that Jen was unconscious, although it was hard to tell about that because not much light penetrated from the room to the balcony. In fact, she still looked like she was out cold.

But she was sliding across the balcony anyway.

"Hey!" Dority yelled. He made a lunge for her, but he was too late. She slipped right over the edge and dropped out of sight. "Al! Al, the girl's gone!"

Instantly, Swearengen was at Dority's side in front of the window. He drove a fist between Dority's shoulder blades. "Gone! Then go after her, you fuckin' idiot!"

The blow staggered Dority. He caught his balance. There was something about the way Jen had moved across the balcony that was spooky. But Al Swearengen's wrath was a lot scarier than anything that might lurk in the darkness, so with his skin crawling, Dority took a deep breath and climbed out the window.

CALAMITY had known that she couldn't help White-Eye Jack. If she climbed into that room, Swearengen and Dority were liable to kill her. But maybe she could do something for the girl, she had thought as she clung to the carved fretwork railing on the front of the balcony. Her legs were still wrapped around the porch post below her.

There was an opening in the railing just to Calamity's right. She hesitated when Dan Dority appeared in the broken window and reached through to try to retrieve Jen. But then Dority drew back and raised the window instead, so Calamity took advantage of the opportunity and acted while she still could. She reached through the opening and stretched her arm toward the sheet that somebody, almost surely the Kid, had wrapped around the girl. Straining, Calamity got hold of the trailing edge of the sheet. She pulled it toward her, got the best grip she could, and then began hauling Jen across the balcony. She worried that the sheet would just come unwrapped, but it stayed tucked in and brought Jen with it. Sweat rolled down Calamity's face as she pulled the whore's deadweight toward her. A lifetime of hard work had given her plenty of strength.

As soon as she could reach it, she grabbed hold of Jen's ankle and used it to pull the girl. Jen's legs reached the edge of the balcony and slid over. Calamity reached higher on the body and got hold of the sheet again. Dority yelled, "Hey!" and Calamity gave the sheet a jerk. Jen slipped right off the balcony.

Given time, Calamity could have caught her and climbed down with her, but it all happened too fast. Jen fell toward the street. Calamity clamped down hard on the sheet, trying to hold her up. The sheet held for a second and then ripped in two. Jen fell the rest of the way to the street, landing with a soggy thud.

At least Calamity had been able to break her fall somewhat. Calamity let go and dropped to the ground, landing agilely beside Jen's sprawled shape. She caught her balance, then reached down and got her hands under Jen's arms. With a grunt, she lifted the whore and draped her limp form over a shoulder.

It occurred to Calamity to hope that the whore hadn't died from all this hoo-rawing around.

Carrying Jen, Calamity scuttled toward the alley next to the Gem and disappeared into the darkness there. Swearengen would send somebody after them, if he didn't give chase himself. He wasn't going to let the gal go without a fight. She needed help, Calamity knew, or this could still turn out to be a disaster.

The White-Eyed Kid needed help, too, because he was still up there in Swearengen's hands.

And although you could say a lot of things about Al Swearengen, nobody had ever claimed that he was the forgiving sort. . . .

SWEARENGEN sat down on the edge of the bed and opened and closed his knobby fists while Dority climbed out the window to see what had happened to Jen. The more he thought about it, the more certain Swearengen was that Calamity Jane had been part of the plot to steal the girl away from him. She would pay for scheming against him. By God, she would pay.

Rage burned brightly inside him. All his life, people had been trying to steal what was rightfully his. He had been poor in his life, heartbreakingly poor, and he had fought hard for everything he had ever gotten. He knew that when you wanted something, you had to take it, and you used every weapon at your command to get it. You didn't waste even a second of time feeling guilty about anything you did, because the others who were out to get you sure as shit didn't waste any time feeling guilty. You had to fuck them before they fucked you. Kill them before they killed you, if it came down to that. But he was going to win, no matter what it took, because he had lost enough in his life.

He looked at the White-Eyed Kid, who still lay senseless on the floor. The white-hot flames of Swearengen's anger had cooled a little, but he was still mad. The Kid had defied him, and like Calamity Jane, the Kid would pay.

Johnny Burnes stuck his head in the door. "Al?" he asked tentatively. "You need anything?"

Swearengen didn't answer the question directly. He asked one of his own. "Order been restored downstairs?"

"Uh, yeah, I reckon. Folks are drinkin' and gamblin' and pawin' the whores again. Some of 'em are comin' upstairs. And the mess from that fracas is all cleaned up."

Swearengen nodded. "Good."

"So . . . you don't need anything?"

"Not right now," Swearengen said. He felt like he was stuck in the middle of something, not knowing what to do next. It was a bad feeling, an unfamiliar feeling. But he just had to wait until Dan Dority returned, to see if Dority brought the girl back with him.

If not, Swearengen would take all his men and anybody else who wanted to earn some money, and he would tear Deadwood apart until he found her. He would level the camp to the fuckin' ground if he had to.

A hesitant footstep in the doorway made him look up. Dan Dority stood there, and from the frightened look on the man's face, Swearengen knew he had failed.

"I . . . I'm sorry, Al," Dority said hastily. "I looked all around, but I couldn't find her. It's like she just . . . just disappeared or something."

So there it was. Jen was gone. Somehow, despite all his best efforts, she had escaped from him.

No, she had been stolen from him, he corrected himself. He had seen how groggy she was when the Kid was trying to get away with her. She hadn't been awake enough to do anything on her own. And after falling through that window, she would have been even more senseless. Someone had taken her, and his brain went back to his suspicions of Calamity Jane. If she and the Kid had been partners in this rescue attempt, then it was likely Calamity Jane now had the fugitive whore with her.

"Tell Johnny to take some of the boys and go looking for Calamity Jane," Swearengen ordered. "She'll either have Jen with her, or she'll know where she is."

"You think so?"

"She had to be in on it with the Kid. Tell Johnny to find her, goddamn it!"

Dority jerked his head in an anxious nod. "Sure, Al, sure. I'll tell him. You want me to look for Calamity, too?"

"No, once you've told Johnny what to do, come back up here. I've got something more important for you to do."

"What's that?"

Swearengen looked down at the unconscious young man lying at his feet and said, "You're going to take the fuckin' White-Eyed Kid out somewhere and kill him."

Chapter Nineteen

～✦～

BILL Hickok sat at his usual table in the Bella Union, his back to the wall, in the company of friends and acquaintances. He had a decent hand of cards, and the pile of greenbacks and coins in front of him, his winnings from previous hands, was a nice respectable size. A glass of whiskey sat on the table, close at hand, and several drinks already resided warmly within his belly. The women who made up the Bella Union's corps of calico cats were reasonably attractive, and he enjoyed looking at them even though he had no real desire to be unfaithful to his wife Agnes with any of them. From time to time, one of the women laughed, and he enjoyed the sound of that even more. Everything taken into consideration, one might have said that at this particular moment in time, all was right with the world.

Then Calamity Jane came in the saloon's rear entrance, looked around hurriedly, and spotted Hickok across the room. His fingers tightened on the cards as she started toward him.

He should have known that this moment of calm had been too good to last.

She came up to the table and said urgently, "Bill, I got to talk to you."

He laid his cards carefully facedown on the table. "I'm in the midst of a convivial game, Calam," he told her. "Perhaps it could wait until tomorrow."

"No, it can't," she said, shaking her head. "No fuckin' way."

California Joe sat across the table, having come into Deadwood for a night of entertainment after toiling on his gold claim all day. He had known Calamity longer than Hickok had, and he said testily, "Damn it, woman, can't you see we're busy here?"

Calamity ignored him and leaned closer to Hickok. "Bill, I hate to ask a favor of you, but I need some help."

He sighed. Most of the time, Calamity acted as if the two of them were bosom friends and had been for years, instead of barely knowing each other. However, she was a woman—though hardly much of one and certainly not a respectable one—and the way Bill Hickok was constituted, he had a difficult time refusing a plea for help from a woman. He decided that he could at least find out what was bothering her.

"What is it?"

She leaned still closer, so that he could smell whiskey and seldom-washed flesh and . . . was that bear grease? . . . and then she whispered into his ear, "I got a whore in the alley out back."

Hickok's rather bushy eyebrows lifted in surprise. "I'm surprised at you, Calam. I didn't think you had resorted to pimping. At any rate, I'm not interested—"

"Damn it, I don't mean for you to go out there and fuck her!" Calamity burst out. "She's hurt and in trouble."

"And you mistake me, perhaps, for Sir Galahad?" Hickok murmured. He wouldn't stand by and see some woman injured, but on the other hand, he didn't want to get involved in some whore's sordid squabbles, either.

"I'm in trouble, too," Calamity went on, "and so's the White-Eyed Kid!"

Hickok sat up straighter. That put a different face on the

matter. Jack Anderson was a good, loyal friend, and loyalty given demanded loyalty returned.

Hickok wasn't the only one at the table who was fond of the Kid. Colorado Charley Utter and his brother Steve were there, too, and Charley said sharply, "What's all this about, Calamity?"

"Oh, hell." Calamity looked around at the grim-faced men. "I wanted to keep this sort of quietlike. . . ." She took a deep breath. "You remember on the wagon train up here from Fort Laramie, there was a whore called Silky Jen?"

"The one White-Eye Jack was fond of," Hickok recalled. "Of course. What about her?"

"She was supposed to go to work for Al Swearengen over at the Gem. She ain't been workin', though. Swearengen's been holdin' her prisoner in one o' the upstairs rooms, beatin' the shit out of her, and treatin' her worse than even a whore ought to be treated."

Hickok thought about what Calamity had said about having a whore out in the alley. "Calam," he said, "did you steal that girl away from Swearengen?"

"Well . . . sort of. The Kid found out about what was goin' on, and he got some crazy fuckin' romantic notion in his head to rescue her. I figured I'd give him a hand. I don't like that cocksucker Swearengen much."

"So the two of you took the girl away from him, and now you're afraid he's after you, is that it? Is Jack out in the alley with Silky Jen?"

Calamity shook her head. "No, it's just the gal, and she's in piss-poor shape, I gotta tell you, Bill. But the Kid . . ." She swallowed hard. "Swearengen's got the Kid."

The legs of Hickok's chair scraped on the rough floor as he abruptly shoved it back and stood up. "Damn it, Calam," he snapped, "why didn't you say so?"

"I been tryin'! What are you gonna do, Bill?"

Hickok looked around the table at California Joe, Colorado Charley, and Steve, all of whom were already on their feet, too. "We're going to get him back," Hickok said simply, receiving nods of agreement from the other men.

"And God help Al Swearengen if any harm has befallen that boy."

THE jolting as he was carried down the back stairs of the Gem Theater brought the White-Eyed Kid back to consciousness. He wasn't aware at first that he was being carried down the stairs, of course. All he knew was that he hurt like hell and was jouncing up and down for some reason.

By the time he and the man carrying him reached the bottom of the dark, narrow staircase, Jack had figured out, at least vaguely, what was going on. Somebody had picked him up and thrown him over a shoulder, just as he had endeavored to carry Jen away from this place. The difference was that whoever was toting him probably meant him a considerable amount of ill will, instead of intending to rescue him from captivity. The man was large and strong and occasionally muttered a curse under his breath. The voice didn't sound like Al Swearengen's. Swearengen probably wouldn't stoop to such physical labor, either. Jack figured he was the prisoner of Dan Dority.

Even though his head hurt like blazes and he was confused about exactly what had happened to get him in this fix, he was thinking clearly enough to realize that he might be better off if he pretended to still be unconscious. He would bide his time, try to find out what was going on, and then do whatever he could to get out of it.

Dority, or whoever it was, kicked the rear door open and carried Jack outside. The night air was cool at this elevation even in the middle of summer, and it helped clear Jack's head even more. He remembered sneaking into the room where Jen was being held prisoner while Calamity Jane staged a distraction on the first floor of the Gem. He recalled trying to get Jen out the window, only to be attacked by Al Swearengen and then, a few moments later, by Dan Dority as well. After that the details got fuzzy, but he assumed they had beaten him until he passed out.

What had happened to Jen? The last time he had seen her,

she was on the balcony outside the room, having fallen through the window and broken the glass. Had she cut herself? Was she even still alive? The worry made him stiffen involuntarily, and his captor stopped short and dumped him on the ground. The hard landing knocked the breath out of Jack's lungs. He lay trying to get some air back in his body.

"So you're awake, are you?" the man asked, and now Jack could positively identify him as Dan Dority. The starlight that filtered down into the alley revealed that the bartender had removed his apron and put on a hat. He went on. "You are one stupid son of a bitch, you know that? Gettin' yourself killed over some whore. It just ain't worth it, Kid."

"J-Jen . . . ?" Jack gasped out. "Is . . . is she . . ."

Dority scowled down at him. "I don't know where she is. She up an' vanished off that balcony. Al thinks Calamity Jane got her. You know anything about that, Kid?"

Jack closed his eyes for a moment in relief. Jen was out of Swearengen's hands, anyway.

"No," he said honestly. "No, I don't know what happened to her."

Dority hunkered on his heels next to Jack and took out a knife. He put the tip of the blade under Jack's chin and prodded painfully with it. Jack felt a warm trickle of blood down his neck.

"You best tell me the truth," Dority warned. "Al's got men out huntin' for Calamity Jane and the whore right now, but if you can tell me where to find 'em, that'll make things easier on you. I'll tell you true, Kid. Al gave me orders to take you out and kill you, but I reckon if you help him find that girl, he might decide to let you live."

"You think . . . you think I'd want to live . . . if I helped you bring Jen back to Swearengen?"

"Everybody wants to live," Dority said softly. He dug harder with the tip of the blade. "You hear fancy words about dyin' for a cause and givin' up your life for a greater good, but comes the time for a man to take that last breath, he'll trade most anything for another one. A cause, a woman . . . nothin's too much to give up if it means he gets to keep on breathin'."

Fear was like ice in the Kid's veins. All it would take was one little push by Dority, not much effort at all, and that razor-sharp blade would slide right on through his throat and his life would erupt in a gush of hot blood. He was that close to dying.

But he didn't have to decide if he was going to betray Jen or not, and for that, he was thankful. He didn't know where she was. He didn't know whether or not Calamity had her. That hadn't been part of the plan.

"I don't know," he whispered. "I swear, I don't know."

Dority frowned at him for a long moment and then grunted. "Well, if that don't beat all. I reckon I believe you, Kid. That's a shame in a way, 'cause now I got no reason not to go ahead and kill you, the way Al told me to."

Jack expected the man to cut his throat then and there, but to his surprise, Dority stood up and sheathed the knife. Jack lifted a shaking hand to his throat and touched the wound under his chin. Blood smeared his fingertips.

"I'll take you up the gulch and find a ravine to throw your body in," Dority said. "Be a while before anybody finds you, if they ever do. Wolves may see to that." He shook his head and sighed. "Whether you believe it or not, Kid, I don't like doin' this. Tell you what. I'll go ahead and knock you out again, so you won't feel a thing when I kill you. How's about that?" He drew back his foot to kick Jack in the head and struck without waiting for an answer.

But Jack wasn't there anymore. He'd summoned up all the desperate strength he could muster and rolled away just as Dority swung his leg. The kick missed, throwing Dority off balance. The burly bartender slapped a hand against the rear wall of the Gem to steady himself.

Jack kept rolling. He had spotted something from the corner of his eye, a dark heap against the wall. As he came up against it, he recognized it as a stack of firewood. He wrapped his hands around a short length of wood and un-coiled from the ground, swinging the firewood as he wheeled toward Dority, who was rushing after him. The wood crashed into the side of Dority's head and sent his hat flying. He stumbled and ran into the wall.

Jack dropped the wood and turned to run. Avoiding Dority's kick and striking that blow had taken almost everything out of him. His head was spinning and his muscles had gone limp. His legs didn't want to work right. He careened away from Dority. Behind him, Dority cursed, pushed himself away from the wall, and thudded after Jack.

Limber-legged, Jack stumbled around the corner of the building into the narrow space beside the Gem. At the far end, he could see light and knew it came from the windows of the businesses along Main Street. He staggered toward it. Dority was close behind him, though, and he didn't think he was going to make it. All he could do was keep running and hope . . .

But even if he reached Main Street, that wouldn't save him. Dority would just catch up to him and pull him back into the alley, into the darkness where he would meet his death. Deadwood was an outlaw town. Men were murdered here nearly every day of the week, and nobody really gave a damn. Nobody would help him.

Despite that, Jack wouldn't give up. He lurched on, and somehow he was fast enough to reach the end of the alley before Dority grabbed him from behind. He squirted out into the street like a watermelon seed, but then he tripped and went down, sprawling hard in the muck.

He almost collided with somebody's legs. Blinking mud out of his eyes, he saw high-topped boots right in front of his face. Jack lifted his head and looked up. . . .

At the grim, towering figure of Wild Bill Hickok. Suddenly, the bleak expression on Hickok's face disappeared, to be replaced by a surprised grin, and the Prince of Pistoleers said, "Why, there you are, White-Eye. We were just looking for you."

DAN Dority blundered out of the alley mouth and came to a sliding, stunned halt at the sight of the men gathered around the fallen Kid. Wild Bill Hickok, even though he didn't dress as fancy as he used to, was instantly recognizable. So was the little dandy, Colorado Charley, and the buckskin-clad, hatchet-faced California Joe. They were three dangerous men, mighty dangerous. Charley's brother Steve was with them, too, and while Dority didn't know much about him, it didn't matter. The other three were hell-on-wheels by themselves.

Hickok's big, long-fingered hands were unnervingly close to the butts of the twin .38s he wore. Like everybody else in Deadwood, Dority had heard rumors that Hickok's eyesight wasn't what it once was. He was damned if he was going to risk his life on a rumor, though. Keeping his hands well in sight, he backed off a few steps.

In a quiet voice, Hickok said, "Steve, help young Jack up to my hotel room and see to his needs, would you?"

"Sure, Bill," Steve Utter replied. Bigger and stronger than his brother, Steve bent and lifted the Kid to his feet without any trouble. He put an arm around the Kid's waist and led him off toward the Grand Central.

Hickok fixed his gaze on Dority and asked, "Did you have business with my friend Jack, Mr. Dority?"

"Uh . . . no," Dority managed to say. "Not at all."

"It appeared to me that you were pursuing him."

"Just wanted to talk to him," Dority said nervously. "I ain't lookin' for no trouble, Mr. Hickok. You got my word on that." His eyes flicked to the retreating figures of Steve Utter and the White-Eyed Kid. Al was going to be mad as hell when he heard that the Kid had gotten away. But surely even he would understand that Dority couldn't go up against Bill Hickok, Colorado Charley, and California Joe.

Hickok sauntered forward, followed by the other two. "I'm not looking for trouble, either," he said, "but I do need to have a conversation with your employer." Hickok inclined his head toward the front entrance of the Gem. "I take it Al Swearengen is inside?"

"Uh . . . yeah. Leastways, I think so. He was a few minutes ago."

"Obliged," Hickok said as he walked past. The casual,

dismissive way he turned his back on Dority stung. Dority knew he wasn't just about to do anything about it, though.

Hickok and his friends went into the Gem with Dority following them. The citizens of Deadwood were accustomed to seeing the famous Wild Bill by now, but his presence was still enough to cause a slight diminishing of the noise inside the place. Hickok's eyes must not have been too bad, because he strode straight toward Al Swearengen as if he had spotted Swearengen right away.

Swearengen had been leaning on the bar, but he straightened as he saw the contingent of frontiersmen coming toward him. He glanced past them at Dority, his eyes narrowing. Dority shrugged. He didn't know what Hickok was up to.

Trying to look more casual, Swearengen picked up the glass he'd been drinking from and nodded to the newcomers. "Mr. Hickok," he said. "How are you?"

"Concerned," Hickok said.

"Oh? What about?"

"A friend of mine. I'll speak plainly, Mr. Swearengen, but we can have this conversation in your office, if you prefer."

Dority looked at Swearengen and gave a tiny nod. Swearengen saw it and said, "All right, that'll be fine. You gentlemen come with me." He added in a harder tone, "Dan, you come along, too."

Dority didn't want any part of what was about to happen, but he figured he was already in enough trouble. He said, "Sure, Al," and joined the group of men that trooped up the stairs to Swearengen's second-floor office.

Once they were in there with the door closed, Swearengen went behind the desk and said, "Have a seat."

"We'll stand, thanks," Hickok said. "This shouldn't take long."

Swearengen slipped a cigar from his vest pocket and put it in his mouth unlit. He shrugged and stayed on his feet, too, saying around the cigar, "Fine. What can I do for you?"

"Promise me that you won't cause any more trouble for the White-Eyed Kid and his friend Silky Jen."

Swearengen took a sharp breath in through his nose.

"The girl works for me," he said tightly.

Hickok shook his head. "Not anymore. She's tendered her resignation."

"How would you know that?"

"She and the Kid are in my hotel room right now, being tendered to by Doc Peirce and Calamity Jane. They're under my protection, Swearengen." Hickok's voice was as hard and cold as flint.

Dority saw the fires burning in Swearengen's eyes. He knew there was a gun in the half-open desk drawer right in front of Swearengen. He wasn't sure what he would do if Al reached for that gun and started shooting. He was behind Hickok and Colorado Charley and might manage to get a shot off at them, but California Joe had edged back a mite and was watching him from the corner of his eye. Dority was sure that if a gunfight broke out and he tried to join in, California Joe would blast his guts out.

Swearengen controlled his temper, though, and said, "I don't have anything to do with the White-Eyed Kid, and if Jen wants to quit working for me, that's her decision. You didn't have to come in here and announce that they're under your protection, Hickok."

"I believe in being careful and making sure everything is understood," Hickok said. "That way everybody lives longer."

Swearengen's teeth clamped down harder on the cigar. He leaned forward and rested his fists on the desk. "I don't care about the fucking whore, and I don't care about the fucking White-Eyed Kid. Clear enough?"

"Perfectly," Hickok returned coolly. "But if anything unfortunate happens to them in the future, anything at all, I'll be coming back to see you, Swearengen."

"If anything happens to them, it won't be my fault."

"I don't care," Hickok said. "The Gem will still be my first stop." He turned toward the door and added, "Come on, boys."

Colorado Charley followed him through the door. California Joe hung back a little and was the last one out, giving Swearengen and Dority a savage grin as he left. A shiver ran through Dority as the door swung closed. The old scout had looked as if he would enjoy nothing better than carving out both of their livers and frying them up for a treat.

Dority turned his head and looked at Swearengen. The fires were back in Al's eyes.

"You let the Kid get away?" Swearengen's voice was a hiss.

"He clouted me with a chunk of firewood, Al," Dority defended himself, trying not to whine. "I was gonna kill him, I really was. He come to, though, and I figured I ought to ask him if he knew where the girl was."

"It doesn't matter now, does it? We know where she is." Swearengen's voice shook with rage. "She's with that fucking Hickok!"

"I'm sorry, Al. I really am." Dority knew he was taking a chance, but somebody had to try to talk some sense into Al's head. "Maybe you better just let it go. No whore's worth gettin' killed over. That's what I told the Kid, and it's still true."

To his surprise, Swearengen nodded. "You're right, Dan. No whore is worth it. I was already starting to think that myself. I let myself get too caught up in that Jen girl. Hell, she's just another piece of ass."

"Yeah," Dority said, pleased that Swearengen was being reasonable. "Just another piece of ass."

Swearengen took the cigar out of his mouth, and suddenly his hand clenched on it, shredding it so that tobacco was scattered over the desk. "But I'll tell you what I won't stand for," he said savagely. "I won't stand for being shown up in my own place by some gunfighter who thinks he can come in here and put the fear of God in me! I don't give a damn any more about the Kid and that whore, but Wild Bill Hickok . . ." Swearengen paused in his tirade to draw a deep breath. "Wild Bill Hickok is a fuckin' dead man."

Chapter Twenty

A L Swearengen was still calm when he came downstairs
the next morning. Although the Gem never closed and
had customers around the clock, the place wasn't very
busy at this early hour. Even so, Swearengen spotted a couple of familiar faces and grunted in satisfaction. Johnny
Varnes sat at a table playing blackjack with a couple of
sleepy-eyed prospectors. Jim Levy stood at the bar, nursing
a mug of beer. Just the gents Swearengen wanted to see.

Despite his surface composure, he was damned near a
raging lunatic inside. Only years of practice allowed him to
control that inner demon so that it didn't show itself most
of the time. He tamped down his anger now as he walked
over to the bar. Dan Dority stood behind the hardwood,
leaning an elbow on the bar. He had his chin propped in his
hand, and his eyes were closed.

With a swipe of his hand, Swearengen knocked Dority's
elbow off the bar. That took the dozing bartender by surprise. He fell forward, and barely kept from hitting his face
on the bar. As he recovered, he said hastily, "Sorry, Al. It
was a long night."

"I know. Gimme a cup of coffee."

There was a small stove behind the bar, with a coffeepot sitting on it keeping warm. Dority filled a cup for Swearengen and handed it across the bar. Swearengen took his coffee black. He sipped the strong brew and then carried the cup across the room to the table where Varnes's blackjack game was going on.

"Game's over," he said to the two prospectors. "Move along so I can talk to Varnes."

The men looked like they wanted to object, but not many people were foolish enough to argue with Al Swearengen. Wild Bill Hickok could get away with it, maybe—in fact, there was a rumor already going around the settlement that Hickok had forced Swearengen to back down during a confrontation the night before—but these miners had sense enough to throw down their cards, push back their chairs, and leave.

Varnes wasn't happy with the interruption, either. "This is your place, Al, so I guess you can do what you want," he said. "But those lambs were ripe for fleecing."

Swearengen took one of the empty chairs and sat down. "You wouldn't win any more than fuckin' chicken feed from those two," he pointed out. "You've got more important business on your plate."

Varnes gathered the cards, squared up the deck, and began idly shuffling. "Oh? What's that?"

Swearengen inclined his head toward the bar and asked, "Have you talked to Levy about that matter we discussed a while back?"

Varnes looked uncomfortable as he fidgeted with the cards. After a moment he shook his head. "I haven't gotten around to it," he said.

"You're too fuckin' nervous to do it, that's what you mean." Swearengen stood up. "Stay there. We'll do this right now, both of us."

Varnes's eyes darted toward the entrance, as if he were considering bolting out of the Gem, but then he nodded and said, "All right. I suppose it's time. Past time, maybe."

Swearengen grunted. If they had found somebody to

kill Hickok before now, then that brown-haired whore would still be upstairs in his room, where she belonged.

But there was no point in whining about that, even to himself. He fortified himself with the rest of the coffee and then walked over to the bar where the tall, cold-eyed gunman stood.

"Mr. Levy," Swearengen greeted him. "Top of the morning to you."

Levy looked over at him and nodded. "Swearengen."

"I was wondering if you'd be kind enough to join me and an associate of mine for a drink."

Levy lifted the mug of beer in his hand. "Got a drink already."

"We have a business proposition for you," Swearengen said bluntly.

For a moment, Swearengen thought Levy was going to brush him off. But then the gunman shrugged and said in his tight-lipped way, "Reckon it wouldn't hurt to listen."

He finished his beer and followed Swearengen over to the table where Varnes sat. Swearengen motioned for Dority to bring them a bottle and glasses. Varnes stood up and extended his hand. "Mr. Levy," he said. "It's an honor to meet you, sir."

Levy pointedly ignored the gambler's hand and gave him one of his customary curt nods instead. Varnes lowered his hand and looked insulted for a second, but he controlled the reaction and forced a smile back onto his narrow face.

When they were all seated at the table and had drinks in front of them, Swearengen said to Levy, "You know Wild Bill Hickok."

"I know *of* him," Levy corrected. "I've never exchanged words with the man."

"He has quite a reputation with a gun," Varnes said.

"Of course he does. People write dime novels about him." Scorn dripped from Levy's voice. "Those scribblers generally don't know their ass from a hole in the ground."

Swearengen leaned forward, keeping his voice pitched

fairly low. No one was sitting near them, but he didn't want this conversation overheard. "Hickok's earned his rep. He cleaned up Hays City and Abilene. That's what's got us worried."

Understanding dawned in Levy's eyes. "You're afraid he'll do the same thing here."

"It's inevitable," Varnes said. "With a man like Hickok in town, sooner or later the so-called respectable element will approach him and ask him to take the job of marshal. If that happens, it's only a matter of time until he causes trouble for us."

Levy picked up his glass, took a sip of whiskey, and said, "So you want me to kill him for you."

A few seconds of tense silence went by as Swearengen and Varnes looked at him. Then Varnes cleared his throat and said, "That's right. The business owners from this end of town are willing to put up a sizable pot—"

"Not enough," Levy interrupted with a shake of his head.

"I haven't even told you how much we're talking about yet!"

"It doesn't matter," Levy said. "There's not enough gold in the whole damned gulch to pay me to draw against Hickok."

"You think he's faster than you?" Swearengen challenged. "You're afraid of him? You could always bushwhack him."

Levy's head turned slowly toward him, and when Swearengen saw the look in Levy's eyes, he wished he had been a little more discreet in his choice of words.

"No, I'm not afraid of him. I could beat him and I know it. That's why I'm not interested in your offer. That and the fact that I hear his eyes are going bad. It wouldn't be a fair fight. As for bushwhacking him . . ." Levy shook his head. "Hickok deserves better than that." He pushed his chair back. "I'm just about the sorriest fucker you'll ever find, and I don't mind admitting it. But I'll be goddamned if I'm going to shoot Wild Bill Hickok in the back."

Levy stood up.

Varnes said quickly, "If you'll just give us a minute—"

"Our business is over," Levy said. He turned and walked back to the bar.

Varnes stared disconsolately across the table at Swearengen. "He was our best hope for getting rid of Hickok. Now what do we do?"

"Find somebody else," Swearengen said. "There must be somebody in this fuckin' burg who's stupid enough, fast enough, and lucky enough to go up against Hickok and have a chance."

BELLAMY Bridges said, "Ahhhh!" and closed his eyes. His back had arched as he orgasmed, but now he relaxed against the somewhat lumpy mattress underneath him. Ling straddled his hips and rested her hands on his chest. Bellamy reached up and took hold of her arms, pulled her down so that he could hug her. He still felt a little guilty about carrying on like this with Ling so soon after Carla's death . . . but life had to go on, after all.

"Sleepy," Ling murmured as she rested her head on his chest. "Stay here?"

"Yeah, you can stay here," Bellamy told her. "But I can't. I've got work to do."

Ling clutched at him. "No work. Too early. Nobody come fuckee suckee."

Bellamy laughed and said, "There may not be any customers right now, but that doesn't mean there's no work to do."

Ling whined a little more, but Bellamy rolled her off him and got up, leaving her lying there on the tangled sheets. He got dressed, and by the time he was ready to leave, Ling was snoring softly. He closed the door quietly on his way out of the room.

The door of Laurette's office was open. Bellamy leaned a shoulder against the jamb and looked at her as she sat behind the desk, counting money. "It was a good night," she said as she glanced up at him and then returned to what she was doing. "Could have been better, though."

"I'll see what I can do about that."

"Going to pay a visit to Turner?"

"That's right."

She looked up at him again and said, "Be careful."

"I will be. But I'm not worried about Turner."

He tugged his hat down a little tighter on his head as he left the Academy. He walked toward the east end of Deadwood, where the Chinese community was located. Before he got there, he reached a new building made of lumber so raw it seemed that it had been sawed only yesterday. A sign over the door read simply TURNER'S. That was all that was needed. Everybody in town was already aware that it was the newest whorehouse in Deadwood.

Nobody was going in and out of the place at this time of day. Bellamy tried the door and found it unlocked. He walked inside and looked around. The parlor was barely furnished. In comparison to the Academy, it looked positively spartan. Men didn't come to Turner's for the atmosphere, though. They came for the prices.

Laurette had been outraged when she'd heard about them. "A dollar for a regular fuck!" she'd exclaimed angrily. "A fuckin' dollar! That's outrageous! What do they charge for a French job, four bits?"

That was exactly right, but having her guess confirmed hadn't made Laurette feel any better.

"I can't compete with that," she said. "Nobody can. Something's got to be done about it."

That was when her wild-eyed gaze had fallen on Bellamy, and she had given him the job of going down to talk some sense into Turner's head.

"It's got to be at least three bucks for a straight poke," she'd said. "Four or five would be better."

"Wouldn't it be even better if he just closed down and left Deadwood?" Bellamy had asked.

"Well, sure. The less competition the better. But hell, this town's a gold mine for a whoremonger. I don't know why Turner would up and leave, unless—" She had stopped short and looked for a long moment at Bellamy. Then, smiling slowly, she said, "You go have that talk with him. Who knows, maybe he *will* decide to leave town."

Bellamy had waited until morning, when Turner's place wouldn't be busy. That appeared to be understating the case. The building was deserted, as far as he could see. He called, "Anybody here?"

"Hold your horses," a woman's voice replied from somewhere in the rear. A moment later, she came sauntering up a hallway. She had blond hair and was short and a little heavy. She wore a robe, but it hung all the way open and revealed that she was naked underneath it. Bellamy thought the nipples on her thick breasts were the largest he had ever seen.

She came into the parlor and yawned. "Damn, slick, it's mighty early. You sure you're up for it?"

"Are you the only one here?" Bellamy asked.

"The only girl, you mean?" She sniffed and looked offended. "What's the matter, am I too fat for you? Gimme a try, mister. I'll squeeze the dick right off of you."

"That's not what I meant—" Bellamy began.

"All the other girls are asleep, and that's where I oughta be." She yawned again. "Tell you what, if you can get off in a hurry—"

"That's not why I'm here," Bellamy said. "I want to see the man who runs this place."

"Turner, you mean?" She jerked a thumb over her shoulder. "He's out back, splitting some firewood. What do you want with him?"

"That's my business," Bellamy said.

The woman shrugged, making her breasts wobble. "Suit yourself. As long as I can get some sleep, I don't care." She turned her back on Bellamy, but then some perverse streak made her pause and pull up her robe, baring her fleshy rump to him. She shook it and said, "You don't know what you're missing, though."

Bellamy didn't respond to the taunt. He just walked past her, down a hallway toward a rear door.

When he stepped outside, he saw why he hadn't heard the sound of an ax splitting wood as he came up to the place. Turner might have come out here to perform that chore, but at the moment he was sitting on a stump, sipping from a silver flask. Fortifying himself with whiskey for the task to come, Bellamy thought.

He was a big man with heavy shoulders, thinning brown hair, and bushy side-whiskers. Turning bleary eyes toward Bellamy, he said, "Mornin'. What can I do for you, mister? If you're lookin' for girls, I got the finest in Deadwood inside."

Judging by what he had seen, Bellamy doubted that, but he wasn't here to talk about the quality of anybody's whores. He said, "I hear you've got good prices."

Turner took another nip from the flask. "Yes, sir. Dollar a fuck, best price in Deadwood. And just 'cause the price is cheap, don't mean the pussy is. It's all prime stuff."

"You've been touting it all over town, too."

"Well, why the hell not? I'm proud of the service I offer, mighty proud."

"It won't do," Bellamy said flatly.

That made the smile disappear from Turner's face. He frowned as he said, "What do you mean? This is a free country, ain't it? A man can charge whatever he damn well pleases!"

"Not when it undercuts everybody else's profits. You've got two choices, Turner: You can fall in line with the other houses, or you can get out of Deadwood."

The big man stood up and set his flask on the stump where he had been sitting. The ax he had planned to use to split wood leaned against the stump, but he didn't reach for it.

"Who sent you down here to threaten me?" Turner demanded. "The fella who runs the Gem?"

"It doesn't matter who sent me. I'm here to tell you to leave."

"You said I had two choices."

"I lied," Bellamy said. "Close down. Get out. Keep living. Simple as that."

Turner's face purpled with rage. "You little bastard! I won't be talked to like that! I fought the Rebels at the Wilderness and Spotsylvania—"

"That doesn't have a damned thing to do with this," Bellamy cut in. "Take your fat, ugly whores and get out."

"Damn you!" Turner shouted. "You can't talk to me like that!" He grabbed up the ax and whirled toward Bellamy.

Bellamy moved his coat aside, leaving his hand close to the butt of his gun. He didn't draw the weapon, but rather just stood there, waiting. Turner halted abruptly after taking a step. He read the menace in Bellamy's stance.

"You'd shoot me down?"

"Come at me with an ax and I will. Nobody will care, either. It would be self-defense."

"What if I won't leave?" Turner blustered.

"Then I'll shoot you anyway. And again, nobody will care."

Turner seemed to shrink under Bellamy's cool gaze. Despite his size and physical strength, he couldn't stand up to the threat of the gun on Bellamy's hip. "What if I stay and raise my prices?" he asked in a thin voice.

"Raise them to ten dollars and you can stay."

"Ten dollars?" Turner sputtered. "Nobody's gonna pay that for a fuck when they can get it for less in a dozen places!"

"That's your problem. There are other camps. You can go to Montana City or Fountain City or Anchor and charge whatever you want. But not in Deadwood."

"This ain't right," Turner muttered, his eyes downcast.

"You've got the rest of today to pack up," Bellamy said. "Be gone by tonight."

"And if I ain't?" Turner asked, summoning up a shred of defiance.

"Then I'll come see you again."

The big man heaved a deflated sigh. "All right. I'll go inside and tell the missus to start packin'."

Bellamy frowned. "Your *wife* works in a whorehouse?"

Turner's chin lifted. "She's the best gal I got. You must've seen her when you come through the house." A sly look appeared on the man's face, harbinger of a last, fading hope. "If you want . . ."

Bellamy didn't wait for him to finish. He just shook his head and walked off. "Gone by tonight," he threw over his shoulder.

Laurette would be pleased. With her to handle the thinking and him to take care of enforcing her decisions, they made a good team. It was Laurette's goal to rule Deadwood like it was her own personal kingdom.

Before they were through, she just might do it.

Chapter Twenty-one

❧❧

IT was difficult to keep track of the days in Deadwood, Bill Hickok discovered. One might think that Sunday would be easy to distinguish because that was the day church services were held, but there was no church in Deadwood, only the box on which Reverend H. W. Smith stood to deliver his message, and the reverend preached the Gospel every day, day in and day out, standing on the crate that served as his tabernacle.

From saloon to saloon, Hickok drifted, playing cards, drinking—but seldom getting drunk—and enjoying the company of his friends. There was a newcomer in Deadwood, a young man named Leander Richardson, who was acquainted somehow with Colorado Charley and therefore became acquainted with Hickok as well. He obviously looked up to Wild Bill, and spent most of his time hanging around the edges of the circle that included Charley, California Joe, Bloody Dick Seymour, and the White-Eyed Kid.

Fortune had smiled at last on the Kid, assisted, of course, by Wild Bill Hickok and Calamity Jane. Silky Jen was still in rather bad shape, but was improving with every day that went by. Hickok had ensconced the young couple in his hotel room at the Grand Central, figuring that they could use the comfort and privacy of the place more than he could. After giving up his room, he had taken to sleeping in one of the wagons that belonged to Charley Utter. He knew better than to ask to share Charley's tent. The fastidious little man didn't want anyone intruding on his neatness and order, not even his best friend, the illustrious Wild Bill.

It was a pleasant life, yet haunted by doubt and regret, both of which had been virtual strangers to Hickok during his long and eventful life. He had promised Agnes that he was going to Deadwood to search for gold, to secure a comfortable future for them. And yet he had turned down a partnership in a perfectly good claim with California Joe, and instead of looking for a claim of his own, he was whiling away his days in saloons and theaters. He knew he should have been more industrious . . . but it seemed to him that in his case, there was no point to industry.

His dreams were haunted by death.

He didn't know if they were premonitions or visits by earthbound spirits or simply the product of too much whiskey and rich food. But there was a growing core of coldness somewhere deep inside him, despite the heat of summer, and he suspected that he knew what it meant. His time on this earth was drawing to a close.

But he would not admit that. Not yet. Things might still change. It was possible. Just look at Silky Jen. Her bruises were healing, and according to the White-Eyed Kid, she no longer flinched when he touched her hair or her shoulder. Hickok had advised the lad to take things slowly. The poor girl had endured a great deal, and it would take time for all of her injuries to heal. The spiritual ones would doubtless require more patience than the physical ones. The Kid had sworn to do whatever he had to in order to make things right for her, and Bill believed him.

Dick Seymour had returned to Deadwood, and Brant Street had taken the second run of the Pioneer Pony Express. Steve Utter was off somewhere working on the arrangements for the freight line, and Colorado Charley would likely join him soon. A couple of men named Bullock and

Star came in from Montana Territory with several wagon loads of hardware and announced that they were establishing a store. Almost immediately, the frame of the building that would house it began to go up. Another doctor and several lawyers arrived in the camp. "Camp," in fact, was no longer a suitable word to describe the place. Deadwood was a town now, and was well on its way to becoming a city. Whether it was legal or not, there would be no stopping its growth. A bustle of activity went on twenty-four hours a day.

But it went on almost unnoticed around Bill Hickok, who played cards and sipped whiskey and dreamed his dreams of death when he rolled up in his blankets in the back of Colorado Charley's wagon.

COLORADO Charley was fuming when he came into the dining room of the Grand Central Hotel. Hickok sat at one of the tables with Dick Seymour, the White-Eyed Kid, and Leander Richardson, with the remains of breakfast in front of them. The Kid was getting ready to go upstairs and take a plate with him for Jen. Lou Marchbanks's cooking had done wonders for the girl, the Kid claimed.

Hickok caught Charley's eye and motioned him over to the table. Charley's face was flushed with rage, and Hickok commented, "Land's sake, Charley, you look like you're about to have a fit of apoplexy. Why don't you sit down and have a cup of coffee instead, and maybe something to eat?"

"No time, no time," Charley said distractedly. "I got to go kill somebody."

Hickok's eyebrows rose in surprise. "Why, Charley, it's not like you to go around threatening folks with death, especially this early in the morning. What's happened to get you so worked up?"

"What's happened?" Charley thrust his hand into a pocket and brought out a crumpled piece of paper. "I'll show you what's happened." He smoothed out the paper and slapped it down on the table in front of Hickok. "*That's* what's happened!"

The others around the table craned their necks to see

what was printed on the paper in large, somewhat blurred letters. Hickok helped them out by reading the words. "Initial Run of the Frontier Pony Express . . . Fast, Dependable Delivery of Mail to Fort Laramie, Cheyenne, and All Points North, South, East, and West . . . Reasonable Rates . . . August Clippinger, Proprietor."

Charley jabbed a finger at the flyer, which had obviously been ripped down from wherever it had been posted, and grated, "Fuckin' Frontier Pony Express!"

"I don't see the word *fucking* printed on there anywhere," Hickok said dryly.

Charley smacked a palm on the table. "You know what I mean! The bastard stole it! He stole my idea!"

"Seems like there was already a Pony Express," Dick Seymour pointed out. "Pretty well known, too."

Dick had been rather brooding and withdrawn for some reason ever since he'd gotten back from his ride to Fort Laramie, so Hickok was glad to see a grin on his face as he twitted Charley a little. Charley wasn't so pleased. He said, "God damn it! This ain't funny. This Clippinger son of a bitch is tryin' to steal my business out from under me."

"Any successful business will always have its imitators, Charley, you know that," Hickok said. "I'm sure this fellow Clippinger won't prove to be any real competition to you."

"Damn right he won't, because I'm goin' down to the stable where his office is and shoot the son of a bitch." Charley looked around the table. "Who's with me?"

"I, uh, have to go see to Jen," the White-Eyed Kid said.

"I'll go," Dick replied. "I reckon it is a pretty low thing the fella is doing."

Richardson leaned forward. "I'll go if Wild Bill is going," he declared.

Hickok said, "You and I have been friends for too long for me to let anything happen to you now, Charley. I'll come along to see that you keep that temper of yours under control."

"Just don't get in my way when I go to shoot the bastard," Charley warned.

The four men left the Grand Central and started down

the street. Along the way they ran into Dick Street and Charlie Anderson, the Kid's brother. Both young men fell in with them, so the group numbered half a dozen as it approached the livery stable, which now had another sign hung out front that read FRONTIER PONY EXPRESS.

A short man with a round face and a neatly trimmed goatee greeted them. He wore a beaded buckskin jacket and a hat with a rattlesnake band. "Gentlemen," he said, "what can I do for you? Have you come to mail some letters?"

Charley brandished the flyer. "Is this yours?"

"Why, I believe it is," the man drawled in a voice that said he came from Virginia or some other place in the South. "August Clippinger, at your service."

"I'm Charley Utter, the man you stole this whole idea from!"

Hickok figured that Clippinger already knew who they were. Charley cut a distinctive figure, and Bill wasn't so overly modest as to think that folks wouldn't recognize him wherever he went. Clippinger didn't seem shaken, though. He had probably been expecting just such a visit.

"Better not make such rash statements, my friend," he said. "August Clippinger is no thief. I merely foresaw a need in this fine community and moved to fill it."

"There ain't no need for your two-bit Pony Express!" Charley flared. "Deadwood's already got mail service. The Pioneer Pony Express has already made a successful run, and my rider will be back any day now from another one!"

"First isn't necessarily always the best, nor the one that lasts."

Charley stepped forward and poked a finger against Clippinger's chest. "Listen, you smug son of a bitch—"

Clippinger took a rapid step backward and called, "Durkin! Winchell! Prescott!"

Three rugged-looking men hurried out of the shadowy interior of the barn. "What is it, Boss?" one of them asked.

Clippinger had lost his smooth, affable façade. "These gents are causing trouble. Run them off for me, will you?"

The three men started forward with scowls on their faces, but one of them stopped suddenly and shot out an arm to hold back the other two. "Uh, Mr. Clippinger," he said. "That tall hombre is Wild Bill Hickok."

Clippinger paled. "I'm not looking for a gun battle," he said hastily.

"Nor am I," Bill said. "I assure you, I'm here just to see that no one gets hurt too badly."

Clippinger squinted suspiciously at him. "You ain't going to start shooting?"

"Not unless someone else reaches for a gun first."

Charley Utter looked sideways at Hickok. "I thought you was gonna back my play."

"You don't need me, Charley. I'd just hold you back."

"Yeah, I reckon that's true," Charley snapped, clearly not caring if his words stung or not. He swung back toward Clippinger and said, "Take that sign down and forget about runnin' a Pony Express."

"Mind your own business," Clippinger shot back at him, "and get away from mine, you dandified little fucker."

Charley's hands balled into fists, but before he could throw a punch, Dick Seymour stepped forward and said, "Allow me, Charley."

With that, he slammed a hard right fist into Clippinger's face.

The brawl was on.

Clippinger was rocked back by the blow to the face. He yelled through bloody lips, "Get 'em!" The three men who worked for him lunged forward, to be met by Dick Street, Charlie Anderson, and Leander Richardson. The combatants stood toe-to-toe, slugging it out. Clippinger, who wasn't as soft as he looked, grabbed Dick Seymour and wrestled him to the ground. People on the street began to take notice of the battle and gathered around, shouting encouragement to the participants. The only two who weren't taking part were Hickok and Charley Utter. Hickok put a hand on Charley's arm and drew him back a few steps. "Let them have it, Charley," he advised. "They're full of youth and energy."

"Piss and vinegar's more like it," Charley said. He looked like he wanted to be right in the middle of the fra-

cas, but he held back. "Watch out, Dick!" he shouted to the
Englishman. "He's tryin' to gouge you!"

The knot of fighting men surged back and forth in front
of the stable. Whenever one of them got knocked into the
crowd, those helpful spectators grabbed him and shoved
him back into the fray. Preacher Smith wandered up and
began shouting, "Brethren! Brethren! This violence is most
ungodly!" He was ignored.

Drawn by the commotion, A. W. Merrick of the *Black
Hills Pioneer* hurried up and started asking questions of
those on the periphery of the fight, wanting to know who
was involved and what they were brawling over. When he
spotted Hickok and Colorado Charley, he bulled his way
through the crowd to their side. Looking from Charley to
the sign that read FRONTIER PONY EXPRESS, he said, "Oh,
ho! Feuding Pony Expresses!" He pulled a pad of paper
and a pencil from his pocket and began scribbling notes for
a story. He asked, "What's your part in this, Mr. Hickok?"

"Interested bystander, that's all," Bill replied.

"You don't think you ought to break it up?"

Hickok shook his head. "My town-taming days are
over. I've said that more than once since I came to Deadwood, and it's still true."

Merrick looked like he doubted that, but he turned his
attention back to the fight.

Several more minutes of hard fighting went by. Most of
the men were bloody and staggering by now. Dick Seymour had thrown off Clippinger and was currently sitting
on top of the stocky entrepreneur, throttling him. Clippinger flailed and thrashed but couldn't shake loose Dick's
grip. His tongue stuck out, and he was starting to turn blue
and purple in the face.

Hickok liked Bloody Dick and didn't want to see him
strung up for murder by a group of vigilantes. He stepped
forward and grabbed Dick's collar, pulling him up and off
Clippinger. Hickok shoved Dick at Charley Utter and
snapped, "Hang onto him!" Realizing that he had just told
the newspaperman that he wasn't going to break up the

fight, Hickok hesitated. Then, thinking that somebody wa:
going to get seriously hurt if he didn't step in, Hickol
shrugged, drew his right-hand Colt, and blasted a couple o:
shots into the air.

The loud reports put a stop to the fighting, all right
Some of the men ducked, thinking they were being shot at
and then looked around sheepishly when they realized tha
wasn't the case.

"That's enough," Hickok said, his powerful voice carrying along the street. "This isn't going to settle anything."

"Indeed it's not," A. W. Merrick said as he stepped forward. Then, with a journalist's flair for the dramatic, he wen
on. "The best way to settle such a dispute is with a race."

"A race!" Several men in the crowd took up the cry. "A
race between the Pony Expresses!"

Colorado Charley held up his hands and said, "Hold on
Hold on, damn it! I was here first—"

The shouts from the crowd drowned him out. The idea
of a race had caught the fancy of Deadwood's citizens, and
now it took fire.

Hickok holstered his gun and said, "Looks like you're
stuck, Charley. You're going to have to take on Clippinger
and try to beat him that way."

Still red-faced from being choked, Clippinger came up
and glared defiantly at Charley. "How about it, Utter?" he
demanded. "One of your riders against one of mine, and
the winning line gets to carry the mail between here and
Fort Laramie!"

Charley scowled and grimaced and muttered curses for
a few seconds, but finally he stuck out a hand and said
"You're on, damn it! And may the best man win, which'l
be me! You can fuckin' well count on that!"

A cheer went up from the crowd. Everybody liked a
race, and once all the details were worked out, this was going to be the biggest thing to hit Deadwood yet.

JOHNNY Varnes stood on the porch of the Gem Theater with
Al Swearengen and said, "Did you see that?" Both of them

were looking down the street at the area where the brawl had taken place. The crowd was beginning to disperse now.

Swearengen stood with his hands in his pockets and rocked back and forth slightly on the balls of his feet. "You mean the way Hickok plowed right in there and broke up that fight?"

"That's exactly what I mean. You just wait, Al. The next issue of the *Pioneer* will have a story about that. I saw Merrick talking to Hickok. He's going to write about how the famous Wild Bill stepped in and quelled a disturbance. The story probably won't say anything about how it was Hickok's friends who started the ruckus in the first place."

"And reading about that will just remind people even more that Hickok used to wear a badge," Swearengen mused.

"You think it won't?"

"I didn't say that."

"We've got to act fast," Varnes insisted. "If we don't do something soon, Hickok will be appointed marshal of Deadwood, and then it'll be too late."

Swearengen looked narrow-eyed across the street toward Miss Laurette's Academy for Young Ladies. They had heard the commotion inside the Academy, too, and come out to see what was going on just as Swearengen, Varnes, and others from the Gem had done. Laurette Parkhurst still stood on the boardwalk over there, with that kid gunfighter of hers standing next to her. Swearengen remembered the way Bellamy Bridges had gunned down the gambler who had been cheating him. He had heard, as well, that Bellamy was responsible for running that fellow Turner out of Deadwood at gunpoint. Obviously, the kid had nerve, and at least a little skill with a gun.

"Don't worry, we're going to do something," Swearengen said to Varnes. "And I think I know just who we're going to get to do it."

Chapter Twenty-two

❦

FLETCH Parkhurst was sitting in the Grand Central dining room having dinner when Dan Dority came up to him. "Al wants to see you again," Dority said.

Fletch frowned. "I don't think your boss and I have any business that needs tending to."

Dority looked uncomfortable as he said, "Look, I'm just deliverin' the message, Fletch. Al did say that it's important, though. Said to tell you it's about Miss Laurette."

The frown on Fletch's face deepened. Swearengen knew that Laurette was his mother, although that wasn't general knowledge around Deadwood. He wasn't quite sure how Swearengen had found out, but he didn't doubt that the man had spies all over the settlement.

He had to ask himself just how much he really cared what happened to Laurette. After all, she had abandoned her family, including him, when he was very young. Though Fletch had forced his way into a partnership with her in the Academy, it had been a business arrangement for the most part. She had certainly never demonstrated much in the way of maternal feelings for him.

And yet, she *was* his mother. He wasn't quite sure why

Swearengen thought he would be willing to work against her. Fletch didn't want to spend the rest of his time in Deadwood being pestered about it, though. Maybe he ought to try one more time to set Swearengen straight.

"All right," he said as he got to his feet. "I'll talk to him. But this is the last time."

Dority held up his hands, palms out. "Hey, that's between you and Al. I'm just the messenger."

"So I shouldn't kill the messenger, is that what you're saying?" Fletch asked.

Dority's eyes widened. "Damn right!"

Fletch shook his head and chuckled. He followed Dority out of the Grand Central and down the street to the Gem.

On the second floor of the theater, Johnny Varnes came into Swearengen's office and sat down. "Have you talked to Parkhurst yet?" the gambler asked.

Behind the desk, Swearengen shook his head. "No, but I sent Dan to bring him over here. He ought to be here soon."

"I hope this works," Varnes said nervously. "I talked to Charlie Storms."

Swearengen looked surprised. "Storms is in town?"

"That's right. I put the proposition to him."

"Damn it," Swearengen growled. "We should have talked about that first." Although he was irritated with Varnes, Swearengen had to admit to himself that approaching Charlie Storms about killing Hickok wasn't a bad idea. Storms was primarily a gambler, but he had a reputation as a fast gun, too.

"I know," Varnes said, "but it doesn't really matter, because Storms turned me down flat. We're getting to the end of our rope, Al. That's why I hope this idea of yours works."

Swearengen nodded. "Go back downstairs," he told Varnes. "We'll see what happens."

Varnes left, and Swearengen leaned back in his chair to see if Fletch Parkhurst answered his summons.

When Fletch and Dority came into the Gem, Dority pointed toward the second floor and said, "You know where Al's office is. He said for you to go right on up."

"All right." Fletch paused before heading for the stairs and said quietly to Dority, "This wouldn't be a trap of some kind, would it?"

"A trap? What the hell do you mean by that?"

"I'm just wondering if you don't want to take me up there because I'm going to be walking into an ambush."

Dority shook his head vehemently. "I don't know nothin' about any trap. Al just said he wanted to talk to you, that's all."

"I hope you're telling the truth, Dan. And you'd better hope that if it *is* an ambush, I'm killed right away. Otherwise, I'm going to make a point of living long enough to come back down here and put a bullet or two in *you*."

Dority swallowed and shook his head. "I'll go up with you, just to prove it. Come on."

But Fletch thought Dority looked decidedly nervous as they climbed the stairs. It must have occurred to him that Al Swearengen might not necessarily let him in on everything that was planned.

No murderous gunmen were lurking in the upstairs hallway, however, and the only door that opened as Fletch and Dority walked along it was to allow one of the whores and her half-drunk customer to stumble out into the corridor. The prospector had a big grin on his whiskery face, and the woman just looked bored.

Dority went to the door of Swearengen's office and rapped on it. "Come in," Swearengen called from inside.

Dority opened the door, poked his head in long enough to say, "Here's Fletch Parkhurst, like you wanted, Al," and then stepped back to let Fletch stride past him into the office. Behind the desk, Swearengen stood up and smiled a greeting. He looked a little like a picture Fletch had seen once in a book, a picture of a big fish called a shark.

"Sit down, Fletch, sit down," Swearengen said. "Cigar? Drink?"

"No, thanks to both," Fletch said as he took a seat in front of the desk. "What do you want, Al? I'm still not interested in working for you."

"And that's not why I asked you to come see me."

Swearengen sat down as Dority closed the office door. With an intent look on his face, Swearengen leaned forward and clasped his hands together on the desk. "I need your help, Fletch. Deadwood needs your help."

"I told you—"

Swearengen held up a hand to forestall his protest. "Look, it's no secret that there's bad blood between your mother and me. She thinks I paid those boys to bust up her place a while back. That's not true, but I don't blame her for sending young Bridges over here to pick a fight and gun down one of my customers."

Fletch was convinced that Swearengen had indeed paid several miners to start a brawl in the Academy, as a result of which there was a lot of damage and several of the girls had been injured. It was equally true that Laurette was behind the gunfight Bellamy had had in the Gem. But he wasn't here to argue about either of those things, and evidently neither was Swearengen, because the man went on. "I've seen feuds like this before, in other towns. Sooner or later they get out of hand. Buildings get burned down, and folks get shot."

"Are you threatening to burn down the Academy or to have my mother killed?" Fletch asked coldly.

"Hell, no! I'm saying I don't want anything like that to happen. Deadwood's big enough for both of us. I want to work out a truce with her, and I want you to be my . . . ambassador, I guess you'd call it. I want you to set up a meeting with her, so we can have a fuckin' peace treaty, like the government's got with the Indians." Swearengen chuckled. "Only we'll keep our treaty."

The declaration took Fletch by surprise. He never would have expected to hear peace overtures from Swearengen.

"Look, I've heard the rumors," Swearengen said. "I know you're on the outs with Laurette. But you're still her son, and I reckon she'll listen to you."

"That's a big assumption," Fletch said.

"You can do it. You can talk her into being reasonable. You can help see to it that Deadwood doesn't break out into a war that'll just get innocent folks hurt or killed. How about it, Fletch?"

It all sounded appealing enough. But agreeing to help Swearengen meant trusting the man as if he weren't a treacherous snake. Fletch wasn't sure he was prepared to go that far. This might still be a ruse of some sort.

"Where would you have this meeting?" he asked.

"Anywhere Laurette says. She can pick the place. Or you can, if you're more comfortable with that."

"You won't come in with a bunch of hard cases and try to bully her into going along with whatever you want?"

Swearengen shook his head. "I'll come alone, if that's what she wants. You can be there, and she can even bring along Bridges."

Fletch frowned. It certainly sounded like Swearengen was being straight about wanting to negotiate a truce. Distrusting him was a hard habit to break, though.

"I'll go over and talk to her," he said. "That's all I can promise. She may tell me to go to hell, and take you with me."

"Fair enough. At least then I'll know that I tried to make peace."

Fletch grunted. "Al Swearengen, peacemaker. Somehow the role doesn't quite suit you."

Swearengen looked squarely at him and said, "We all do what we have to do to survive."

THE evening's business was already well under way in the Academy when Bellamy saw Fletch Parkhurst come in through the front door. Bellamy was standing hatless in a corner of the parlor, sipping a drink. Several of the girls were sitting around on the divans in various stages of undress, while others were already occupied with customers in the rooms.

Bellamy set his drink aside and hooked his thumbs in his gun belt as he stepped over to confront Fletch. He nodded and said, "Hello, Fletch. Haven't seen you around here for a while. You come looking for a girl?"

Fletch smiled faintly, as if that were a far-fetched notion, and shook his head. "Not unless you consider my mother a girl, and I'm afraid she's long past that stage. I need to talk to her."

The request took Bellamy by surprise. He knew that there had been some sort of falling-out between Fletch and Laurette, although he wasn't sure of all the reasons behind it. Still, Laurette had never said that Fletch was banned from the place or anything like that. With a shrug, Bellamy said, "Sure, she's back in the office. Come on."

He walked with Fletch down the hallway to the rear corridor where Laurette's office was located. The door was open, so Bellamy didn't have to knock. He said, "Miss Laurette, somebody to see you."

She was sitting at the desk, not really working on anything, just sitting and staring straight ahead. When Bellamy spoke, she gave a little shake of her head and looked up at him. There was a glass of brandy on the desk in front of her, and Bellamy suspected there was a little tincture of laudanum in it, too.

"Hello, Fletch," she said to her son without smiling. "Come for your share of the profits?"

"I told you, I don't care about that anymore," Fletch said as he moved past Bellamy into the room. "I *am* here on business, though."

"Well, it can't be because you want a whore. I never saw anybody more resistant to a woman's charms than you."

"I'm resistant to *your* charms, Laurette."

"Well, I should hope so. I'm your mother, after all."

Bellamy said, "Should I go back to the parlor?"

Fletch looked over his shoulder. "It doesn't matter to me. You might as well hear this, too."

"Stay here, Bellamy," Laurette snapped. "And you, Fletch—if you've got something to say, spit it out."

"Al Swearengen sent me."

That made Laurette sit back in her chair and stare at Fletch in disbelief. Bellamy was pretty surprised, too.

"You're working for Swearengen now?" Laurette asked. "You'd turn on me that much?"

Fletch shook his head. "I'm not working for him, although he asked me to a few days ago and I turned him down. I'm just here as a favor to him . . . and, in a way, to you."

"I didn't ask you for any fuckin' favors. Never have and never will."

"He wanted me to come over here and ask you to have a meeting with him."

Laurette snorted. "A meeting? With Swearengen? That'd be like having a meeting with a goddamn rattlesnake! What's the point?"

"He wants a truce between the two of you. A peace treaty, he called it."

Laurette shook her head. "I don't believe it. Swearengen wouldn't do such a thing."

Fletch took off his hat and turned it over in his hands. "That's the way I felt at first," he admitted, "but now I'm not so sure. He said that Deadwood was big enough for both of you, and that if this rivalry goes on, there'll be more trouble and folks will get killed."

Laurette slapped a hand on the desk. "So he's threatenin' to have me killed!"

"Maybe he's afraid *you'll* have *him* killed," Fletch pointed out. "Maybe he's got a point. There doesn't have to be trouble between the two of you. Deadwood's growing fast. It seems to me like you're both making money hand over fist. If you're both getting rich, why fight?"

Bellamy knew it wasn't his place to get involved in this discussion, but he said anyway, "Swearengen seems like the sort of man who would fight just because he likes to win, not because he has to."

Fletch half-turned to look at him. "Yeah, but when you get right down to it, I think he's greedier than he is anything else. He wants to do whatever will make him the most money with the least trouble. When you look at it like that, what he's proposing makes sense."

"Maybe," Laurette said, although she didn't sound convinced. "But if he thinks I'm gonna waltz in over there at the Gem and find myself in a trap, he's crazy."

"No trap. He said he'd meet with you wherever you

wanted." Fletch paused and then went on. "I was thinking about the dining room of the Grand Central Hotel."

Laurette took a sharply indrawn breath. "You're saying that the town's leading madam and its biggest whoremonger ought to sit down together where all the respectable folks go to eat?"

"I thought you might like that idea," Fletch said as he watched a smile spread slowly across his mother's face.

Chapter Twenty-three

⌒⌒

JOHNNY Varnes was worried. He had gone along with Swearengen's idea to propose a truce with Laurette Parkhurst, so that they could recruit Bellamy Bridges to gun down Wild Bill Hickok. Varnes had seen Bridges in action. He knew the young man was fast and accurate, even though he had only started practicing with a handgun in recent weeks. Some men just had a natural talent for killing. Evidently, Bellamy Bridges was one of them.

And to think that he might never have discovered that talent if he hadn't come to Deadwood . . . !

But while Swearengen and Laurette were talking, they might discover that Varnes had approached both of them about paying someone to get rid of Hickok, back in the days when they had still been bitter enemies. Varnes didn't know how that would make them feel about *him*. If they joined forces, would they then turn on him?

He couldn't say, but he fretted over the possibility. He made sure that he was in the dining room of the Grand Central when the two of them sat down for their face-to-face meeting. If anything went wrong, he wanted to know it as soon as possible, so that he could be ready for it.

It was the middle of the afternoon. The lunch crowd was gone, and it would be a while before folks started showing up for supper. None of the other tables were occupied when Al Swearengen came in and sat down. A waitress started over toward him, but he stopped her before she got there by saying, "Just bring a pot of coffee, please." He could be a polite, cultured man when he wanted . . . or at least he could appear to be like that, Varnes thought as he came through the doorway between the dining room and the hotel lobby.

Swearengen grunted at the sight of him. "What are you doing here?"

Varnes sat down at another table, took a deck of cards from his coat, and began laying out a hand of solitaire. With a smile, he said, "I just thought I'd be on hand if you needed me, Al."

"I won't," Swearengen said bluntly. "But I reckon you can stay, if the lady doesn't have any objection."

Varnes nodded and concentrated on the cards in front of him. He knew that he shouldn't have come here; his presence was liable to provoke the very conversation he hoped would be avoided. And yet, he was unable to stay away. So much was riding on what happened here today, and he wanted to witness it firsthand.

A few minutes later, Laurette Parkhurst came into the dining room, dressed in an elegant, dark green gown. A hat of the same shade perched on her auburn curls. Fletch and Bellamy followed her and sat down at another table, while she came to the one where Swearengen was sitting. The waitress had brought the coffee, and Swearengen had poured a cup for each of them.

He got to his feet, behaving like a gentleman for once. With a polite nod, he said, "Good afternoon, Mrs. Parkhurst."

"Mr. Swearengen," she returned coolly.

"Please, sit down." He made no move to hold her chair for her. That would have been pushing things.

Laurette seated herself and clasped her gloved hands together on the table. "Let's get to it," she said. "I hear you want the trouble between us to end."

"That's right. You don't need to send Bellamy over to the Gem to start any more gunfights."

"I never did that," Laurette snapped.

Careful, Varnes thought. Damn it, be careful, Al.

Swearengen held his hands up, palms out. "Sorry," he muttered. "I didn't mean to accuse you. See, that's what we've got to get past, all this bein' suspicious of each other. There's no reason we can't cooperate."

"Except for the fact that we're in the same line of work, and our businesses are right across the street from each other."

"I sell liquor, too, and I don't worry about the Bella Union or the No. Ten. Seems to me like Billy Nuttall is doin' better than either of us."

She frowned. "I wouldn't go so far as to say that. Still, I got to admit it sort of bothers me, havin' Nuttall's places on both sides of me."

"If we join forces, then together we're as big as he is," Swearengen pointed out.

Laurette's frown deepened as she thought about what he'd said. "Maybe. Maybe you're right, Al. But going in together . . . that means I'd have to trust you." She shook her head.

"I'm not sure I can do that."

"For that matter," Swearengen said, "how do I know I can trust you?"

"I reckon if this is gonna work, we're both gonna have to make what they call a leap of faith, aren't we?"

"I'm willing if you are," Swearengen said. He extended a hand across the table. "I'll even shake on it."

"You'd shake on a deal with a mere woman?" Laurette asked mockingly.

"Trust me or not, but believe me when I say that I've never thought of you as a mere woman. From the first day you came to Deadwood, I've known that if I had any real competition in this town, it was you."

That was smooth, thought Varnes. And although he was somewhat surprised, he could see that Laurette was beginning to accept it. She liked the flattery, even from a man such as Swearengen. She hesitated a moment longer and then reached out to take his hand.

"It's a deal . . . for now," she said. "But I'm gonna be keepin' a close eye on you, Al."

"I wouldn't expect any less from you, Laurette."

Good God! The two of them were going to be billing and cooing at each other if they kept this up. But he was happy that things were going so well. With any luck, Wild Bill Hickok would soon be dead, and then Swearengen and Laurette could cut each other's throats, for all Varnes cared.

Because once the threat of Hickok was eliminated, Varnes was giving some serious thought to double-crossing both of them. . . .

BELLAMY wouldn't have believed it if he hadn't seen it with his own eyes. Al Swearengen and Miss Laurette were not only getting along, they had even agreed to work together. Snow must be falling in hell. Bellamy had heard Laurette rant for hours about how everything that had gone wrong for her since coming to Deadwood had been Swearengen's fault.

And yet, Bellamy was already learning that if there was one thing you could say about whores, it was that they were adaptable. They could change at will, bending whichever way the wind was blowing. And even though Laurette no longer entertained customers herself, she was still a whore at heart. If she could make more money by cooperating with Swearengen, and have fewer problems to boot, she was going to do it.

"Come over to my place tonight," she had said to Swearengen before they left the Grand Central Hotel. "You can have the best girl in the place, free of charge. Sort of seal the deal, I guess you could say."

"I appreciate that," Swearengen had told her, "and I'll take you up on the offer."

Now it was evening, and Laurette had assembled the girls in the parlor so that Swearengen could have his pick of them.

Bellamy stood off to the side as Swearengen inspected them
He was uneasy about the whole thing. He knew Laurette
didn't really trust Swearengen; she was just pretending to so
that she could get as much as possible out of this new deal
Bellamy didn't trust the owner of the Gem Theater, either
He just wasn't as good at concealing that as Laurette was
That's why he scowled as Swearengen picked Ling and led
her off to one of the rooms in the rear of the house.

Ling had become Bellamy's favorite. She would never
be able to make him forget Carla, but she was sweet and
seemed to genuinely like him. And she was beautiful and
good at what she did, there was no doubt about that. Bellamy had heard rumors that Swearengen liked to treat his
girls rough. If Swearengen hurt Ling, then he'd kill the son
of a bitch, no matter what kind of deal Miss Laurette had
with him.

Laurette must have noticed his reaction, because she
said, "Bellamy, come with me." He went, but not before
casting a final glance after Swearengen and Ling.

Once they were in Laurette's office, she said, "Who put
a burr under your saddle?"

"I don't like Swearengen," he said bluntly. "I don'
trust him."

Laurette gave an unladylike snort. "You think I do?
He's an evil fucker. I know that. But if teaming up with him
gives me the chance to get rid of some of the other compe
tition in Deadwood, I'm willin' to do it for a while. Hell
I've gone to bed—so to speak—with worse."

Bellamy wasn't sure that was possible. He said, "How
are the two of you going to eliminate the rest of the com
petition?"

She shook her head. "I don't really know yet. We ain'
worked it out. But Swearengen's smart, don't you ever for
get it. I may not like him, but I know he can come up with
something."

Bellamy hooked his thumbs in his gun belt. "All I know
is that every time I see him, I want to shoot him."

"Well, you ride herd on that impulse, you hear?" Lau

rette demanded. "Wait until we've gotten everything we can out of Al Swearengen. Then maybe you can kill him."

Bellamy nodded. That sounded pretty good to him.

Later in the evening, Ling came out of her room with Swearengen sauntering behind her, a self-satisfied smirk on his face. Bellamy looked Ling over, searching for any signs that Swearengen had mistreated her, but she seemed to be all right. She smiled at Bellamy and nodded.

Swearengen came up to him and clapped a hand on his shoulder. Bellamy forced himself not to flinch at the man's touch. It wasn't easy to control the reaction, but he thought he managed.

"Come on back to your boss's office with me, Bellamy," Swearengen said. "Got something I want to talk to you about."

Bellamy suppressed the impulse to ask Swearengen just when it was that they had become friends. Laurette wanted him to get along with the man, so he would try his best.

They walked back to the office together, where Laurette greeted them by asking Swearengen, "Well, what did you think, Al? That pretty little chink gal is a mighty fine fuck, ain't she?"

Swearengen nodded. "Fine as can be. You can be proud of having her work for you, Laurette. That's not why I came back here, though."

"Want some brandy?"

"Don't mind if I do."

They were so friendly it made Bellamy sick. He folded his arms over his chest and leaned back against the wall.

Once she had poured the drinks for them, Laurette asked, "Just what was it you wanted, Al?"

"I've been thinkin' about what we need to do as our first act together, to get us off on the right foot."

Laurette chuckled. "I sort of thought that's what lettin' you fuck one of my girls tonight amounted to."

"I appreciate that, but I'm talking about something that can make Deadwood safer for us for a long time."

Now Laurette looked interested. "What might that be?"

"We have to get rid of Wild Bill Hickok," Swearengen said.

Laurette's eyebrows rose in surprise, and Bellamy straightened out of his casual pose against the wall. "Get rid of Hickok?" he blurted out. "What do you mean?"

"The same thing most folks mean when they talk about getting rid of somebody, kid," Swearengen said dryly. "He needs to be killed."

Laurette toyed with her glass of brandy for a moment before she said, "I've heard something about this before."

"From a gambler named Johnny Varnes, I'd wager."

She nodded. "That's right."

Swearengen said, "Varnes is just like everybody else. He looks out for his own hide first. He views Hickok as a threat, and I don't blame him. And I'm not surprised that he approached you with the idea just like he approached me."

"Kind of underhanded, ain't it? Varnes had to know that you and me didn't get along, but he tried to partner up with both of us anyway."

"Nothing wrong with playing both ends against the middle, as long as you can get away with it," Swearengen said.

"I still don't like it."

Swearengen waved a hand. "Don't worry about Varnes. He's strictly a nobody. You and me, we're going to be a lot bigger than that before we're through."

"Yeah . . . and gettin' rid of Hickok *is* a good idea, no matter who came up with it."

"That's what I thought."

"I've been thinkin' that something ought to be done about that damn preacher. He annoys the hell out of me, the way he stands out in the street, bellowing and running off some of my customers who are too embarrassed to come in with him standin' right there."

Swearengen nodded. "I feel the same way about him. But the preacher won't ever be any more than an annoyance. Hickok's a real threat."

"I see what you mean."

They seemed to have forgotten that Bellamy was standing there. He couldn't believe they would just sit there, so cool and calm, and talk about having Wild Bill Hickok killed. Why, Hickok was a living legend! The Prince of Pistoleers! Bellamy had heard stories about Wild Bill Hickok for . . . well, almost as far back as he could remember.

"I still don't see how you're going to do it," he said. "Wild Bill is famous. Nobody with any sense is going to try to kill him."

Swearengen looked up at him. "Why not? Think about it, kid. Has Hickok shot anybody since he's been here?"

Bellamy frowned in thought, and after a moment he had to say, "Well . . . no. I reckon not."

"How long has it been since Hickok's last gunfight? Two years? Three? *Five?*" Swearengen shook his head emphatically. "I don't know that he's killed anybody since that shoot-out with Phil Coe in Abilene, and that was a long time ago. He's just living on his reputation. Resting on his laurels, they call it."

"Those are some pretty good laurels," Bellamy said dubiously.

"Maybe so, but you've heard the same rumors I have. Hickok can't see good anymore. He's all bluff. People are afraid to go up against him because of who he is, not because he can really outdraw anybody anymore."

Bellamy still wasn't convinced, but he could see that Swearengen had a point. Somebody who was young, and fast with a gun, might indeed have a chance against Hickok.

"The man who killed Wild Bill Hickok," Swearengen said softly, "would be famous all over the West. Hell, he'd be famous all over the country."

"You sound like . . ." Bellamy swallowed hard. "You sound like you're saying it ought to be me."

"I think you could do it."

"I do, too," Laurette said. She was beginning to look excited at the idea.

This was all going too fast for Bellamy. Only a few weeks earlier, he had been a prospector, working the claim up the gulch with Dan Ryan. A couple of months before that, he had been back on the farm with his family.

But men sometimes grew up fast on the frontier. He had

heard that, and now he knew it to be true. Just this summer, he had known his first love, and he had killed his first man. He had seen that lover gunned down in the street, and he had killed another man. He had a natural talent for handling a gun; he couldn't deny that.

There was only one way for a gunman to make a reputation: He had to go up against other men who were fast on the draw and beat them. Only after he had done that would men begin to step aside from him and folks talk around him in whispers.

"What do you think, Bellamy?" Laurette asked.

He looked at her, not knowing how he would have gotten through the horrors of recent days without her. He felt almost as close to her as he would have to his mother.

"You want me to do this?"

"I think it's worth considering."

Slowly, Bellamy nodded. "I can do that. I can think about it."

"Just don't think too long, kid," Swearengen said. "Once Hickok pins on a marshal's badge, it's a whole different story. Then he's got the power of the law behind him." Swearengen paused and shrugged. "Not that we can't work around that if we have to. And a tin star never stopped a bullet yet."

Chapter Twenty-four

~~

FLETCH had taken to sleeping in one of the upstairs rooms at the Bella Union. Billy Nuttall didn't mind, since he and Fletch were friends and Fletch gave the house a cut from the card games he sometimes ran on the Bella Union's first floor. Usually, it was nearly dawn by the time he turned in, and he slept until after noon.

He had just stretched out to try to go to sleep when the soft knock came on his door.

He rolled over and put his hand on the butt of the gun that lay on the night table. "Who is it?" he called. As far as he knew, nobody wanted to kill him right now, but if a shot came through the door, he would be ready to return the favor.

The reply to his question was unexpected. "Ling."

Fletch sat up and swung his legs out of bed. Wearing only the bottoms from a pair of long underwear, he went to the door and opened it. Ling slipped inside. She wore a plain gray dress, very unlike the more provocative outfits she sported in her job.

"What is it?" Fletch asked her. "Is something wrong at the Academy?"

"Something is very wrong," Ling replied in her precise English. Around the Academy, with the customers and with Laurette and Bellamy, Ling spoke as if she barely understood the language. Fletch was the only one who knew just how intelligent and articulate she really was. "I overheard Bellamy, Miss Laurette, and that man Swearengen talking in Miss Laurette's office."

"You eavesdropped, you mean."

"Call it what you will. What I heard has me very concerned, Fletcher. Miss Laurette and Swearengen are trying to convince Bellamy to have a fight with Wild Bill Hickok."

That news rocked Fletch almost like a physical blow. "A fight?" he repeated. "You mean a gunfight?"

"Exactly. They want Mr. Hickok killed, and they believe Bellamy can do it."

"Good Lord!"

It sounded ludicrous on the face of it . . . and yet, there was a possibility that Bellamy might prevail in a showdown with Hickok. Fletch had witnessed Bellamy's skill as a gun-thrower. Bellamy was fast, accurate, and surprisingly cool-headed. Those three elements were vital. The cool-headedness was perhaps the most important of all. If Bellamy could keep his nerves steady and not be overwhelmed by the fact that he was going up against the most famous gunman in the West, there was a chance he might triumph.

But even if he survived that showdown, there would be another, and another, and another. If Hickok fell to Bellamy's gun, his friends would take up the cause. And then there would be all the men who didn't know Hickok or Bellamy, but who wanted to make a name for themselves. The quickest way to do that would be to down the man who had killed Wild Bill Hickok.

One way or another, drawing against Hickok would be the same as signing his death warrant for Bellamy.

Ling reached out and grasped Fletch's arm. "Is there any way you can prevent this?" she asked.

He smiled ruefully. "You've gotten fond of Bellamy, haven't you?"

"He is . . . such a boy. Such a sad little boy. I thought at first merely to comfort him, but over time . . ." She shrugged. "I would have rather it had been you I comforted, Fletch. You know that. But it was not to be."

"No," Fletch said. "It wasn't. And I'm sorry about that, too."

Her fingers dug harder into his flesh. "But you will help him?"

He nodded. "I'll do what I can. Do you know when this gunfight is supposed to take place?"

"Bellamy has not yet told them that he will fight Mr. Hickok. He has promised only to consider it."

"Well, thank God he's showing a little sense. I'll go see him and try to talk some more sense into his head."

"You will go right now?"

"Sure. Why not?" He gave her a brief hug. "Don't worry, Ling. Not even Bellamy is crazy enough to do something like this. He'll see that, once I point it out to him."

She nodded, but he could tell that she was still worried.

To tell the truth, so was he. He hoped he could make Bellamy see reason, but he didn't really know the younger man all that well. They had been on their way to being good friends, when everything had gotten fouled up. Now, Fletch wasn't sure what Bellamy was capable of.

But he figured he would soon find out.

"**I** got to go visit all the places Dick'll stop along the way and make sure they'll have fresh horses ready for him," Charley Utter said to Hickok as they strolled along Deadwood's Main Street toward the Grand Central Hotel. It was early, a little before dawn on July 31st, 1876. Leander Richardson trailed along behind them, as he usually did these days, ever since he'd been introduced to the famous Wild Bill. Charley went on. "Why don't you go with me, Bill?"

"I don't know, Charley. I still have to locate a suitable claim. . . ."

"Oh, hell, you ain't gonna prospect for gold!" Charley said. "We both know that. I reckon you had the best intentions in the world when you come up here, but if you'd wanted to be a miner, you'd have gone in with California Joe."

Hickok sighed. "It's true. The gambling dens have seduced me with their cards and their whiskey and their smoky atmosphere."

"Then you could use some fresh air," Charley insisted. "Ride to Fort Laramie with me."

"When are you leaving?"

"Tomorrow, I reckon. The race won't be for another week or so."

"I'll think about it," Hickok promised.

"You do that. I think it'd do you good to get out of Deadwood for a while, Bill."

"You're undoubtedly correct," Hickok murmured.

He had been up all night, playing cards in the No. Ten, which had become his regular spot over the past few days. It was smaller and less fancy than the Bella Union, but there was a friendly attitude about the place that was hard to beat.

Right now he was tired, but before turning in, he thought he might have a bite of breakfast with Charley and the hero-worshipping young Richardson. There would be time after that for sleeping.

Plenty of time, thought Hickok . . . but was his time running out?

FLETCH let himself into the Academy. The front door was open, but the parlor was deserted. At this hour, business had died away to just about nothing, and most of the whores had finished off their last customers of the night and were asleep. Fletch knew that his mother would still be awake, though. She would be in her office, counting the night's take.

She looked up when she heard his footstep in the doorway. "You again," she said with a sniff. "Swearengen send you?"

"No, I told you I don't work for Swearengen. My part in your little arrangement was concluded when you agreed to meet with him. I'm here strictly on my own."

"Well, what do you want?"

"You're going to get Bellamy killed. You know that, don't you? One way or another, he won't survive what you and Swearengen are doing to him."

Laurette's eyes narrowed. "Nobody survives this life. Bellamy can make up his own mind what he wants to do. And how the hell did you find out about it, anyway?"

"That doesn't matter." Fletch slipped his Colt out of its holster. "What's important is that you're going to tell Bellamy to forget about it."

He had thought hard about the situation on the way over here and decided that it wouldn't do any good to talk to Bellamy, despite what he had promised Ling. Bellamy was too proud and too stubborn to listen to reason, no matter what Fletch said. The way to save Bellamy's life was to convince Laurette to rein him in and tell him to forget any crazy notions of drawing against Wild Bill Hickok.

She glared at him across the desk as he lifted the revolver. "Have you lost your mind?" she demanded. "You can't come in here and point a gun at me like that!"

"I'm doing it," Fletch said. "And I'm telling you that you're not going to get Bellamy killed."

"What the hell does it matter to you what happens to him? It ain't like you two are brothers or something!"

"Aren't we?" Fletch said. "He seems to have adopted you as his mother. He just doesn't know what a viper he's taking to his bosom."

She snorted. "There you go with that crazy talk again. Look, in case you haven't noticed, I ain't scared of that gun, and I ain't scared of you. I don't believe for a second that you'd shoot your own ma in cold blood."

"You don't know that, though."

"The hell I don't!" She came to her feet and leaned over the desk, resting her fists against its top. "You're soft! You've always been soft! I knew that as soon as you were born and I looked in your eyes. A mother can tell those things. I knew right off that you didn't have what it took to survive. I'd have tied you up in a tow sack and throwed you in the river, if it was up to me! That's what you do with something that's worthless."

The scornful, acid-laced words made Fletch's pulse pound in his head. "Shut up," he hissed.

"No, I won't shut up. Why the fuck do you think I left as soon as I could? I knew you'd grow up to be a spineless mewlin' little bastard like your pa. He was never good for anything, and neither are you. You just sit around and play cards all day and all night. Can't even get it up to fuck a woman!" She was furious now, her green eyes blazing, caught in the grip of years of pent-up emotions. Her hand went to the bosom of her dress, yanking it down and ripping it as she bared her breasts. "Here you are, you god-damn little baby! Come suck your mama's teats!"

Fletch was frozen inside, chilled by the horror of what he was seeing and hearing. His mother barely looked human now. Greed and hatred and ruthless ambition had transformed her into one of the harpies out of legend, and almost before he knew what he was doing, his finger began to contract on the trigger of the gun that was pointed at her heaving breasts.

"Fletch!"

The shout made him jerk sharply to his right. The gun in his hand exploded, the report deafening in the close confines of the narrow, shadowy hallway. He saw Bellamy Bridges standing at the other end of the corridor, saw splinters leap from the wall beside Bellamy's head as the slug from his gun struck it.

Then orange-red muzzle flame lit up the corridor and more shots hammered on Fletch's ears as something else hammered his chest once, twice, three times. He had barely seen Bellamy's draw, it had been that fast and smooth. Instinct and reflexes had taken over, and the gun was up and out and had exploded three times in little more than the space of a heartbeat. The impact of the bullets drove Fletch against the doorjamb. He bounced off, the gun slipping from his suddenly nerveless fingers as he did so. He heard it thud on the floor.

Laurette screamed.

Now Fletch was hot and cold at the same time. A consuming heat blazed in his chest, but it was no match for the cold seeping in from his extremities. He looked down at his chest. He hadn't put on a vest before he came over here, just his coat, so he could see the white breast of his shirt as it quickly turned dark red from the blood. The flames that he felt inside began to flicker out as he raised his gaze to Bellamy, who was staring at him open-mouthed over the gun, the gun with smoke still curling from its barrel. Then Fletch turned his head and looked at Laurette, who stood there with her sagging breasts still exposed, her hands pressed to her face in shock.

He leaned against the wall and felt himself sliding down it. "Mother . . ." he whispered.

That was the end of it, the end of all things. He was gone.

AT breakfast in the Grand Central Hotel, a waitress had just set a platter of Lou Marchbanks's wonderful flapjacks and ham and fried eggs in front of Bill Hickok when he lifted his head. His eyes might be going back on him a bit, but there was nothing wrong with his ears. He had heard shots from somewhere down the street, one sharp report and then three more, coming swift on the heels of the first.

"Someone's just crossed the divide," he muttered.

Colorado Charley nodded solemnly, but Leander Richardson looked confused. "What do you mean, Bill?" he asked. "Are you talking about those shots?"

"That's right."

"But I don't understand," Richardson insisted. "Maybe it was just some prospector lettin' off steam. How do you know somebody got killed?"

"Trust me, kid," Colorado Charley said. "If there's anybody who knows that sound well enough to recognize it, it's Wild Bill Hickok."

Epilogue

~~~

THE fatal shooting of a gambler inside a whorehouse failed to cause many ripples in the fabric of Deadwood's day-to-day life. People died all the time. Fletch Parkhurst had been fairly well liked in the camp, but really, when you got right down to it . . . he was just another gambler. A. W. Merrick didn't even put a note about his death in the *Black Hills Pioneer,* although Preacher Smith, as usual, gave a fine sermon at the brief and sparsely attended burial service on the afternoon of July 31st. Miss Laurette and her girls were there, but the Celestial was the only one who cried very much, the preacher noted. Miss Laurette remained dry-eyed throughout the funeral.

The only surprising thing was that she was escorted by Al Swearengen. The two of them seemed much closer than before, surprising since they had been at each other's throats only a few days earlier.

Perhaps they had somehow learned forgiveness, Preacher Smith thought.

Bellamy Bridges didn't attend the service at Deadwood's cemetery, but he was waiting at the Academy when Laurette got back there. He was hollow-eyed, gaunt, and haggard, but composed. He followed her into the office and asked, "Do you and Swearengen still want Hickok killed?"

Laurette unpinned her hat and set it on the desk. "I reckon we do," she said, not knowing what to expect from Bellamy. He had been shaken by what had happened early that morning. Fletch had been his friend, despite their disagreements. Just like Fletch had been her son, despite everything that had gone wrong between them. She felt grief at his loss. She told herself that she did. She planned to go on telling herself that she did.

"He'll be dead within the week."

"Hold on, Bellamy. There's no need to rush into this. You need to wait for the right time and place. It ain't a simple thing to kill a man, especially not one like Wild Bill Hickok."

"It was simple enough to kill Fletch. Just draw and fire. That's all I did."

"You saved my life," she said. "He was going to shoot me."

Bellamy turned away. "Hickok will be dead within a week," he said again.

Later, as evening fell, the man himself strolled along Main Street. As he passed the Grand Central Hotel, he looked in through the dining room window and saw the White-Eyed Kid and Silky Jen sitting at one of the tables. Hickok smiled. It was nice to see that the girl was feeling good enough to come downstairs now. Her hair was brushed and shone in the lamplight. She wore a clean dress, and there was no paint on her face. She smiled and even laughed a little as the Kid said something to her, and outside on the boardwalk, Hickok moved on.

Somehow, he had given the slip to Leander Richardson, who bid fair to becoming as big a nuisance as Calamity Jane. Calam had her good points, of course—she was kindhearted despite her rough exterior, and she had helped rescue Jen from Al Swearengen—and Hickok was sure that young Richardson had much to recommend him as well. For the moment, though, he was enjoying the comparative solitude. Deadwood was still a busy place, of course. The street was crowded with men and horses and mules. Across the way, those two Montana men, Bullock and Star, were working on their new hardware store despite the fading light. Their hammers rang in the early evening stillness. The sound of progress, Hickok thought, but more than that, the sound of a wager. Bullock and Star were betting that they could make a go of it here, just like all the other people who had come to Deadwood. Just like Charley Utter, recently departed on his trip to complete the arrangements for the big race with August Clippinger's Frontier Pony Express. Charley was betting that Bloody Dick would win that race, and Hickok certainly wouldn't count the young Englishman out.

He paused and looked back at the warm yellow glow coming from the window of the Grand Central's dining room. White-Eye Jack was a gambler, too, but the stakes were even bigger in his game. He had bet on his love for Jen, and against all odds, he had won.

"Good evening, Mr. Hickok."

He turned his head and saw the tall, angular shape of the preacher. Smith had slipped up on him. That wasn't good. A man of God shouldn't be able to sneak up on him when Indians and Confederates and outlaws had never been able to in the past.

"Evening, Preacher."

"Are you out for a constitutional?" Smith asked.

Hickok shook his head. "On my way to the No. Ten. I thought I would play a few hands of cards with my friends."

"You're going to gamble."

Bill Hickok put his head back and laughed. He clapped a hand on Smith's shoulder. "All men are gamblers, Preacher," he said. "They wager when they get up in the morning that they'll still be alive when it comes time to lay their head on the pillow that night."

"Well . . . I suppose you could look at it that way. I prefer a sure thing, myself. I speak, of course, of Our Lord and Savior, and the home He has prepared for us in Heaven."

"I know what you mean, Preacher. I reckon that time's

coming for us all. But until then . . ." Hickok waved as he moved off along the boardwalk. "Until then, the cards are waiting for me, and who knows that the next turn of them will bring?"

Author's Note

❧❧

As with the previous book in this series, many of the characters in this story actually came to Deadwood, Dakota Territory, in the summer of 1876, and many of their actions took place as described here.

Richard "Bloody Dick" Seymour is known to have been a buffalo hunter and trader with the Indians before traveling to the Black Hills to become a rider for Charley Utter's Pioneer Pony Express. History tells us nothing about his past other than speculation that he was the son of an English nobleman, so I have taken it upon myself to invent a life for him on the other side of the Atlantic, as well as fleshing out the details of his life in America. The best, indeed, almost the only source of information about his early days in this country is the book *Medicine Creek Journals: Ena and the Plainsman,* by D. Jean Smith, which casts some light on his days as a buffalo hunter and trader and his acquaintance with Ena Raymonde. Seymour is also mentioned several times, although not in great detail, in the memoirs of Colonel William F. "Buffalo Bill" Cody.

Also as before, special thanks to Samantha Mandor and Kimberly Lionetti for helping to make this series possible.

MIKE JAMESON

Tales from

DEADWOOD

*The first in a new series of fictionalized tales,
based on real-life characters, that show
Deadwood as it really was—
and might have been.*

Deadwood is the infamous and lawless
cesspool where a man is as likely to strike
it rich as he is to lose everything.
Now, the legendary Wild Bill Hickok—
who has lost his eyesight—and
Calamity Jane are coming to start
their own trouble.

0-425-20675-0

**Available wherever books are sold or at
penguin.com**